Br

Murder Mystery Weekend

Detective Inspector Skelgill Investigates

LUCiUS

Text copyright 2018 Bruce Beckham

Kindle edition first published by Lucius 2018

Paperback edition first published by Lucius 2018

For more details and Rights enquiries contact:
Lucius-ebooks@live.com

Cover design by Moira Kay Nicol

EDITOR'S NOTE

Murder Mystery Weekend is a stand-alone crime mystery, the eleventh in the series 'Detective Inspector Skelgill Investigates'. It is set primarily in and around the English Lake District – a National Park of 885 square miles that lies in the rugged northern county of Cumbria – and the Scottish capital, Edinburgh.

THE DI SKELGILL SERIES

Murder in Adland
Murder in School
Murder on the Edge
Murder on the Lake
Murder by Magic
Murder in the Mind
Murder at the Wake
Murder in the Woods
Murder at the Flood
Murder at Dead Crags
Murder Mystery Weekend
Murder on the Run
Murder at Shake Holes
Murder at the Meet
Murder on the Moor
Murder Unseen
Murder in our Midst

Glossary

Some of the local Cumbrian and Scots dialect words used in 'Murder Mystery Weekend' are as follows:

Ah kent yer faither – I knew your father
Auld Reekie – 'Old Smoky' (=Edinburgh)
Beck – mountain stream
Cuddy – donkey
Cuddy wifter – left-handed
Deek – sly look around
Donnat – idiot
Happen – possibly, maybe, it seems
Hunner – hundred
Janny – janitor
Jings – an exclamation
Keks – trousers
Ken – know; you know
Lass – girl, young woman
Lug – ear
Ma sel – myself
Mash – making a pot of tea
Mithered – bothered
Owt – anything
Polis – police
Skelp – slap
Sommat – something
Tup – ram (male sheep)
Tupping – what rams do
Yowe – ewe

And DS Leyton's Cockney!

Apples – stairs ('Apples and Pears')
Blow the gaff – reveal a secret
Bottle – arse ('Bottle and Glass')
Cream-crackered – exhausted

Dog – phone ('Dog and Bone')
Gaff – property/home
Geezer – man
Mincers – eyes ('Mince Pies')
Trouble – wife ('Trouble and Strife')
Two-an'-eight – state (of upset)

1. FIRST DAY OF SPRING

Friday, morning

Since early self-awareness March 21st has held a special meaning for Skelgill. The sun has crossed the equator and is on its way back to breathe life into Cumbria's stalled landscape. Dog violets raise expectant lilac faces from decayed autumn leaf litter; tench stir from winter torpor, detecting a degree or two of warmth; the first chiffchaff, newly alighted bankside, taps out tentative chopsticks from a crack willow, announcing the auspicious date. Skelgill's birthday.

From his boat, far from madding crowds, he turns *his* face to the sun, still low over Barf, though it is late morning. Bassenthwaite Lake is becalmed, reflecting the scene: two Barfs, two Bishops, two suns that cause him to close his eyes; that warm hint of summer, a frisson – hard to define which senses it fleetingly captivates – a promise of something that, truth be told, never really materialises; it is like a distant vista, smudged and mysterious, that becomes familiar and mundane when finally entered.

Still, who knows what spring will bring, surely something? Afloat, the plaintive bleat of new lambs reaches Skelgill's keen ears. This little paradox reminds him it is the cusp of Pisces and Aries, the last and first signs of the zodiac. No mystic – only ever pragmatic – there are nonetheless aspects that please him – the celestial fish, guiding his vocation, his angling bent – and the ram – hereabouts a much-revered creature – who would not wish to be endowed with its legendary traits?

And the tups have been busy – though it must be said that October is the time for tupping in the Lakes; now, five months on, their carnal heroics bear fruit. Skelgill is fishing the shallower southern reaches fed by Newlands Beck; onshore bloated yowes graze the floodplain, the area known as Green Mire, an alluvial semi-wilderness where an uneasy truce was long ago drawn up between man and Mother Nature. Inundations are recurrent; vegetation untameable; there is treacherous swamp and bog. Such obstacles were turned to advantage – five centuries ago foundations were sunk into the stable underlying moraine; whence arose the isolated edifice of Greenmire Castle – a proper castle with towers and turrets and arrow-slit windows – if bijou by the standards of more noteworthy northern bastions, Alnwick, Bamburgh and Carlisle. Today, with enough ghosts passing within its walls to fill a couple of box sets, it serves as an exclusive country residence for hire by the well heeled.

Well heeled, but not always well behaved. For some minutes Skelgill has been conscious of a disturbance on the lake. The boat that slid out from Peel Wyke – *his* Peel Wyke – did not escape his sharp eyes. The tiny secluded inlet, albeit a public launching point, is rarely frequented by anyone other than he. Now his grey-green irises seem to mirror the cold surface as he watches the craft; he estimates a closest point of approach of fifty yards; he pulls down the brim of his *Tilley* hat.

There are nine people aboard – four couples, around his age at a guess, and the elderly boatman, crouched in the stern, whom he knows. It is a traditional clinker-built Lakes longboat with an electric outboard fitted; its progress is steady and silent, unlike its occupants, who sound ginned up to the gills and are now popping corks between bursts of raucous laughter. The boatman gives a somewhat apologetic tip of his head; Skelgill reciprocates – they might be motorcyclists exchanging the biker's nod. The passengers are preoccupied with their booze and banter, until one of the females, distinctive as the only redhead, notices him and cries out to ask whether he has caught anything.

Skelgill makes a noncommittal hand gesture – but suddenly he must suppress an irrational juvenile urge to shout back that it is his birthday. Jolted, he reminds himself that is precisely why he is here – why he does this every year on this same day – takes a day's holiday – not to celebrate, but to *escape* from any such attention. Since attaining the grand old age of thirty – announcing he was henceforth 'retiring' from birthdays – he now refuses to count or advertise or acknowledge the event – declaring himself suspended in time, in his prime. His pals in his local call him *Peter Pan*. Water off a duck's back, it bolsters his determination not to decline.

When he looks up from his moment of introspection he realises the woman has lost interest in his reply, if she had any in the first place. The wake from the passenger boat laps against his starboard side, gently rocking the craft. The rhythmical splosh of the ripples subsides, and with it the sound of the party; they are nearing the spindly landing stage for Greenmire Castle – the next phase of their adventure beckons and a hush of anticipation descends. *"Live Like A Lord"* – he has seen the ads for bespoke luxury breaks – most recently in a high-end field sports magazine whilst waiting for dental torture. Over water is the expensive way to arrive ('pushing the boat out', Skelgill had mused) – instead of bumping by car along the rough track across the flood plain from Thornthwaite. But they can obviously afford it – passing at dawn he noticed a dew-coated line of prestige marques parked outside *The Partridge* – the old coaching inn where perhaps they had rendezvoused last night – no expense spared. The cars bear Scottish plates, though the redhead sounds English, well spoken, if not exactly posh.

2. 'A MURDER IS ANNOUNCED'

Sunday, morning

'They all come from Edinburgh, Guv.'

Skelgill does not respond, but in any event DS Jones is not watching him; she continues.

Will Liddell, 40 – address in The Grange. Father of two children: a girl and a boy, from his first marriage. Venture capitalist. He's footing the bill for the entire weekend.

'Kevin Makepeace, 35 – accompanied by but separated from *Felicity Belvedere, 38.* One child, a girl, lives with the mother in the Ravelston district; father's address given as Newington, Edinburgh. Kevin Makepeace is employed as a marketing manager by one of Will Liddell's companies. Felicity Belvedere is an architect, currently works part time.

'Mike Luker, 38 and wife *Belinda, 39* – live in the Murrayfield area. Two daughters. Mike Luker is a financial advisor. Belinda Luker is a qualified lawyer but currently a housewife.

'Derek Duff, 40 – some kind of businessman. Wife *Suzy, 38,* housewife. Four children. Address Blackhall, Edinburgh.

'Finally, *Scarlett Liddell, 28.* Deceased.'

Skelgill, driving, stares ahead implacably. There is half a minute of silence.

'Is she a redhead?'

DS Jones looks up from the roughcast report from which she has been adeptly skimming salient facts, knowing Skelgill's limited patience.

'It doesn't say, Guv. Why do you ask?'

Skelgill shakes his head – he gives the impression that he will not reply – but then he does.

'I reckon I saw her – them, anyway – crossing Bass Lake on Friday morning. The castle must have hired Abel Thurnwyke – must have put his boat in up at the sailing club.'

'That would fit with when they registered, Guv. They're due to stay until tomorrow morning – though I don't suppose they'll want to – not now.'

'What do we know about it?'

DS Jones dutifully turns a page.

'In a nutshell – they assembled for pre-dinner cocktails on Saturday evening – it was arranged as one of these 'Murder Mystery' nights. Scarlett Liddell didn't appear. Eventually they went to look for her – and found her hanged in her bathroom. There was a 1920s dress theme – she'd looped her feather boa over a coat hook on the back of the door. They administered CPR – Mrs Duff is a trained first aider – meanwhile someone dialled 999 – the paramedics took over and tried to resuscitate her – but she was declared dead on arrival at Cumberland Infirmary.'

'Who found her?'

'The husband was first. But only by a matter of seconds, it seems. Her bedroom door was locked and they'd had to get in through the interconnecting dressing rooms, from his bedroom.'

'And the PM?'

Skelgill refers to a preliminary post mortem ordered by the Coroner – a standard procedure in the event of a sudden or unnatural death.

'It confirms compression of the neck, consistent with hanging. The time of death corresponds to when they discovered her – although there's a margin of error of about half an hour.'

Again there is a period of silence before Skelgill responds.

'So where's the issue?'

'There's no one single thing, Guv – the pathologist has highlighted a couple of advisories – when taken together, just enough to sow a seed of doubt.'

'Aye.'

Skelgill's acknowledgement has sufficient a hint of a question in it to prompt his subordinate to elaborate.

'The marks on her neck were slightly abnormal – more widespread than might be expected – as if she had thrashed about.'

'You would, wouldn't you?'

Skelgill seems to be biting at his cheek. He turns his head away however as they cross Derwent Bridge, and seems to be distracted by external factors. The trout fishing season opens on Monday. DS Jones meanwhile is frowning, head down still.

'Also, Guv – and I don't know what to read into this – she was fully dressed in her outfit, and made up like she was ready to go – but she had on no underwear.' She glances up, and adds a quick proviso. 'There was no evidence of sexual assault.'

Skelgill's features contract – he looks for a moment like he is about to quip – but it might be to cover a trace of embarrassment. In the event he settles for something rather cryptic.

'Some things you never get to the bottom of.'

DS Jones furrows her brow – he might almost be joking – but she too looks like she has something to say – and then thinks the better of it. She knows her superior dislikes unfounded speculation. Instead she states a fact.

'The toxicology report indicates she'd drunk the equivalent of a bottle of medium-strength wine.'

Now it is Skelgill's turn to raise an eyebrow – his sergeant's tone is neutral, though he wonders if she is disapproving – on this subject she is a lot closer to teetotal than he. But he is thinking it is more likely a case of steady topping-up than a sudden binge, if what he saw on Friday morning was anything to go by.

'Let's ask the butler, eh?'

*

'*A Murder Is Announced?* – yes, Inspector – it is one of Agatha Christie's most popular – perfect for a house party event – you know the plot, of course?'

Skelgill looks nonplussed – he casts a brief glance at DS Jones, seated beside him on a capacious chesterfield sofa, one of a pair set perpendicular to a hearth in which embers smoke. DS Jones appears to respond with a faint nod. Skelgill turns back to the woman who has posed the question.

'Should I?'

'Oh – well – if you don't, I shouldn't like to spoil it for you – you will certainly want to read it one day.'

Skelgill scowls doubtfully.

'Does it have any bearing on what happened?'

The woman, who is sitting opposite them with her legs crossed, folds her hands together upon her lap, intertwines her fingers and regards them thoughtfully. Skelgill notices the nails are bitten down severely. After a moment's deliberation she answers.

'No – I shouldn't say so, Inspector.' She looks him in the eye, a curious twisted expression, it seems. 'I think you shall have to discover your own clues.'

Skelgill is finding the woman's manner hard to read – there is a strange kind of eccentricity, inwardly focused – as if she is unaccustomed to showing empathy – which is odd given her apparent role as hostess. Her bearing is more that of a rather awkward schoolgirl – not yet 'finished' as regards decorum, as was the way back in the day. And she *looks* girlish, too – long dark hair pulled into bunches – plain and a little plump, no obvious make-up – and yet she is dressed in a calf-length tartan skirt of beaver, orange and magenta, brown leather boots, and a formal white blouse beneath a cerise cashmere cardigan. Girlish, yes she is – and yet old before her time.

As for her statement about clues – it contains an incongruous presumption: that they are here to investigate something more sinister than they know – to all intents and purposes (despite DS Jones's minor caveats) a straightforward case of suicide.

Skelgill senses he is in danger of becoming sidetracked. He opts to rewind. He reaches for a clip of papers that DS Jones has placed in front of her on the large square coffee table.

'Madam – I've been off duty the past two days – so if you'll bear with me I'm just catching up with the report submitted by the uniformed officer that attended last night.'

The woman nods acceptingly. Skelgill squints at the typed page, which tells him he is facing Lavinia Montagu-Browne, 34, described as 'general manager' in PC Dodd's transcribed notes. It is perhaps the aristocratic-sounding name that prompts his first question.

'So – are you the owner?' He raises a palm to indicate their surroundings – the room itself is built a half-storey above ground level, long and rectangular, with small deep leaded windows set into exposed stonework, and most of its walls lined with bookshelves.

'All of my family's properties are held in a trust, Inspector – one is merely a caretaker for a subsequent generation. But I have complete responsibility for Greenmire Castle, and the hospitality business.'

Skelgill nods; she seems to have understood what he is driving at. However, he taps the page with the back of his left hand.

'So – Thomas Montagu-Browne –'

'Is my half-brother.'

Her interjection is swift and practised – as though she is used to correcting the assumption that the person must be her spouse – or even her twin. He is listed as having the same age.

Skelgill is still scowling belligerently at the words on the page, like a student reacting unfavourably to his tutor's criticism. They tell him that catering, room service and cleaning are subcontracted, with temporary staff drafted according to needs. Yesterday afternoon and evening this took the shape of a male chef and two female assistants.

'Just the two of you live here.'

'That is correct – it provides maximum efficiency – we do not experience week-round occupancy. There are various advantages

16

– for example we can enlist a guest chef from one of the Lake District's many prestigious restaurants. And we are not tempted by cheap foreign labour – the ad hoc housekeeping provides local jobs for local people.'

Skelgill hands the document back to DS Jones.

'The lady who committed suicide – Mrs Liddell – when did you last see her?'

Lavinia Montagu-Browne does not seem perturbed that he has put her directly in the spotlight.

'The group returned for afternoon tea at 4.30pm. They had been over at Greystoke – at the forest adventure centre. They arrived together and all eight were in the drawing room. I mingled with them for a few minutes to make sure that everybody was content and that the timetable was still on schedule. Tom remained to dispense drinks, and a waitress served tea and cakes. I left to place the Murder Mystery envelopes with each person's role and instructions on the dressing tables in their rooms. Then I had other matters to which to attend.'

'Did you notice anything about Mrs Liddell – that seemed unusual – even with hindsight?'

She regards him evenly.

'They were all in high spirits – laughing and joking about their escapades on the rope swings – I don't recall Mrs Liddell or anyone else acting out of the ordinary. Of course, one doesn't know one's guests intimately. They would better be able to tell you that.'

Skelgill remains silent for a moment.

'She was drinking alcohol?'

'Oh, Inspector – I think they were all partaking of what you might call sherry *chasers* with their Earl Grey.'

Skelgill nods. He is conscious that DS Jones beside him is taking notes in surges of shorthand.

'So what happened next – after tea?'

'I imagine they drifted off to their rooms – I checked the drawing room at around 5.30pm and it was empty. Tom and I cleared away glasses and tidied up, as they would be using it after dinner.'

'So you last saw Mrs Liddell at 4.30?'

'I didn't see anyone in fact after – say, 4.35pm – until – until what you might call the commotion. From the drawing room I went to liaise with chef, supervise the table setting, and finally to prepare for the Murder Mystery.' She hesitates for a moment. 'I was to play the part of the intruder.'

Skelgill looks baffled.

'Could you explain that, madam?'

Lavinia Montagu-Browne glances at DS Jones.

'The crux of *A Murder Is Announced* is when the party is assembled for drinks. The lights fail, and in the ensuing melee the door bursts open. An anonymous voice calls out and shots are fired. The room has more than one exit – and so of course there is conjecture over whether someone slipped out under cover of darkness and re-entered to commit the crime.' She indicates with first her left and then her right hand. 'As you can see, in addition to the central door behind us, the library has a door at each end, opening onto the respective staircases. So this room makes an ideal setting.'

Skelgill is now glowering darkly. He feels the weight of an improbable whodunit descending upon his shoulders, and the alarming prospect of having to explain such fiction to the Chief. He gives an involuntary shudder. An antique bracket clock on the mantle strikes the quarter hour; it has a mahogany casement and a large enamel face with a clearly delineated chapter ring and the words *Bennett*, and *Cheapside, London*. Skelgill seems to wait for the sound to diffuse before he speaks.

'So you didn't see anyone until this – this *shooting* scene?'

'Oh, no, Inspector – it did not get that far. They were to meet here in the library for classic cocktails from 7pm – my part was scheduled for 7.30 – but somewhere in between – I should say about ten minutes before I was due to make an entrance – they discovered Mrs Liddell.'

'Where were you then?'

'I was waiting in my office – we have staff quarters through in the new wing. Tom came running to tell me to call an ambulance.'

'So it was you that did that?'

The woman leans forward; she seems pleased with herself.

'Mobile phones do not work within the castle walls, Inspector – a blessing, some would say.' She pauses as though she invites his agreement – but before he can remark she continues, again her manner becoming somewhat arch. 'I understand there was an element of confusion.'

'In what way, madam?'

'Several of the party believed that Mrs Liddell was acting her role in the Murder Mystery.' Again she glances tellingly towards DS Jones. 'Tom of course knew otherwise.'

Skelgill, too, looks at his subordinate – she anticipates his thoughts.

'The 999 call was timed at 7.23pm.'

Lavinia Montagu-Browne nods approvingly.

'After that I ran up to the room. I could see that the woman giving heart massage knew what she was doing – I suggested that the others – excluding her husband, naturally – should come back down and wait in here.'

'And did they?'

'Yes – they were all in shock, of course – in fact a strange euphoria overcame them – but I think it helped to be relieved of the responsibility. And the paramedics arrived within minutes to take full control. Sadly they could not save her. They brought Mr Liddell back from the hospital about two hours later. Alone.'

Skelgill senses a certain ghoulishness in the woman's manner – as if this is just another inevitable chapter in the castle's morbid history. He straightens his posture and begins to cast about the library, looking first to one end and then the other, where the aged oak doors that Lavinia Montagu-Browne has pointed out are set into the bookcases, in mirror image of one another.

'Could you explain to me about the arrangement of the bedrooms, please, madam.'

She regards him with a look of satisfaction, as one rather revelling in having their expert knowledge slowly drawn from them.

'You have no doubt noticed that this part of the castle – the late medieval – is tall and narrow. It was built with defence rather than ostentation in mind. It does not have a central grand staircase, but a stone spiral stair in the two corner towers. Above us are four floors, each with two bedrooms. The bedrooms interconnect via dressing rooms, while their main doors open on opposite stairs. We have six additional bedrooms in the Victorian wing, but they are not in use this weekend.'

Skelgill is looking puzzled.

'So, what – each person had their own room?'

She smiles – for the first time, he realises – and rather coyly, displaying small childish teeth, emphasising the girl-like impression.

'Our guests are generally intrigued by the prospect of the Lord's and Lady's bedchambers, Inspector.' She smirks, and there is a hint of innuendo in her tone. 'It is part of our unique attraction. The rooms are decorated and fitted accordingly. And of course it means the ladies can dress in privacy and appear downstairs in their full finery.' Now she looks to DS Jones, as if to gain womanly corroboration for the significance of this arrangement. But Skelgill has drawn his own conclusion.

'So the females – and males – have separate staircases?'

'In practice that is correct, Inspector. The ladies' rooms give on to the west tower, the gentlemen's to the east.' A small crease appears between her eyebrows, which are unplucked and come close to joining. 'Of course, there are occasions when the composition of the guests does not accommodate an exactly even split. Indeed the most recent incident in Lady Anne's chamber involved a small child.' She gives the semblance of a laugh, just a small sound from her nose.

Skelgill's tone is guarded.

'What do you mean by Lady Anne's chamber?'

'That is what we call the bedroom in which Mrs Liddell slept. It is probably our most haunted room.' Her voice becomes a little hushed, and she gazes reflectively at her hands; her fingers tighten their grip on one another. 'Anne de Flamville was a sixteenth century noble – a troubled young woman – more or less exiled to the Barren North. She was found floating face down in the lake.' She looks up with a jerk of her head, and speaks more briskly. 'Not one of my ancestors, Inspector – Sir Horace Montagu-Browne acquired the castle in the early 1900s. The heyday of the whodunit, you might say.'

Skelgill's countenance tells of his unease with the direction of travel – but curiosity gets the better of him.

'And this affair with the bairn – what was that about, madam?'

'Oh, yes – nothing sinister – but typical of the sort of thing we experience. We hosted an extended family for their Christmas break. The principal married couple were using the two top-floor rooms for their children. They put their youngest child – just a toddler, eighteen months – to bed in Lady Anne's chamber. They locked the connecting door so her siblings would not disturb her. The parents were directly below. In the morning they were woken by the faint sound of crying – but when the mother went up the stair she found the outer door locked as well. They imagined one of the brothers had crept in and was playing a prank. But when the other children were summoned they were all present and correct.'

Skelgill is impatient for the outcome.

'So, what did you do?'

'Well, by enormous good fortune the key was perfectly aligned in the keyhole – I was able to push it out with my spare – and we gained entry. Otherwise there would have been a challenging job for the fire brigade.'

'And the bairn was on her own?'

'Certainly.'

'She locked herself in?'

'Aha – that, Inspector, is a matter of conjecture. The parents insisted she had never before climbed out of her cot – and certainly not whilst zipped into a sleeping bag – it would have taken some extraordinary gymnastic vault! And then to crawl

like a caterpillar to the door and to reach up and engage the key –
in their modern home they have no such locks. But, of course,
she was too young to provide an account of her actions.'

Lavinia Montagu-Browne regards Skelgill and DS Jones in
turn and, content with their bemused looks, gives a snort of
triumph. Clearly the principle of strange goings on is something
to be celebrated, as far as she is concerned. She unclasps her
hands and pats her thighs, as though she rests her case.

'Would you like to see Lady Anne's chamber just now – or I
imagine you will want to speak with Mr Liddell – and, perhaps –
my half-brother?'

Skelgill takes a moment to formulate his response.

'Aye – all of what you've just said, madam – in that order.'

3. LADY ANNE'S CHAMBER

Sunday, midday

'O n the advice of your constable I have kept it locked – the interconnecting door as well.'

While Lavinia Montagu-Browne stoops to insert the blackened iron key, Skelgill exchanges a sharp glance with DS Jones. That PC Dodd took such a precaution – without exactly going to the lengths of declaring the bedroom a crime scene – suggests that something about the situation had troubled him, albeit that his report did not stray from the plain facts. His visit, in the wake of the ambulance, had taken place during the period while Will Liddell was absent.

'So nobody has been in – since when, madam?'

The woman rises to face him.

'I should say it was 8.30pm last night – I showed the officer around the empty suite and he was with me when I locked up.'

Skelgill nods.

'And this external door – it was unlocked at the time?'

'Yes?'

She looks puzzled. Skelgill realises she is probably unaware of the account they have received – that the room was locked prior to the discovery of Scarlett Liddell's lifeless form. He sees no requirement to enlighten her.

'Mr Liddell hasn't needed to retrieve any personal effects?'

She regards Skelgill a little suspiciously.

'No – I have kept both sets of keys – we have a secure cupboard in my office.'

'What about yourself, madam – have you been in?'

For fleeting moment a frown clouds her features. 'Oh no – I quite understand – you would want the suite left undisturbed – don't forget I am something of an amateur sleuth when it comes to whodunits, Inspector – or, at least, when it comes to laying down clues – and red herrings.'

Skelgill looks discomfited by the prospect.

'Madam – it is standard police procedure to treat all apparent suicides as suspicious deaths in the first instance. It's our job to provide sufficient evidence for the Coroner to bring a verdict of suicide, in order for a death certificate to be issued. It's in the family's interest – and that of the wider public.'

'Of course, Inspector – let me guide you – I can perhaps highlight the salient points.'

But Skelgill steps across in front of her. He holds out a restraining palm, in the manner of a traffic cop.

'I'm afraid I'll have to ask you to leave us to ourselves for the time being, madam.'

Lavinia Montagu-Browne looks for a second like she is about to stamp her foot – but in the event she does not attempt to argue. Rather grudgingly she presses the key against his palm – and then digs into the pocket of her skirt and produces a slightly smaller one, which she also hands over.

'For the interconnecting door.'

'We shan't be long, madam. We'll come and find you to organise seeing the others when we're finished.'

She nods obediently, though there is a distinct look of disappointment in her dark eyes. She takes a couple of paces backwards, obliging her to step down from the cramped stone landing onto the spiral stair. She seems reluctant to depart.

'Inspector – in case I don't get the chance – my half-brother, Tom. I ought to warn you that you may find his manner rather awkward.'

'Aye?'

'He suffers from a form of autism – he's highly intelligent – but he finds discourse uncomfortable – especially if he is being questioned – he may come across as rude, cantankerous – or perhaps unreasonably obstructive – but it is just his manner, you understand?'

Skelgill stares at her for a moment; he senses DS Jones is watching him, no doubt interested in his reply.

'There's nowt so strange as folk, madam.'

*

Skelgill's first impression is of a large bedchamber, low ceilinged and gloomy, despite south and west facing windows – undersized and recessed into the thick stonework, like those of the library. A four-poster bed – unslept in, though the counterpane is disarranged and a pillow has been pulled out from beneath the covers – dominates the room. He looks for lights – but there are only individual table lamps and a standard lamp in one corner. He switches them all on. He turns in time to see DS Jones squat to gather up a loose white bundle from the carpet between the bed and the external wall – for a split second he thinks it is a cat – until she raises one arm and lets the item unravel – it is the feather boa. He strides across and takes it from her. He examines the fabric of the item minutely, scowling like a biologist presented with some new species to classify.

'This is braided cord these feathers are stitched to.' He whistles through his teeth. 'You wouldn't snap that in a hurry. Non-stretch as well.'

He passes it back to DS Jones – two-handed she expands it like a hank of wool: the ends are tied together to form a continuous loop.

'She must have twisted it round her neck, Guv – then looped it over the hook.'

Skelgill is baring his teeth.

'Let's have a deek.'

They move into the bathroom. Sure enough on the back of the door is a solid brass hat-and-coat hook. A white towelling robe lies crumpled on the floor in the corner, more or less beneath. Skelgill grabs hold of the longer spur and gives it a couple of hard tugs – the device is secured by four slot-head screws, size 6 he guesses – it feels to him that if it were a climbing hold he could trust it with his weight. It is set just above his eye level; he is five or six inches taller than his colleague.

'Stand there – try it – see if this stacks up.'

DS Jones makes a face of exaggerated trepidation. But she passes the boa over her head like a garland, twists it once and then reaches up to loop it over the hat spur. She turns easily to face him.

'It's long enough, Guv – possibly too long.'

'If she'd put in a few more twists – that would have shortened it. Like if you spin yourself round.'

With a rueful grin, DS Jones ducks out of the noose.

'I'll skip that part of the experiment, if you don't mind.'

However, she backs against the door, beneath the hook, and bends her knees to demonstrate a second point.

'There's not a huge margin of error, Guv – she would have needed to make her legs give way – in which case her weight would still have been partially supported.'

'Or jerk them off the ground completely.'

DS Jones frowns as she tries to imagine whether such a contortion would be possible. Skelgill meanwhile starts to make a cursory inspection of the contents of the bathroom. An array of toiletries has been neatly merchandised upon a glass shelf; it has the look of a beauty counter in an upmarket store. His face is grim – lotions and potions that do not smell of ground bait are anathema to him.

'She may not have meant to kill herself, Guv.'

Skelgill – despite himself – is examining a packet of "anti-aging serum", scowling as he wrestles with the hyperbole printed on the box. He makes a distracted grunt of acknowledgement. DS Jones continues.

'The forensics course I attended in January – there was a module on suicide investigation – the statistics indicate that roughly half of all people who make an attempt are actually in the 'cry for help' category. An early-intervention programme at a university in the USA reduced the death rate by 55%. Also, a significant proportion of suicides are accidental – Guv?'

Skelgill is still holding the wrinkle-reducing balm – though now he has his face pressed close to a vanity mirror.

'Aye?'

'Usually it's an overdose, or –' She hesitates. 'Or in some instances a sex game gone wrong.'

Skelgill puts down the cosmetic, but he does not meet his colleague's gaze. He lowers his head distractedly, and digs his hands into his pockets – but then he pulls them out again and swivels on his heel and strides out of the bathroom. He speaks over his shoulder.

'Keep an open mind, eh, lass?'

DS Jones takes a few moments to look about the bathroom. She satisfies herself there is nothing more of significance. She carries the boa with her – and places it on a chair beside the main door. Skelgill, meanwhile, has disappeared into the dressing room. She enters to find him unlocking the interconnecting door. It opens to reveal a second, identical door, flush with the first. Skelgill knocks but does not wait for a reply and immediately tries the handle – however, the door is locked – he drops to one knee and places his left eye against the keyhole.

'The key's in it.'

He rises and knocks again, more vigorously – and calls out, "Mr Liddell?" – but there is no answer, or sound of movement.

'Perhaps they're all down at lunch, Guv?'

A picture of thick-cut honey-cured ham and ale-steeped wholegrain mustard on lavishly buttered farmhouse bread suddenly hijacks Skelgill's thoughts. He can feel his mouth beginning to water. He swallows, and shakes his head to dispel the image – inadvertently giving the impression that he gainsays his subordinate. He turns his attention to the interior of the dressing room. It is more of a walk-in wardrobe – equivalent in depth to the bathroom, being part of a continuous partitioned section, but shorter in width, a floor space of about eight feet by five. There is a freestanding cheval glass, and a brass clothes rail running the length of one side and shelves and pigeonholes on the other. DS Jones begins to browse carefully through little stacks of exotic-looking garments filed neatly in several of the latter.

'There's no shortage of underwear, Guv.'

Skelgill does not reply. He is looking at a set of matching wheeled designer luggage, arranged in descending size order beneath one end of the hanging rail, on which an extensive collection of skirts, dresses, slacks and blouses is displayed.

'Never mind three nights – you'd think she'd come for three weeks. Look here – there's the thick end of a dozen pairs of fancy shoes.'

But DS Jones seems disinclined to disparage. Her expression has become one of introspection. It is as if this act of physical immersion in Scarlett Liddell's decadent wardrobe has recalibrated her insight – after all, the dead woman was close on her own age. And it tells of a lifestyle to which most young women would surely aspire. When she responds her tone betrays some other emotion – and certainly not envy, it is more a note of wistful frustration.

'There must be thirty thousand pounds' worth of clothes here, Guv.'

Skelgill detects something of her conversion; he swivels to face her.

'What are you saying?'

DS Jones turns out her full lower lip in an exaggerated gesture. She takes down a silk dress from the rail and holds it in front of herself before the mirror and strikes a model's pose.

'You'd think all this would make you happy, Guv.'

Skelgill's gaze is fixed on her reflection, his eyes wide – though he does not reveal the source of his reaction, nor offer to expand upon her supposition. Instead he steps past her, back into the bedroom. He crosses to a Queen Anne walnut dressing table topped by a misty triptych mirror, which is set before the south-facing window. The first thing that strikes him is the presence of two glasses – one a traditional martini glass with a residue of yellowish liquid, and the other an empty sherry glass. He scans the various grooming accessories – but the item that he reaches for is a black envelope embossed with a gold leaf art deco pattern and the name *Mitzi* printed in matching Rennie Mackintosh type. The envelope is open – Skelgill withdraws a card designed in the same style – also black, with the text reversed out in gold. He does not attempt to read it.

'Look at this.'

DS Jones approaches and takes the card as he offers it. She reads aloud.

'You are Mitzi, housekeeper and cook, a refugee from war-torn Europe. You are paranoid, believing someone is out to get you. When the lights go out in the library and shots are fired, you are in the dining room, polishing the silver. The door is locked on the outside. You become hysterical and begin screaming loudly.'

DS Jones turns the card over, but the flip side is blank.

'Is that it?'

'Seems to be, Guv. Perhaps they get more instructions as they go along. Or maybe they just improvise.'

Skelgill looks away, rather disinterestedly.

'What happened – in the book?'

A smile forms upon DS Jones's lips.

'I'm afraid I can't tell you, Inspector – you will certainly want to read it someday.'

She does a passable impression of the upper-class accent of Lavinia Montagu-Browne.

'Very funny, Jones.'

'Actually, it's a clever plot. One of her classics, like the lady said.' DS Jones glances again at the description on the card. 'I don't see any connection – other than maybe the locked door – but locked doors were Agatha Christie's stock in trade.'

Skelgill appears unhappy with what he is about to say. It is through gritted teeth that he speaks.

'This *Mitzi* character – does she get bumped off?'

DS Jones shakes her head.

'In the first instance it's the intruder that is killed – shot, apparently by his own gun.' She grins once more. 'And that's not a spoiler, Guv – in fact it probably tells you that in the blurb. I suppose from the point of view of this party – Lavinia

Montagu-Browne playing the victim keeps all of the guests involved the game.'

Skelgill is making a series of pained faces – some of them it seems for DS Jones's benefit – for it prompts her to question him directly.

'What is it, Guv?'

'Happen I'll just buy this book – take it up to the Chief – tell her I've got this new way of solving crimes. Never mind sending folk on fancy courses – you find a story that's vaguely like your case – hey presto!' He snaps his fingers. 'The butler did it.'

DS Jones shows her amusement with a broad smile, flashing her even white teeth.

'Actually, Guv – you're describing Miss Marple's method. Though it's not always the butler.'

Skelgill strides over to the window on the west side. He leans into the recess, supporting himself upon the heels of his hands on the deep sill. He contemplates the outlook.

'How come you're such an expert on Agatha Christie?'

'Oh.' DS Jones is checking under the bed. 'My Gran is a massive fan – she's got the entire collection. I used to read them when I was a teenager. There are so many that Gran insists you don't need any other books. By the time you've finished the last one, you've long forgotten the first – so you can just start again. *The Mysterious Affair At Styles.'*

Skelgill seems pensive. It is half a minute before he speaks.

'Aye – I'm a bit like that with my *Wainwrights* – amazing how much slips your mind.'

He remains looking out of the window. Though he is silent, his lips seem to be moving. Perhaps he is testing himself on the names of the visible fell tops and landmarks. There is a good view of the slopes of Barf ("insignificant in height, but hostile and aggressive" according to Alfred Wainwright), and the Bishop, the whitewashed rock pinnacle that baffles many a passing visitor. Beyond is Lord's Seat, maintaining the lofty theme. The day is cool and bright and breezy, and fair weather clouds are roughly reflected in the quite choppy waters of Bassenthwaite Lake. Above the ridge a buzzard sails downwind, shadowed by a small murder of crows. Skelgill pulls away from the window, ducking low to avoid catching the back of his head. He casts about the room, but in a general, rather vague way.

'We'd better lock up – and get those spare keys off her ladyship.'

DS Jones aims a sharp glance at her boss. The significance of what he says does not escape her.

'Do you want to get forensics in?'

Skelgill shrugs dispassionately.

'Happen they'll find something we've missed. Even if it's just for the record.'

He stoops to pick up some small object from the rug. It looks like a large hairgrip – he bridges it between his thumb and the tip of his ring finger, and turns it absently with the fingers of his other hand. Then he gestures loosely at the dressing table, where the two glasses stand – usually the first port of call for fingerprints. Now DS Jones is looking at him still more acutely.

'Think it *is* a crime, Guv?'

Skelgill manufactures a wry grin.

'Can't tell you, lass – that would be a plot spoiler.'

4. WILL LIDDELL

Sunday, early afternoon

Along with the library, on its south side, the medieval heart of Greenmire Castle boasts on its raised ground floor a dining room with windows facing west, and a drawing room; and to the east a billiards room and a study. It is to the last of these that Lavinia Montagu-Browne has directed Skelgill and DS Jones.

A youthful face – that could be taken for the countenance of a man ten years younger – turns up towards them as they enter without knocking. That the face is also expressionless strikes Skelgill as odd, although not in any way that he can put his finger on – is it the face of a man still in shock from his traumatic experience (quite plausible) – or the face of a man with something to hide? That Skelgill should entertain the latter idea can be based on no facts that they have encountered – but it forces him to consider whether he has subconsciously gleaned some information upon which Will Liddell's unnatural reaction suddenly casts a light.

However, as they make introductions and convey their commiserations, and Skelgill explains the necessity for their interview, it is a feeling that begins to dissipate – for the man's expression does not markedly change. Perhaps after all it was not an unguarded response but simply his way of being – a rather unemotional, apparently humourless manner, a man not tending to loquaciousness, but one from whom information has to be patiently drawn. Perhaps it is a learned business trait, where the first rule is to give nothing away to one's adversary, especially in times of setback – or perhaps it is a similar ethic ingrained much earlier in life. That is something with which Skelgill can identify.

He notices the man's eyes flick appraisingly over DS Jones as she takes her seat, and while she is preoccupied with extracting her notebook and pen from her shoulder bag. It is a natural enough thing to do, though DS Jones is wearing close-fitting black stretch jeans, and it seems the man's gaze lingers as she settles herself and crosses her legs.

Their seating arrangement is of several comfortable Georgian wing armchairs, old in style but new in condition, in keeping with the ambiance of quality that pervades the upmarket establishment, crowded around a coffee table. On this lies an expensive laptop that Will Liddell has gently pressed shut before rising to receive them.

His boyish appearance is furthered by his medium height (on moderately stacked heels), neat build, short dark hair cut in no particular fashion of the day, and features that neither seem to have enlarged with puberty nor subsequently settled with the onset of early middle age. He has a narrow, serious mouth, pale unblemished skin, no obvious cheekbones – indeed it is a doughy characterless visage housing small sky-blue eyes that rove about without great urgency. There are dark half-moon shadows beneath, which can be put down presumably to a night of broken sleep. Only the nose perhaps, leaves anything of a lasting impression, drooping and broader at the tip than the rest of the features might easily accommodate. Skelgill notices he has a modest paunch beneath a *Pringle* sweater worn over a polo shirt; and, without looking overweight, a general fleshiness that goes with good eating. Overall, it is the look of someone unwinding in the members' lounge of a prestigious golf club.

And his accent supports this notion, it is what might disparagingly be called 'Edinburgh English', the lingua franca of FPs of the Scottish capital's myriad private schools, the professional class, and does not really sound Scots at all. In such tenor he responds to Skelgill's request to describe the discovery of his wife's body.

'I was concerned that Scarlett was late coming down to the library. We needed to be in our positions by 7.30pm. I went up but her door was locked and I could get no answer. I had handed my cocktail to Suzy Duff and she offered to come back up with me, the other way. We climbed the opposite staircase and went through my room, and the dressing rooms. Scarlett's suite seemed deserted – until I looked in the bathroom –' He swallows. 'And there she was.'

Will Liddell reaches for a glass of what looks like plain tap water. He sips, and replaces it. Skelgill is reminded that he is thirsty. It has not escaped his attention that they have not yet been offered refreshments (never mind his fantasy ham sandwich).

'And what did you do, sir?'

'I said to Suzy to call an ambulance – urgently. I lifted Scarlett through onto the bed – unwound the feather boa – I couldn't break it.' He looks at his hands, as if there might be marks. 'Then Suzy was performing CPR – until the paramedics came and took over. After a while they put her on a stretcher. I went with them to the hospital. But they couldn't save her.'

Skelgill detects a glance in his direction from DS Jones – it is just a casual movement – but he knows she is concerned by something in the man's reply. However, he accepts the explanation at face value, and moves on.

'Was there anything about your wife – her past behaviour – that might explain what she did?'

'Absolutely nothing.'

Skelgill is surprised by the sudden vehemence of Will Liddell's reply.

'Nothing at all, sir?'

'Naturally I have been running over all this.'

'Was she taking any medication? For depression, for instance?'

'No. But I imagine you will have access to her medical records.' There is just a hint of irritation in the man's tone – perhaps that his testimony is being challenged.

'What about non-prescription drugs, sir?'

Within the strictures of his rigid countenance Will Liddell seems to bridle. Plainly he takes offence at Skelgill's euphemism.

'Scarlett wouldn't touch so much as a cigarette.'

'The preliminary toxicology report indicated she'd had quite a lot to drink.'

'No more than anyone – it is the nature of these events. And perfectly legal.'

The exchange has become rather terse. Skelgill shifts in his seat, and looks around – though there is little of note in the rather gloomy study – the oak panelled walls are hung with ornately framed portraits – why did they paint them so black? Was life so dark? However, the room is at least cheered by a fire that smoulders in a grate just across from them. Skelgill can see a means of improvement – he has to resist the urge to go over and rearrange the logs. He returns his gaze to Will Liddell.

'What exactly *is* the nature of this event, sir?'

The man's expression distinctly softens; indeed he seems almost to demand sympathy.

'It was my birthday – on Friday – you know, *The Big Four-O?*'

Skelgill senses again that DS Jones is looking at him – no doubt expecting him to announce the coincidence – to make some remark that will claim the date for himself. But though he is certainly jolted, and has to wrestle with competing thoughts, it is a more oblique rejoinder that comes out on top.

'First day of spring.'

The man looks blankly at Skelgill – and in this small action tells Skelgill a good deal about himself – confirming the impression conveyed by his attire and demeanour, and in a broader sense the very fact of his coming to Greenmire Castle – that he is not an outdoorsman of any shape or form – but a metropolitan type (in the majority, it must be said) for whom the countryside is something with which to engage superficially, in the same category as a cinema complex, a shopping mall, or even a holiday to a hot climate where luxury hotels line up along fake beaches of imported bulldozered sand and craned-in palm trees. And, too, that they found him on his laptop in a room he has commandeered as a private office – when Skelgill is certain that in similar circumstances he would be tramping the fells, immersed in the elements, wind tugging at his hair and rain lashing his face, Mother Nature assuaging his agonies. Will Liddell does not answer.

'So – the other couples that are staying, sir – I take it these are your friends celebrating your birthday with you?' The easing of Will Liddell's features is replaced by a subtle frown, as if he finds the question intrusive. It prompts Skelgill to qualify his reasoning. 'Rather than being your wife's friends – that's what I mean, sir.'

There is a pause before the man responds.

'We're *all* friends. But if you're asking for a common denominator, we each have a daughter in S2 at the same school. St Salvator's Academy.' He scrutinises them in turn for signs of recognition, his gaze resting longer upon DS Jones. 'Wester Coates – Edinburgh.'

Skelgill is nodding comprehendingly.

'So in fact you're all mutual friends?'

Still the man seems needlessly reticent.

'On the whole. There are certain other connections.'

'Such as what, sir?'

His description comes in economical terms.

'Derek Duff, I've known since university. Mike Luker is a financial advisor to my holding company. Kevin Makepeace works for one of my subsidiaries.'

'What about your wife, sir – is there anyone in the group that was a particularly close friend of hers?'

'Naturally, she got on well with all of them – she got on well with everyone. But she hadn't known them as long as I have.'

'When were you married, sir?'

'It would have been two years this coming June.'

Skelgill inserts a respectful pause.

'I understand her family live mainly in Paris, sir?'

He glances at DS Jones and she nods in confirmation. However, it is Will Liddell that now interjects.

'They will be flying over tomorrow.'

His lips twist as if he experiences a bitter taste – it seems he does not want to dwell on this aspect of the tragedy. Skelgill spreads his long palms in a conciliatory gesture.

'We'll have a trained bereavement counsellor look after them, sir. I appreciate some of these questions are awkward – but we need to be prepared for the sort of queries the family will have. It's only natural for people to want to understand why something like this has happened.'

Will Liddell has been sitting still and upright, an almost combative pose with his clenched hands laid on his thighs; now he folds his arms.

'It could not have been prevented.'

'What makes you so certain, sir?'

'It was totally out of the blue – and out of character. How can one anticipate something like that?'

Skelgill rocks his head slowly from side to side – it is not a normal gesture of his; he might be gingerly testing strained neck muscles.

'Is it possible she was just messing around, sir – that it was some kind of tragic accident?'

Again it seems that Will Liddell is angered – but closer inspection reveals that in fact he has some enthusiasm for what is surely a long shot. He stares penetratingly at Skelgill.

'For a split second that was what I thought – that she would jump up and cry, "fooled you!" – there had been jokes all day and speculation about who would be murdered.' But now his expression sours once more and he lowers his gaze despondently. 'But you couldn't act that.'

The three sit in silence for a few moments; until Skelgill clears his throat; his tone is matter of fact.

'How did you meet your wife, sir?'

Will Liddell looks up – again he seems discomfited by what is an innocuous question.

'She worked in one of my companies.'

'And she worked with you, personally?'

'She was recruited by their export marketing department.'

'So what brought you together – if you don't mind my asking, sir?'

Will Liddell looks like he does mind – but he must conclude there is no good reason to withhold his response.

'I was investing in a company in Marseilles – our personnel manager identified her as a fluent French speaker – she was co-opted onto the acquisition team based in our corporate unit.'

Skelgill nods. He realises further probing risks trespassing upon ground that is perhaps too close to home, that might be interpreted as prying for its own sake, rather than pursuit of knowledge that will justifiably help him to do his job. Besides, in this regard there are alternative avenues of approach.

'Coming back to this weekend, sir – was there anything that occurred that on reflection might have had a bearing on your wife's suicide – even the smallest thing, as it may have seemed at the time?'

Will Liddell does not answer – he looks blankly at Skelgill and shakes his head. He seems determined that on this point he has no more to add. Skelgill tries again.

'For instance did she get into any argument – or did she see or hear something that might have upset her?'

Still the man is unforthcoming.

'At risk of sounding repetitive, Inspector – there's nothing I can tell you. If there were, I was not aware of it. The whole idea of this weekend was for everyone to have a good time, and that was what Scarlett was doing. When last I saw her she was laughing and joking with the other girls.'

'Where was that, sir – what time?'

'After we'd arrived back from Greystoke – it must have been about five o'clock. We had afternoon tea in the drawing room. She was still there when I went up to my room.'

Skelgill looks puzzled.

'You didn't have any contact with her after that, sir?'

'I took a bath. Then I lay on my bed to deal with some emails.' He makes a small hand gesture towards his laptop. 'I fell asleep – we'd already had a couple of late nights. When I woke up it was seven o'clock – that was when we were due downstairs. I dressed in about a minute flat.'

The account appears to end here. Skelgill presses for more detail.

'Did you not think to check on your wife, sir – to see that she was ready?'

Will Liddell's features seem to be frozen; only his small mouth moves, like a ventriloquist's dummy.

'I did check on her.'

'How did you go about that?'

'I went through her dressing room. The bedroom was empty – silent. I called her name in case she was in the bathroom. The door was ajar – but there was no answer.'

'But you didn't look, sir?'

'I assumed she'd gone down – or was getting ready in one of the other girls' rooms – they'd been discussing their outfits and hair and make-up – I wouldn't have been surprised if they'd got together to apply the finishing touches.'

Now Will Liddell looks to DS Jones – as though seeking confirmation that his suggestion is plausible. However, she returns his gaze implacably. Skelgill watches the silent exchange.

'So the interconnecting doors – they were unlocked, sir.'

'Yes, of course.'

'But the stair door of your wife's room – you didn't try that?'

'I had no reason to, Inspector – it didn't cross my mind. I don't think anyone has been locking their doors – why would we? Besides, I was cutting it fine and my watch and cufflinks were in my room. I went back that way and directly down to the library.'

Skelgill is silent for a few moments. When he speaks, it is more ponderously than is usual.

'So if I'm reading this right sir – unless we get any contrary information from your fellow guests – sadly, it seems likely your wife had already taken her own life when you called her at 7pm or thereabouts.'

A shadow clouds Will Liddell's features – a trace of concern? – that he perceives responsibility is being heaped on his shoulders. His eyes flick questioningly from one detective to the other.

'She could have been somewhere else. It was twenty minutes later that we found her.'

'Were you not surprised when she wasn't in the library?'

'Yes, possibly – except *no one* was there – other than Kevin Makepeace – and Tom, the butler chap, serving the cocktails. Kevin buttonholed me about some project he's running – there's been a problem and he obviously wanted to let me know he's got it taped. Then the others started to appear and I was distracted – but as time went on I realised only Scarlett was missing.'

'That was when you were speaking with Mrs –'

'Suzy Duff.'

Skelgill nods. The man's account has now turned full circle. His own manner becomes more casual, his tone less probing.

'Have you discussed with your friends, sir – why it might have happened?'

It is a moment before Will Liddell provides an answer.

'They have tried to console me, naturally. But they could probably see I was best left to my own devices.' It takes just a subtle change around his eyes and mouth for his expression to convey displeasure. 'Besides – they are probably in shock – it's not an ideal time to have a rational discussion.'

Skelgill seems prepared to take the hint.

'I quite understand, sir.'

He turns to DS Jones – seamlessly she picks up the dialogue.

'Mr Liddell – it might be helpful if we could examine your wife's mobile phone.'

'How would that help?'

'We have to satisfy ourselves that there were no suspicious circumstances – it's our legal obligation, as Inspector Skelgill has explained. If there is no indication of a problem on her social media accounts, then that will go a long way to closing the case. Alternatively – it might provide an explanation for what she did. Which surely you would want to understand, sir?'

Though Will Liddell's eyes remain cold, there is something in his manner that relents. He stares for several seconds at DS Jones.

'It is in my room – inside my briefcase. I picked it up from her bedside last night – took it in the ambulance. You're welcome to it, Sergeant. The screen is cracked.'

DS Jones crosses her wrists casually over her thighs, and bends at the waist. Her voice is calm and unthreatening.

'What made you take it with you, sir?'

He continues to gaze at her but does not immediately reply. Then he too leans forward but as he does so he drops an elbow onto the arm of his chair and bows his head, and shields his eyes with his palm.

'I thought she'd want it – when she recovered.'

5. SOUTHWAITE

Sunday, 5.30pm

I f Skelgill were a man actively to seek coincidences (which he is not; connections are his bag), it would strike him that there is a modest one in the river that he overlooks while he kills time waiting for his colleagues. The Petteril – a relatively anonymous but productive trout stream – has its source up near Penruddock, and its waters wander for a day or so about Cumbria, ultimately to supplement the mighty Eden above Carlisle. However, though he has covered not dissimilar ground, this is not the coincidence he might mull over. Instead, it is that the river's erratic course takes it through both his present location, beside the hamlet of Southwaite and – earlier in its journey – through Greystoke, a quiet backwater that has been mentioned more than once today. But such multifarious coincidences dog a man whose job it is to detect. Another: below is a trout stream; the season opens tomorrow. Another: he is starving; the motorway service station is two minutes' drive. Or is that a *connection*?

*

'Sorry for the delay, Guv – I had to wait twenty minutes for that Tom geezer to show up – turns out he was down at the lake doing something to a rowing boat.'

Skelgill does not rise as DS Leyton pulls out a chair, but he does admit the courtesy of lifting onto an adjoining table his tray with its scoured plate and loosely discarded alloy cutlery and drained stainless steel teapot, extensively littered with torn packets of salt and sauce and sugar. He makes no discernable sign of acknowledgement towards his sergeant, but remains tilted to see around his stocky frame. He squints across the refectory.

'DS Jones is getting us some fancy coffees – she won't be a mo.' (Skelgill nods once.) 'She's filled me in on the drive up. How'd you get on, Guvnor? Reckon we've got a wrong 'un?'

Now Skelgill pushes back against his plastic seat and folds his arms; for the first time he looks properly at his colleague; his features contort into a shrewish expression, showing his top front teeth.

'I'll keep my powder dry – while I hear what you pair have got to say.'

DS Leyton shrugs patiently and settles himself at the table. He neither expects nor receives any commendation for interrupting his family Sunday lunch, and postponing until some indeterminate time partaking of his wife's homemade rhubarb crumble. He obeyed with stoicism the summons from Skelgill to take over from him at Greenmire Castle while his superior acted upon a call from Carlisle – from the hospital – to be precise, from the resident pathologist.

'DS Jones spoke to the ladies – I saw the blokes. Quite a posh crowd, eh, Guvnor? Must cost a pretty penny – hiring that place. Imagine – people once lived like that.'

'Some still do, Leyton.'

Now DS Jones appears at DS Leyton's side bearing a tray, and he applies Skelgill's supposition.

'Nice one, Emma – I could get used to being waited on. All I've got waiting is a sink full of dishes.'

Skelgill eyes the tray – he looks like he might still be hungry.

'You should eat out more often, Leyton – saves on the washing up. It's cheap enough if you know where to go.'

Now DS Leyton grins. On their travels about the county, if it is not a river or pond that Skelgill is pointing out, it is an obscure eatery, backstreet café, mobile burger bar – or hotel kitchen, where one of his many dubious relations is employed, trained to dispense leftovers from the tradesman's entrance. On reflection, it is probably not a bad strategy from a budgetary perspective – and it cannot be as unhealthy as Big Brother would have it – for despite his appetite his superior carries barely an ounce of fat on his wiry frame. Now, as he shifts aside to enable DS Jones to deposit the tray of promised coffees, he sees Skelgill's lupine eyes fasten upon a plate of cookies.

'Aye – well I shan't keep you, Leyton.'

Skelgill possibly nods his thanks as DS Jones lifts one of the mugs across and pushes the plate closest to his reach. He selects a biscuit, snaps it in two, and promptly dunks a sharpened end into the chocolatey froth of his drink.

'Top line – anything?'

DS Jones glances a little apprehensively at her fellow sergeant. Though she is undoubtedly enjoying a much steeper career trajectory than he (indeed, his might be said to have stalled – probably to his contentment), by dint of service he is the more senior officer. However, it is she that has been coordinating matters – and he gestures willingly that she should speak for both of them. She folds her arms onto the edge of the table, and looks up at Skelgill with a furrowed brow.

'Nothing concrete, Guv – but – well, maybe enough to keep an open mind at this stage.'

Skelgill is eyeing her suspiciously – she seems to be hedging her bets.

'We went through a series of questions with each of them – to cover their movements, what you might call 'state of mind' issues, and then past history. Necessarily it was a little superficial, given the time constraints. And they were all keen to leave – understandably, they want to get back to their kids.'

Skelgill is now nibbling distractedly at the remaining fragment of cookie. He does not appear to identify with the sentiment. After a moment he nods for her to continue.

'Probably the most significant point is that no one saw Scarlett Liddell after she left the drawing room at about 5.20pm.'

She turns briefly to DS Leyton for confirmation – he nods supportively. She goes on.

'The four women all left together and went to their individual rooms. There's a route through the central hallway to the foot of the tower – both towers, actually. Technically, Felicity Belvedere

— that's Kevin Makepeace's ex-wife — was the last person to see her alive, because she was on the floor below. She says Scarlett Liddell continued on up the staircase. The last thing she heard was the slam of the door — and nothing thereafter.

'As for reconvening in the library, Felicity Belvedere says she knocked on Belinda Luker's door — she thinks about 7.10pm — and they continued together. They knocked on Suzy Duff's door in passing, but there was no answer. She had gone down a few minutes before and was talking to Will Liddell when they arrived. Suzy Duff said she brought it to Will Liddell's attention that hadn't his wife better come soon — and that was when he went to chivvy her along. Up to a point their accounts correspond — that he came back down saying the door was locked and there was no answer — so she volunteered to go up with him in case Scarlett Liddell was indisposed — she said with *women's trouble* — to which he agreed.'

Skelgill is frowning over the rim of his mug. He has his head tipped back in an effort to avoid the froth. It is not an easy manoeuvre for a man endowed with his physiognomy — he lowers the mug to reveal only limited success. He smears the sleeve of his jacket across the tip of his nose.

'And where they *don't* correspond?'

DS Jones regards him reflectively.

'I suppose it's more omission than divergence. I noticed when Will Liddell described to us finding his wife he made it sound like Suzy Duff was with him the whole time — as though she had telephoned for help on the spot. He didn't mention that she left the room. She says she raced down to the library — screamed at the others — and it was the butler Tom Montagu-Browne that shot off to raise the alarm — then she ran back up with the rest of them — that's when she realised she was the only first aider.'

'Did she unlock the door?'

'She says she can't remember — but that she supposes she must have done. Certainly she used the women's staircase — for want of a better description.'

'How long was she gone from the bedroom – Lady Anne's room?'

'She thinks about a minute – or two at the most. The time it took to descend and ascend four flights. It wouldn't take long, Guv – she looks quite a fit woman.'

'What was Will Liddell doing when she got back?'

'He'd laid his wife on the bed – removed the feather boa – but was just staring at her helplessly – "in shock" was her description.'

Skelgill is pensive – he glowers at the plate of surviving cookies.

'What about the rest of them?'

DS Leyton flicks out a hand.

'Help yourself, Guv – I've had chicken dinner – plus I'm on pain of death if I don't eat the missus's pudding.'

Skelgill darts an admonishing scowl at DS Leyton – but nevertheless he takes him up on his suggestion. Meanwhile DS Jones supplies an appropriate response to the question.

'It was only a couple of minutes more before Lavinia arrived in the room – she took control – at least as far as shepherding everyone but Will Liddell and Suzy Duff back downstairs. She broke out the vintage brandy to calm their nerves.'

There is a short contemplative silence. DS Leyton is first to speak.

'The Liddell geezer probably *was* in shock, Guv – it does funny things to you. I got some award once – out of the blue, called up to the stage in assembly. I mean, *me* – winning an award! It was all a blur – couldn't remember a thing afterwards – apparently I even made a flippin' acceptance speech!'

Skelgill looks irked that his sergeant has digressed – but curiosity gets the better of him.

'What was the award?'

'Most improved player, Guv – you know the old thing – make the fat kid the goalie – that was me.' He shakes his head reflectively. 'Bit harsh on the others really – reckon I had a head start – far as room for improvement was concerned.'

46

DS Jones is regarding her colleague benevolently, but Skelgill's expression is more one of pity tinged with horror. However he eschews the open goal (viz. room for improvement) and instead drags the discussion back on track.

'How do the men's movements stack up?'

DS Leyton snaps out of what appears to be fond reverie. He has his pocket notebook on the table, and he flips it open to the current marked page. 'They all went up to their rooms to have a rest after tea – get their glad rags on. Kevin Makepeace was the first one to go downstairs – said he was bang on the gong at 7pm. Seems like he gets on okay with his ex – but reckons he didn't have any interaction with her – kept to their own rooms. The other two – Mike Luker and Derek Duff – similar story – except they'd both had their adjoining doors wide open. But they'd agreed the chaps would go down separately from the ladies. They went about five minutes before their wives – maybe 7.05pm – said Suzy Duff was the first woman to arrive, just after them, then the other two women a few minutes later.'

He looks up questioningly, first at Skelgill – who regards him blankly – and then at DS Jones, who gives a nod of encouragement. He runs the fingers of one hand through his tousle of dark hair and makes a laboured expiration of breath, vibrating his rubbery lips.

'If what you're looking for, Guv, is that someone went to Scarlett Liddell's room before seven o'clock – seems to me like they'd have needed to slip past Will Liddell, one way or another.'

Skelgill's subordinates regard him with anticipation – they seem to suspect he has some particular calculation in mind. But his expression is one of dissatisfaction. As he sees it, the permutations are plentiful – and therefore constitute unedifying speculation. They cannot even be sure that each guest has given an accurate account of their movements. Rather than dwell on such imponderables he moves the conversation forward.

'What are they saying about Scarlett Liddell?'

DS Jones is first to respond.

'I have a ream of notes – but in a nutshell it's, *"complete shock – out of character – can't think why she did it."* But I get the feeling everyone is treading on eggshells right now – if only out of respect for Will Liddell.'

'So there's more to it.'

'Reading between the lines – quite possibly – I mean, so far as their relationships go.' She is nodding in response to Skelgill's statement. A strand of her naturally streaked honey blonde hair becomes displaced; she blinks and brushes it away. 'Felicity Belvedere and Belinda Luker were both circumspect. I think they would have preferred not to engage at all. Suzy Duff was more forthcoming – for instance she referred to them expecting Scarlett Liddell to make her "usual grand entrance", once everyone else had arrived.'

Skelgill gives a small shrug, as though he is indifferent to such a narcissistic trait. He looks at DS Leyton.

'What did the husbands have to say?'

DS Leyton gives a rueful grin. 'Nothing so complicated, Guv. Nice girl – *beautiful* girl – not a bad word. Just that Will Liddell had fallen on his feet after his divorce.'

Skelgill raises an eyebrow at this latter remark. He is thinking how gravity seems to favour men with fat wallets in this regard. However it prompts his next question. He directs it at DS Jones.

'Any mention of the ex-wife?'

DS Jones shakes her head.

'Not as such, Guv. As Will Liddell said – this social group stems from having daughters in the same year at school – Year 7 now – so the adults have had ample time to become familiar. They meet for dinner parties, and there have been several trips like this one – including skiing during school holidays with the kids. Obviously, for most of that period, it was the first wife that was present – not Scarlett Liddell.'

Skelgill ponders these words. But he trusts his sergeant to have sniffed out anything salient. Since she has nothing to add, he does not trouble himself with inventing further questions. Instead he turns to DS Leyton.

'How about Tom Montagu-Browne?'

'Some cranky cove, he is, Guv.' DS Leyton makes a distressed face. 'Hope he's got better flamin' manners when he's

48

doing his butlering. You'd think I'd accused him of strangling Scarlett Liddell and stringing her up!'

Skelgill glances at DS Jones – perhaps she did not relay Lavinia Montagu-Browne's cautionary words about her cantankerous relation. With a note of irony in his voice he plays along with DS Leyton's hyperbole.

'What was his alibi?'

'What? Well – I didn't exactly ask him outright, Guv. I couldn't very well go round treating everyone like murder suspects.' DS Leyton sounds rather flummoxed, as though he has taken Skelgill's question more seriously than it was intended. 'I was concentrating on Scarlett Liddell's movements. Tom Montagu-Browne confirmed that she left the drawing room after tea with the other women – 5.21pm, actually, he said it was – and that was the last he saw of her. He reckons if she were moving about the ground floor after that he would have seen her – or anyone else. He was busy between the drawing room, the dining room and the kitchen – then at a quarter to seven he started to mix a tray of cocktails in his butler's pantry – that's got a hatch that overlooks the hall – just before seven took the drinks into the library and waited for the guests to arrive.'

Despite this matter-of-fact account, it is plain to see that DS Leyton shoulders an air of unease.

'So what made your lugs prick up?'

DS Leyton shifts a little apprehensively in his seat.

'I suppose it was more an impression – rather than what he actually said.'

'Aye?'

'When Suzy Duff burst into the library – he said the guests thought that was the Murder Mystery game kicking off – but he didn't hang around to put them right. He went straight to Lavinia Montagu-Browne's office and told her to call 999.'

Skelgill is frowning.

'It's his condition, Leyton. Say something to him – he'll take it literally. That's obviously what he did.'

DS Leyton shakes his head reflectively – as though this does not ring true with his experience of the man.

'Guv – I get that. It's just – I dunno – there's another way of looking at it – I mean – what if he didn't question it – *because he knew what had happened to her?*'

Skelgill is looking increasingly pained.

'Think about it, Guv – if anyone could sneak around without arousing suspicion, it would be him. Plus he'd have access to spare keys.'

'Scarlett Liddell's door was locked on the inside.'

'We don't know that, Guv – we don't even know if the key was actually in the lock.'

Now Skelgill feels he must state his objection to hypothetical scenarios. His tone is unduly severe.

'Leyton – there's a hatful of ways folk could have been in and out of that room. I've already given up thinking about it. So should you.'

DS Leyton looks suitably chastised. He is familiar with Skelgill's attitude in circumstances such as these, and realises he ought to know better. He holds up his hands in a placatory gesture.

'I realise that, Guv – it was just, well –' He makes a growl of exasperation in his throat. Then he seems to give up on the point. 'Like you say – maybe it was just his cranky manner.'

But DS Jones is watching Skelgill intently. For what she sees is not a desire to sweep under the carpet any possible irregularities – but in fact a sentiment underlying his stern countenance that she recognises as *doubt*. As such she provides a prompt – an outlet for his discontent.

'How did you get on at Carlisle, Guv?'

Skelgill – in typically capricious fashion – grimaces uncooperatively. He resettles himself in his chair and slides his coffee mug to a revised position. It is twenty seconds or so before he replies.

'There were a couple of things. The duty pathologist last night was a locum in training. As a matter of protocol the senior pathologist reviewed his findings this morning. She performed a second examination and ran some additional tests.' He pauses, and with furrowed brow stares across the cafeteria beyond his colleagues. 'There was light bruising on the lower forearm – both arms – matching the pattern of being held firmly. It was fresh – caused the same day – hadn't really developed. Easy to overlook.'

DS Leyton is leaning forward eagerly.

'What – like someone restrained her, Guv – held back her arms?'

Skelgill continues to glare vacantly into space; he answers reluctantly.

'Aye – but you're forgetting something. What did they tell us? They were at the rope-swing park at Greystoke all afternoon. I know one of the instructors – he's in the mountain rescue. I gave him a bell after I'd left the hospital. He reckons there's a half a dozen activities where folk have to help one another. For example, if you're a lightweight there's a flying fox that doesn't reach the lower station – your teammates have to lean out, grab you by the wrists – haul you onto the platform.'

Skelgill's own associates look suddenly deflated – that he has supplied them with the oxygen of a breakthrough, and then in the next breath has snatched it away. But DS Jones senses that he has not finished.

'You said there were a couple of points, Guv?'

Skelgill's gaze now returns from the abstract of their surroundings to the specific of his coffee. He breaks a cookie in half and drops both pieces rebelliously into the foam. He lifts the mug but does not immediately attempt to drink. He looks from one to the other of his subordinates, his face severe. He seems to be trying to decide upon whom to address. In the event his eyes fall upon DS Jones.

'She was three weeks pregnant.'

6. REST AND BE THANKFUL

Tuesday, 6.15am

Skelgill has been woken by gibbons.

It is not the anticipated dawn chorus – which in fact began much earlier, and in its lilting familiarity did not disturb him as it drifted on the cool air through his wide-open hotel window. But the jungle hullabaloo, a persistent drawn-out electronic piping that with first light penetrated his dreams brought on a spell of fitful hallucinations. Skelgill, becoming semi-conscious, was reminded that his budget accommodation backs on to Edinburgh Zoological Gardens. Perhaps he should have asked for a room at the front. But – hey – up with the lark – up with the gibbon – what is the difference? He had pulled on his walking shoes and moseyed along the deserted Glasgow road in the direction of the city centre, whence a breach in a wall admitted him into a dense stand of sycamores; above these a heathland of steeply rising gorse and bramble scrub, topped with gnarled Scots pines and oaks and beeches; quite an extraordinary wilderness within the metropolitan limits. Now, plateauing and puffing a little, he has followed his nose through a stone arch, a choke point between zoo security fencing and a golf course – to arrive at a spectacular window upon the 'Athens of the North' – although with typical Calvinist rectitude a signboard merely declares, 'Rest & Be Thankful'. Accordingly, there is provided a bench, above a stone wall, below which another rocky path wends up from the east. The vista is positively vertiginous, telescoping over a sweeping emerald fairway, across the great grey volcanic barnacle cluster of the ancient city, to the silver sands of the East Lothian coastline where – as the information post relates – the Bass Rock stands proud 26 miles hence, its solid white cap an optical illusion, an agglomeration of 150,000 northern gannets. Skelgill sinks down – not in need of the rest, but thankful for the solidity of the bench. He is just pondering why the Bass Rock is so called, and how many mackerel a gannet eats in a year (one a day, two, three?), when he is hailed.

'Good morning to you.'

This only adds to Skelgill's sense of disorientation – the voice is of indeterminate origin; it resounds in the ether. He rises and takes a couple of steps forward. He realises that over the wall, below him on the steep declivity, is an elderly man. Of a rangy build he is clad in an all-black outfit of waterproofs, walking boots and a trapper hat with the flaps tied up, revealing protruding ears matched in proportion by a long bulbous nose, red at the tip, and a wide mouth with spittle at the corners. He stands side on to Skelgill, facing out over the golf course; a small black backpack hangs on the spiked railings. He is performing what Skelgill suspects might be Tai Chi.

'I'm disturbing your peace.'

'You're fine, young man – talking doesn't affect my routine. Besides, I'm used to it – this is a busy spot.'

'Even this early?'

'Och, aye – you'd be surprised how many folk are up and about. I get a lot of Chinese.'

The man is clearly Scottish, well spoken.

'How's that?'

'Jet lag.'

He performs an intricate series of hand and arm movements (aircraft, maybe?), balancing on one leg. Skelgill is about to ask a supplementary question when the man pre-empts him.

'Tourists from China. When they land their body clocks are eight hours ahead. They stay in the big hotel down on the Glasgow road. Wake early – find their way up here.'

'You're kind of describing what I did – except it was the gibbons got me up – not jet lag.'

'Nor do you hail from so far afield.'

The man's intonation invites a response.

53

'Cumbria.'

'Ah – now there's a wonderful place.'

Skelgill can't help some affected modesty, when better decorum would be to return the compliment.

'Happen it's alright, aye.'

The man generously makes a sound of agreement in his throat.

'I used to fish there at one time – must be forty years back. Bassenthwaite Lake. I expect you've heard of it?'

Skelgill feels another wave of light-headedness crashing over him. Should he pinch himself? Did the gibbons really wake him up – or is this still the feverish dream: a torrid flight across the Scottish Highlands, malevolent pursuers, their unearthly cries sapping his resolve? Bass Rock – fish. Fishing – on Bass Lake! Is the old man a ghost that haunts this ancient trackway? Shall Scarlett Liddell be the next apparition? He is wrestling with such fancies, when the man speaks again.

'Are you here for a spring break?'

The question hauls his thoughts back to reality. He wavers. In his profession, this line of conversation can prove problematic. But where a white lie is normally prudent, there is something about the happenstance that defeats his resistance, and he finds himself answering truthfully.

'I'm a police officer.'

'Aha! Cross-border bootleggers?'

He can see the man is half grinning – and half grimacing, as he continues his vigorous routine. There is an irony – some would say hypocrisy – that for public health reasons cheap whisky now costs more in Scotland than England, and Cumbrian purveyors are handily placed to restore the natural equilibrium.

'Holidaymakers. Just tying up a few loose ends. Parents of kids at a local school.'

'Ah – which one – if you don't mind my asking? You know how we Edinburghers are obsessed by our *alma mater*. I'm a Watsonian, myself.'

Again Skelgill hesitates, but can find no reason to withhold the answer.

54

'St Salvator's Academy.'

'Ah – Sallies! Par excellence. All girls, of course. A rarity nowadays.' He makes more mystical shapes in the air. But he might also be directing Skelgill's gaze with a crooked finger. 'You can see the school – over there. In line with the castle rock? Come this side of the verdigris domes – that's Donaldson's – the Deaf School, as locals like to call it. Sallies is the sandstone tower.'

Skelgill squints into the rising sun. A mile or more away, on a bearing that must be precisely due east, he spies the square tower protruding from a zone of bare treetops and grey tiled roofs. It is not a suburb he knows, for the Water of Leith in its wooded gorge borders the north side, and thus there are no through routes.

'Looks like a pretty decent area.'

'Och, aye – Murrayfield, Ravelston, Coates – the lawyers' and financiers' ghetto, you might say. An upstanding community.'

Skelgill notices the man casts him a sly sideways glance – and he wonders if he is being ironic. Or perhaps that Skelgill himself has revealed too much – the implication that he is investigating the Scottish capital's upper-middle-classes – of which the elderly man is likely a member. He nods – though the man is no longer looking at him.

'Where's Blackhall?'

'You can't quite see it from here because of the bank of trees to your left. It forms the north side of Ravelston. Rather more affordable. Nonetheless – desirable – well placed for the local schools – private, that is.'

Skelgill has no immediate rejoinder. Then a flickering movement and whirring sound catches his attention. Close beside him on the wall a nuthatch has alighted and is prising a sunflower heart from a crevice. The man must have scattered seed. He realises that other birds – blue, great and coal tits, and chaffinches – are likewise engaged, while avaricious jackdaws lurk on low boughs, willing the humans to depart.

On such a note Skelgill feels a rumbling – it bears no relation to the igneous topography – but has its origins in his midriff. If he returns now the hotel refectory might have opened. However, he contrives a more serviceable excuse.

'I'd better head back – my colleague will be thinking I've been abducted by aliens – I didn't bring my phone.'

The man takes this as a cue and interrupts his exercise routine and steps up to the wall. He reaches above head height, offering a gnarled hand to Skelgill. His grip is firm.

'David Balfour.'

Skelgill feels a certain reticence creeping over him.

'Er – nice to meet you. I'm – Dan.'

'Well – goodbye.'

It seems to be a perfunctory farewell – yet there is some suggestion they have not seen the last of one another.

'Aye – be seeing you.'

Skelgill turns to move away. But at this moment from the higher path that curves off around the zoo appears a runner – a female; she comes at a lick, despite the uneven ground. She has on a coordinated outfit of lilac and black – but most striking is a shock of flaming red hair, only partly tamed by a headband. Skelgill freezes – while at the speed of light his mind is transported back to the hospital mortuary – it requires a double take for him to remind himself of the facts – *Scarlett Liddell is dead* – and this is Scotland, home of the redheads (if not exactly ten a penny, then certainly one in ten). Besides if Scarlett Liddell were a jogger, he doubts if she came here; he knows enough local geography to understand that the Liddell's residence is in The Grange, over in the Southside.

The woman approaches quickly, not labouring at all, despite the punishing gradient that she must only recently have conquered. She is younger than he, he thinks maybe around thirty. She watches the uneven ground as she skips down a flight of steps formed by railway sleepers. Skelgill backs against the wall to make way. She notices him. She has striking green eyes. They meet his. Her expression is wary. His gaze tracks her athletic form, the figure-hugging *Lycra* – but she dodges left at the end of the wall, leaving only a hint of chic fragrance on the breeze. There is a brushing at his shins – he looks down — two

Cocker Spaniels scamper past, dragging their unruly hindquarters around the sharp turn. Skelgill can feel his heart in his chest. Then he hears the man's voice.

'Good morning, Catriona!'

Skelgill does not catch any reply – nor hear properly when the man hails the dashing spaniels. He draws a deep breath – and sighs – and begins to saunter pensively back down the southerly path. But he has covered maybe twenty paces when a cry stops him dead in his tracks.

'Skelgill!'

He spins on his heel. Sure enough it is David Balfour – he has come round the end of the wall and is stooping to get sight of Skelgill through the early-budding shrub layer of hawthorn and elder. Skelgill stands scowling, perplexed.

'I'm sorry?'

'*Skelgill.*' The man raises a palm to shield his mouth, to project his words. 'That was the chap's name. It's coming back to me now. Fellow that took me fishing on Bassenthwaite Lake. Bit of a joker – had this line he'd trot out – how it was the only lake in the Lake District. And his boat was called *Covenant.*'

7. BREAKFAST IN CORSTORPHINE

Tuesday, 8.30am

'Would you know if you were three weeks pregnant?' Skelgill is looking out of the plate glass that separates their table from a drop of some forty feet, above a steep bank of shrubs and grass where half a dozen rabbits graze, inured to the honking line of city-bound commuter traffic that tries to squeeze past a concertina of double-decker buses that jostle for places at a stop. DS Jones glances up from her pink grapefruit – the question, posed casually, has come out of the blue. Skelgill continues to stare analytically at the jam; however she suspects his concentration is affected.

'I believe you might.' She waits for a moment; Skelgill begins to bite distractedly at the corner of a thumbnail. 'I think some women feel immediately hormonally different. Of course – if you had it in mind in the first place – you'd be sensitive to any signs. Or – you might have done a test – and you can't get a false positive.'

Skelgill, still without looking directly at his sergeant, raises an eyebrow. This was not a subject that came up during their journey last evening – two hours north through the Borders, Skelgill driving rapidly, skimming corners and occasionally lifting off over humps, a route familiar to him, off the tourist trail and largely devoid of traffic, hugging the Tweed. Dusk had folded into darkness, and in turn the motion of the car had lulled DS Jones into sleep. Skelgill had glanced at her from time to time – as they passed through a settlement and the shimmer of streetlamp neon illuminated her high cheekbones and the hollows beneath, the proud nose, only slightly curved, olive skin darkened by shadow. He'd seemed contented with her relaxed form slumbering softly beside him – when deprived of company he might have been peeved. She had woken only at the very last minute – eyes wide – alarmed to find him ignoring 'No Entry' signs to snatch the last parking space beneath the hotel, in Edinburgh's sprawling western suburb of Corstorphine.

That they had embarked at all stemmed from a review meeting with the Chief – and the conclusion that sufficient doubt surrounded the death of Scarlett Liddell to merit further investigation. Calls were put in to the neighbouring Scottish authorities; Skelgill and DS Jones tied up loose ends on current projects (in Skelgill's case by dumping an armful of bulging files in DS Leyton's in-tray); and they set off at the end of the day, in order to begin promptly this morning. Although not present at the meeting, straws in the wind tell DS Jones that this course of action hinges upon Skelgill's determination. That is, a determination that a pregnant Scarlett Liddell would not have committed suicide. While some may argue the exact opposite – that pregnancy provided the likely explanation for her actions – it is plain that Skelgill is having none of it. Why he is so vehement – she can only speculate. But the corollary: without using the actual words, they have effectively embarked upon a murder enquiry.

Of course, a whole spectrum of possibilities stretches between suicide and murder – and such uncertainty probably underlies Skelgill's reticence. A tragic accident before the mirror; a sex game gone wrong; a misguided act involving persons unknown; a moment of madness without murderous intent – all of these and more – many times complicated by unknown relationships and motives. To unravel such a web is their task. But first they must understand its scope.

'What about telling Will Liddell, Guv?'

Skelgill frowns.

'*Asking* him.'

DS Jones raises a hand, correcting herself.

'If he knew, you mean?'

'Aye.'

She nods – her boss makes an important distinction. Just because the man never mentioned his wife's pregnancy doesn't mean he was unaware of it. And therefore if he didn't mention it – then perhaps that is significant.

'So what should I do?'

'There's tests still being done. Tell him we'll have a final report in a few days. Keep your cards close to your chest. Play it by ear.'

DS Jones smiles benignly. That seems clear enough, as clichés go! That she presses him for advice on this point derives from their plan of action. At Skelgill's behest she will interview the three males who were Will Liddell's guests at Greenmire Castle; Skelgill will see their partners. And when Skelgill has an appointment with Will Liddell's ex-wife, she will see Will Liddell himself. While there is a certain logic in this arrangement, she can never be entirely sure of her superior's reasoning (indeed, *reasoning* is probably too exact a word). Thus, she chooses not to seek clarification that may not exist.

And yet now – perhaps in response to her silence – Skelgill reveals second thoughts.

'Sure you'll be alright?'

'Why wouldn't I be, Guv?'

DS Jones tries to appear irked – but it is contrary to her nature; equally she wishes to exhibit self-confidence. However, Skelgill does not pursue the point – instead he casts up a hand, rapping his knuckles against the glass of the window. The suggestion is of a reference to the sky, a pale blue canvas dabbed white with fair weather cumulus that tilt gently to the east.

'Fancy a quick stretch of the legs – get the blood flowing?'

'It already is, Guv – I went to a class.'

'What kind of class?'

'Most places like this have a rolling programme for members – hotel guests can just join in. There's a swimming pool – it was aqua-aerobics.'

Skelgill is looking like she describes his worst nightmare.

'Who does that kind of thing?'

'Well – it was mostly elderly ladies – I was the youngest by a generation – but they seemed to appreciate the instructor.'

'What was so good about her?

'It was a he.'

8. BLACKHALL

SUZY DUFF

Tuesday, 10.00am

'Mrs Duff?'
'Yes? Ooh – oh, dear. It's, erm – isn't it?'
'Inspector Skelgill.'
'You don't look like a detective.'

Skelgill has to wrestle with the urge to query this statement – but he sidesteps the diversion to concentrate upon the more pertinent matter – that Suzy Duff appears to be leaving her home – in the company of a dog – at precisely the time an appointment has been arranged. Indeed, had he not arrived several minutes early – having come on foot and covered the ground more quickly than he allowed – then it seems he would have missed her altogether. Now they stand facing one another in the slabbed driveway of what is a large semi-detached bungalow, with harled walls painted white, shy of a fresh coat, and a roof of grey slate tiles, one of hundreds alike in this neighbourhood, a style characteristic of Edinburgh. There is a car – a fairly ancient tan-coloured *SAAB* turbo, that frankly looks well past its sell-by date (and might ordinarily attract the interest of a bored traffic officer) – and at the side of the property a basketball hoop, its net frayed, and beyond a section of patchy lawn with a rusting trampoline backed by stringy leafless shrubs; though an unruly *Forsythia* is in bright yellow bloom. It is the dog that now prevents Skelgill from forming any more impressions – for it is on an extending lead and it makes a rush at him before its owner can engage the locking trigger. It is an overweight Labrador (a tautology, it always seems to Skelgill) – chocolate, and typically fat and happy – it only wants to shake him down of any treats. He drops to one knee to absorb the impact, and contains its exuberance with firm hands that he knows the dog will understand.

'Rolo! No! Leave the nice man alone! Rolo – down!'

Suzy Duff does her ineffectual best to restrain the creature, but Skelgill is not bothered and the dog soon remembers it has more pressing needs and makes a second surge, this time for the freedom of the open entrance of the driveway. The woman is jerked in stages until she stands beside Skelgill. To his surprise she leans close and brushes at his thigh with her free hand.

'I'm sorry – he's covered you in hairs.'

Rather taken aback Skelgill finds himself having to endure her ministrations.

'Don't fret – I'm used to it. Like me to take him?'

'But – don't you want to come inside?'

Skelgill shrugs. 'I'm fine with walking – here, let's have it. Besides – dogs can't cross their legs like we can.'

He reaches out for the leash and she seems content to yield – and immediately he detects a willingly compliant nature. The dog, on the other hand, knows his own mind – systematically tagging with invisible canine graffiti favoured gateposts and trunks. That Suzy Duff now walks at his shoulder somewhat hinders Skelgill's ability to take in her appearance – but what he has seen is striking for a couple of reasons. The weather might be fair, but sunshine on Leith does not guarantee warmth – there is a chill in the air, borrowed from the adjacent North Sea. Yet she wears only black leggings and trainers, and a thin, close-fitting woollen polo-neck – and certainly no bra beneath – and it is not difficult to guess she is feeling the cold. Her hair looks damp – unbrushed – as if she has half-towelled it dry and given up – in her hurry to get out? Before he arrived?

And yet now she seems perfectly at ease. As they engage in polite if insubstantial conversation about the district he notices she has a habit of turning towards him and placing a palm on his upper arm, as if to communicate a point effectively requires some physical transmission. She is of medium height, and narrow-waisted if curvy build; and she steps out at a brisk pace. He would concur with DS Jones's assessment – that she looks fit, and that the spiral staircase at Greenmire Castle would pose few challenges. As they take a route that sees them veer off the suburban avenue into a walled lane, and sharply uphill, she shows no indication of shortness of breath.

'You can let him off here – it's the beginning of the nature reserve.'

Skelgill scowls but pretends it is the sun getting in his eyes. The contradiction does not elude him – quite how loose dogs and a nature reserve go together – but then perhaps that is why he has not heard a pheasant calling this morning. In any event, the thought passes – for he realises this must be the easterly approach to the viewpoint where he encountered David Balfour, he of the Tai Chi.

'I'm guessing this is your regular route.'

Skelgill tips his head towards dog, which seems to know where it is going.

'It's so handy having this lovely wild area nearby. The woods go on for miles. You can walk all the way to Queensferry Road.'

Skelgill nods. He glances sideways.

'Obviously keeps you in good shape.'

For a second he wonders if he has overstepped the mark. She turns to gaze at him. But the action does afford him his first proper look at her face – she is undoubtedly an attractive woman – her lips are full, she has symmetrical curved brows and large dark eyes – she exudes a voluptuousness that seems inviting. Again she has her hand upon his shoulder; her lips part into a smile that reveals even white teeth. And she affects a certain helplessness.

'That comes with running round after four children.'

Skelgill makes a sharp intake of breath – but it is in the way of suppressing a second compliment – that she does not look like she has borne such a clutch of squabs. He lengthens his stride.

'They all at St Salvator's?'

'Heavens, no – we could never afford it. Just the eldest, Poppy. The other three are at the local primary. I don't know what we'll do when the next one starts at secondary – that was when we moved Poppy out of the state system.' Fleetingly she wrings her hands. 'You see – Derek went to Heriots. I think once you've been to private school, you can't believe you can receive a proper education anywhere else.'

Skelgill makes a vaguely discontented growl.

'Most folk seem to get by.'

For a moment she looks hopefully at him. Then her face sinks resignedly – as though she is quickly reminded of the intractability of the dilemma.

'It's an Edinburgh thing. The national average is single figures – here's it's twenty-five percent of secondary age pupils. In our circle of friends it's almost total. You'd feel like you're depriving your kids if you didn't send them.'

'There must be *some* decent state schools.'

She shakes her head sadly.

'You have to live in the right catchment area. Derek doesn't want to move. It's his family house, you see? Never mind the cost and upheaval.'

There ensues a short period of silence.

'We have your occupation down as housewife – if I recall.'

It is the first question Skelgill has asked that befits a formal interview. However, Suzy Duff seems to interpret it as the natural consequence of the point under discussion.

'If I did go back to work we'd need a full-time nanny. That would absorb most of my earnings. It's a *Catch 22*. We don't have the luxury of grandparents living locally. Or pots of money. Though Derek's ever optimistic. He thinks this could be his breakthrough year.' She emits an exaggerated sigh. 'Then again – he was saying that ten years ago.'

They are by now near the end of the steep track that bisects the golf course. There is the occasional metallic thwack of a ball driven ferociously off a tee – each to their own; as an angler Skelgill knows not to question seemingly pointless hobbies – though he does watch with dismay as two golfers having tapped their balls to within a few feet of a flag pick them up and march off. Looking up he recognises the gap in the wooded outcrop that rises before them to be the viewpoint he earlier approached from the south. As they reach the bench he half expects Suzy Duff to stop, or turn back, but she walks on briskly, a little ahead of him; she shows no sign of flagging, and easily scales the steps the redheaded runner skipped down. The image jogs Skelgill's memory and focuses his quest.

'The constable who contacted you will have explained – I need to ask you about Scarlett Liddell.'

'Sure.' She does not look around, but slows where the path widens so he can come alongside. She waves an arm loosely. 'We can continue on for a while – then loop around via Craigcrook Road – if you don't mind doing the last bit on the pavement.'

'Fine by me, madam.'

This time she seems to detect the hint of formality. Her response is disjointed.

'I suppose – in the case of suicide – you can't just leave it at that – if you have any doubts?'

Skelgill ignores the inquiry. Instead he replies with a blunt question of his own.

'Did she look like she'd committed suicide?'

Suzy Duff abruptly swings round in front of him and places a palm against his chest. Her free hand grasps the sleeve of his jacket. Her eyes are filled with alarm. She pouts imploringly.

'I didn't see her – not initially.'

Skelgill looks positively awkward – he leans back, his brows knitted.

'What do you mean, madam?'

'We went through the dressing room into the bedroom – the door to the bathroom is on the right – with the hinges nearest to you – you know?' (Skelgill nods once.) 'The door was ajar – but obviously you couldn't see inside. Will was first – he looked round the door – he just screamed at me for God's sake to get an ambulance.'

Skelgill shifts his weight from one foot to the other. Suzy Duff is pressing closer – a passer-by might judge them to be a couple caught in the throes of some passionate exchange. He steps around her and moves on, if a little ponderously, for she clings to his sleeve – as if for comfort.

'So – what – you left the bedroom without looking at her?'

'Yes. The way Will said it – I knew he wasn't joking.'

She bites her lower lip, her eyes downcast – she seems to be reliving the moment.

'So – was there part of it – that didn't surprise you – that made you not question what Mr Liddell said?'

'Well – yes, perhaps – but I didn't know what she'd actually done – I mean – she might have just been sick – or fainted and banged her head.'

Skelgill gazes pensively as they walk on, perhaps seeing wood not trees. A jay shrieks with grating anxiety from a great oak up to his left, agitated by a feathered interloper.

'When you got back to the bedroom – you told my sergeant that Mr Liddell had lifted his wife onto the bed – unwound the ligature?'

Suzy Duff is frowning. She nods several times, the amplitude diminishing.

'I could see straightaway she wasn't breathing. There was no pulse – although to be honest I don't know how I could tell that – my own heart was bursting out of my chest.'

Again there is a period of silence before Skelgill speaks.

'Did you think you could save her?' His tone is strangely sympathetic – as if he is saying he understands her actions were futile.

'What else could I do but try?' She gives a frustrated tug of his jacket. "You must have done first aid training, Inspector?'

Skelgill nods, but does not otherwise answer.

'So you know there's always a chance.'

'If you're quick enough on the scene, aye.' Skelgill inhales laboriously. 'I've known folk be kept alive for the best part of an hour by CPR – but that took a team of rescuers doing it in relays.'

Suzy Duff shakes her head in a rather exaggerated fashion, as if she is trying to deter midges from approaching.

'I've never done it before – I went on a course – at the time of my last job. You got extra pay if you were a first aider. I never thought I'd have to use it. I probably made a complete mess of things.'

'Happen you were all too late getting there. That weren't your fault.' He says this with some authority – as though he is quoting the official medical report. 'It's commendable that you tried.'

She squeezes his arm thankfully.

'Well – I appreciate your saying so – it must have been awful for Will – having to go to the hospital – hoping against hope...'

Her voice tails off. They walk on in silence. All around the steeply sloping woods are positively thronged with birdsong – beautiful to the human ear, in reality it is avian testosterone pumping, as cocks vie for hens and sling vicious insults at their rivals; it is not a fitting requiem to the morbid subject of their conversation.

'Madam, coming back to what you said about not being entirely surprised – could you expand on that?'

Her expression becomes one of pragmatism – perhaps she is relieved to move on from discussion of her fruitless life-saving.

'I think it would be fair to say that Scarlett could be a little melodramatic. She liked to be the centre of attention – and temperamental when she wasn't.'

'What reason would she have had for behaving like that?'

Suzy Duff's eyes narrow reflectively.

'Well – I suppose with the trip being for Will's birthday – I guess everyone was making a bit of a fuss of him. After all – he was treating us – what else could we do?' (Skelgill remains silent.) 'You know – it's like with the kids – if you praise one of them another may take it as a slight – the next thing they're teasing the dog or setting fire to the curtains to get attention for themselves. It can be quite subtle – I mean, kids don't even know they're doing it.'

68

Though Skelgill might beg to differ when it comes to arson, he lets the remark pass.

'She was younger than the rest of you.' He throws this in casually – though he suspects it might be inflammatory. But it seems to draw empathy rather than animosity.

'Yes – she perhaps seemed a little immature – but she couldn't help her age – and it was Will's choice, wasn't it – a younger woman?'

'It's no big deal, is it – especially for a female?'

Skelgill has said this before he realises it. He sees she is regarding him with curiosity.

'We older women must have some advantages, Inspector.'

There is a note of mischievous reproof in her voice.

'Aye – aye – of course.' He senses he has backed himself into something of a cul-de-sac. 'Youth's wasted on the young, isn't it?'

Impetuously he breaks away from her grip on his sleeve and retrieves a stick from beside the path. He whistles to get the dog's ear, and sends the missile spinning through the trees, down the steep slope to their right. The dog makes a token charge – but the stick gets caught up in low branches – and the dog finds some musky scent more salient. Suzy Duff watches Skelgill with interest.

'You're left-handed, Inspector.'

Skelgill manufactures a grim smile.

'Aye – a cuddy wifter we call it – a cuddy's a donkey.'

She laughs. 'You don't appear to be handicapped by it.' Now she smiles at him warmly, and her brown eyes shine with admiration. 'I expect living in the Lake District keeps *you* pretty fit.'

He restrains an urge to rise to the compliment, though he shrugs with affected modesty. But the subject enables him to pursue a point that has been niggling.

'You all went to the rope-swing adventure park at Greystoke.' (She nods, readily, showing that she realises he wants to continue questioning her.) 'How did that work out?'

'Oh – well – I was surprised how many groups of adults were there.' She frowns – as if she is trying to recall something of substance that will please him. 'Scarlett's team won – she was quite happy about that – if you were wondering.'

Skelgill's features remain implacable.

'Who else was in her team?'

'Well – we split up the couples. There was Scarlett, with Belinda and Kevin – and my Derek, of course. Then I was with Felicity and Mike, and Will.'

'Who picked the teams?'

'Oh – Will had them prearranged. We were handed coloured helmets and harnesses when we arrived. There was no arguing.'

Now Skelgill nods benignly.

'And how did it go?'

'Actually – I was rather dreading it – I think we all were – except perhaps Kevin; he's something of an action man. He enters triathlons.' (Skelgill raises a sceptical eyebrow; though without good reason.) 'But we had a great time. It really did involve teamwork – you'd never have got around the assault course without hauling and pushing one another. Of course – it became quite competitive – I guess we're all driven in our own ways – but I'd say it was a big success.' She falls suddenly silent. 'Such a tragedy – the way the day turned out.'

Skelgill makes a sound of agreement.

'How well did you know Mrs Liddell?'

'Oh, Muriel – well – oh – no – sorry, you mean Scarlett?'

'Aye, Scarlett Liddell.'

'Sorry – it's just that when you say "Mrs Liddell" I automatically think of Will and Muriel – his first wife?'

'Aye – I have an appointment to see her.'

Suzy Duff snatches a sideways glance at Skelgill.

'So – yes – Scarlett – I don't think I met her until the wedding – she rather appeared out of nowhere as far as I was concerned. Naturally Derek told me something about her – he's been seeing Will for a drink on Sunday nights since they were at university together – so he knew a bit about her beforehand – that Will was getting divorced and that he had a younger girlfriend.'

70

'So that's within the last couple of years you've got to know her?'

'Roughly every six or eight weeks we take it in turns to host a dinner party – the four couples, I mean. And last October – the school week – we all stayed in some converted farm cottages on an estate down at Coldstream.'

'On the Tweed.'

'That's right – the boys were all fishing – Will organised boats and ghillies every day.'

Skelgill's mind is boggling at the prospect – both the luxury of fishing what is arguably Britain's premier stretch of water – and the likely cost, peak season; when even half a day's guided salmon angling is out of the reach of most ordinary pockets. And he wants to ask whether they caught anything. It takes him a moment to get back on track.

'How did Scarlett Liddell cope with the domestic situation – the children – and her husband's ex-wife?'

Now he seems to have found a point of contention. For it requires some consideration on her part to settle upon a response.

'The children live with Muriel – Will has them alternate weekends – I mean – they don't – they *didn't* – exactly see Scarlett as the wicked stepmother – but they're old enough to understand that she might have been the catalyst for their home breaking up – at least, to believe that – if that's what they hear.'

'And was she?'

Suzy Duff now gives an exaggerated shrug of her shoulders.

'That would depend upon whom you ask, Inspector. Only Will and Muriel know what happened between them – but I doubt either could give you an unbiased account.'

Skelgill nods reflectively.

'What about the two Mrs Liddells – was there hostility between them?'

'I think Muriel decided to rise above that. They managed their lives so as not to cross paths. Will or the *au pair* did all the lifts. But Derek told me that Scarlett would get annoyed at Will if he was on the phone to Muriel making arrangements – or if she saw him giving the children extra pocket money – that sort of thing.'

'She couldn't really blame that on Muriel Liddell.'

'Of course not, Inspector. But I suspect life as Will's second wife was not always the garden of roses it seemed from the outside. In a divorce situation like that the father is always going to have divided loyalties – and a divided pay cheque.'

Skelgill seems rather doubtful.

'Happen that's not likely to be an issue as far as Mr Liddell's finances are concerned?'

'I'm sure you're right, in practice. I suppose it's the principle that Scarlett might have struggled with – or maybe just the basic human emotional thing – protect what is yours.'

'It's the law of the land. There's no need to get emotionally involved.'

His terse intonation causes her to look at him questioningly – but she decides not to utter whatever thought has occurred to her.

'Yes – I suppose it is.' There is a pause before she adds a rider. 'Poor Will.'

Skelgill now watches while Suzy Duff calls her dog and clips on the lead – for they have been travelling downhill and have reached an exit from the woods into a rather sterile estate of newly built expensive-looking properties. She heads off to the right, along the smart tarmac of the pavement. Skelgill is a couple of paces behind.

'Talking of emotions – a question I have to ask everyone,' (Suzy Duff turns sharply, an alarmed expression in her eyes, as if she suspects that his timing is deliberate, now that her defences have been lowered) 'do you know if either Scarlett Liddell or Mr Liddell had any involvement with another person?'

'Are you talking about a romantic involvement – an affair?'

'Aye – that sort of thing.'

Suzy Duff's features relax, though she looks away, lowering her eyes as she begins to reply.

'I – I shouldn't have thought so – I mean – to answer your question – no – I don't know of anything like that. They've only just got together – it wouldn't make sense.'

Skelgill watches her for maybe five seconds.

'Madam – it seems to me that Scarlett Liddell's suicide doesn't make sense.'

9. MURRAYFIELD

BELINDA LUKER

Tuesday, 12.00pm

'Coffee, Inspector?'

'I'm a bit of a tea jenny, myself, madam.'

'In which case I shall make you a small pot.'

'Very kind of you, madam.'

That Belinda Luker says 'you' rather than 'us' – and declines to make light of his good-natured colloquialism – serves to reinstate Skelgill's first impression that his presence is somewhat resented. Ringing the front doorbell – a traditional brass pull – of the imposing three-storey stone-built Edwardian end-of-terrace house, and having been obliged to wait a couple of minutes, he was eventually admitted through a side door by a flustered youngish woman in torn jeans, washed-out t-shirt and *Converse* sneakers who was perspiring at the armpits and who did not appear to possess more than a smattering of English. That she had dusters dangling from her belt loops and wielded a spray bleach gun led him to deduce that she is the cleaner. Via the tradesman's entrance he was conducted directly to the kitchen – passing opulently furnished dining and sitting rooms, and other doors, unopened – where the woman indicated he should take a seat at an oblong farmhouse table with two carver chairs arranged neatly on either side. She promptly disappeared down steps into a scullery that runs off in the direction of the rear garden, a sliver of which Skelgill can see through a narrow sash window; it is well stocked with fruit trees and – in bloom – a host of golden daffodils running down beside the boundary wall of stone. The kitchen itself is high ceilinged, with a slatted clothes pulley strung above a traditional *Aga* cooker; the units, polished wooden floor and paintwork are all in new condition and spick and span – perhaps a testament to the daily. A side wall is given over to a regular arrangement of children's artworks – the large centrepiece a daubing of human figures labelled "Mummy", "Daddy", "Tabitha", "me" – and a sad-looking dog with a question mark hovering above it like a lopsided halo. Now it strikes him there are no pets in evidence – and likewise no sign of a basket, or bowls for food and water on the floor.

In contrast to Suzy Duff, Belinda Luker presents a considerably more organised appearance. Her dark wavy hair is glossy and expensively styled, and the same can be said of her outfit, a fine woollen twin set in lobster worn over immaculate white slacks; jewellery of matching lapis lazuli necklace and bracelet. Designer sunglasses of the current vogue perch on her forehead; she looks like she has just returned from, or is preparing to go to, the kind of upmarket coffee morning Skelgill imagines ladies of leisure partake of most days. Her features are fine and regular – certainly she would be considered attractive – though she lacks the warmth exuded by Suzy Duff, and her hazel eyes are severe as she lays out the tea things before him.

'I trust a mug is acceptable?'

'All the better, thanks, madam.'

Skelgill senses a hint of disapproval – as if he has failed a small test that places him in a lower class – or maybe *passed* the test, depending upon through whose prism he is judged.

'You wanted to see me, Inspector.'

She has taken the seat opposite. She has no receptacle for herself, and Skelgill realises she is not about to pour for him. Perhaps she is waiting for the tea to brew.

'You're a lawyer, I understand, madam?'

Now she regards him with more overt suspicion.

'I have not been in practice for several years. The girls and home life occupy a good deal of my time.'

That she adds the proviso – when he does not react – suggests a need for self-justification. Certainly she does not look like the traditional housewife – a glance at her manicured nails is enough – never mind the clanking char out in the scullery.

'What branch of law?'

'Corporate litigation – not your line, Inspector.'

Skelgill makes a somewhat pained face.

'You'd be surprised – fraud's only a posh word for having your hand in the till.'

Now Belinda Luker frowns. He wonders if she is irked – that she finds his manner mildly antagonistic.

'Well, that is certainly true, although incompetence is not yet a criminal offence.'

The woman speaks with near perfect diction – it makes him realise just how strong by comparison is Suzy Duff's Scots accent. Belinda Luker sits a little aloof from the table, rather stiff-backed, her arms folded. Skelgill recalls DS Jones's observation that both she and Felicity Belvedere were reluctant interviewees. Nothing appears to have changed. Now, rather ponderously he pours tea into his mug, and adds milk and sugar – sufficient of the latter to elicit the raising of an eyebrow.

'Madam, you'll appreciate, the Coroner calls the shots in cases like this, plain as the circumstances are.'

She does not respond at first. But in targeting her legal background he gives her little option but to be cooperative. He drinks thirstily, drawing breath over the hot liquid (and further disapprobation from Belinda Luker).

'What exactly is it that concerns the Coroner, Inspector?'

Skelgill, leaning over his mug, glances up inquiringly.

'I should like to know that myself, madam.' At this juncture, one of his sergeants would recognise that Skelgill's alter ego, the 'daft country copper' is on duty. 'We've just been instructed to gather some background information.' He shrugs and looks at her blankly. 'If someone kills themself there has to be a reason.'

'That is certainly logical, Inspector.'

Skelgill shifts position, as though he finds the wooden chair uncomfortable.

'From what we understand, there was nothing happened on the day – or during the weekend paid for by Mr Liddell – so we have to look back further.'

Now Belinda Luker nods – but her expression shows little accord with his statement – he wonders if her antipathy has something to do with his mention of Will Liddell's generosity; in these affluent surroundings he sees little need for such charity. He tries a more direct prompt.

'Scarlett Liddell was a good bit younger than all the rest of you. Do you think that bothered her?'

'I would say she was very strong-minded, Inspector.'

Skelgill regards the woman broodingly for a moment or two.

'Madam – you make that sound a bit double-edged.'

Belinda Luker gives a faint shrug of her neat shoulders.

'She was capricious – though I expect you know that much.'

'Aye – but we all have our moments, don't we?'

'Well – perhaps Will found her a little tiresome.'

Skelgill makes a face that hints at chauvinism.

'It's the way of the world.'

'Will likes the world to operate according to his norms.'

She says this without any rancour, as though it is a natural state of affairs. Skelgill's reply is measured accordingly.

'So what of it – she thought he was controlling – or something like that?'

Belinda Luker's eyes narrow a little.

'I did not know her well enough to judge. I doubt that I met her on many more than a dozen occasions – and always in company of the others. In such circumstances one tends not to engage in personal intercourse.'

Skelgill's eyelids flicker.

'How did you come to be friendly with *Mr* Liddell?'

Still she looks guarded – though this must surely be a less contentious question.

'I suppose technically I was introduced to him through the girls' school. I think the first time I met him was when parents were invited to the dining hall, to experience the quality of the lunches.' She glances across at the wall where the artworks are posted. 'Our eldest daughters are in the same academic year. They became friends – when children are dispersed around a large city they tend to spend time together by having sleepovers. The parents inevitably become acquainted. And then there are school social events and parents' evenings – and supporting hockey on Saturdays.'

'And Mr Liddell does that?'

'Occasionally. His daughter is captain.'

'How about Mrs Liddell?'

'If you mean Muriel – yes – it is she that attends the hockey matches. Lulu is *her* daughter, after all.'

Skelgill is looking rather bemused.

'What about Scarlett Liddell – does she get involved?'

'I would suggest only if she thought there were a risk of Will meeting Muriel. I don't believe that other people's offspring were quite on her radar.'

'Happen that were troubling for Mr Liddell?'

The woman looks unwilling to decipher Skelgill's mild use of his vernacular. But when he might have expected her to agree with the sentiment, she surprises him with her answer.

'I should not think it was too much of an issue.'

'Aye?' That Skelgill means "No?" is clear enough from his intonation.

'I doubt surrogate motherhood was something he would have craved on Scarlett's curriculum vitae.'

There might almost be some innuendo in her tone – but Skelgill responds in a more pragmatic manner.

'Sometimes when a man picks a younger woman it's with the future in mind. Child-bearing age – and all that.'

Belinda Luker, however, seems to want to stick to her underlying theme.

'I should say rather that Will was enjoying his newly found freedom.'

'I suppose it's easy enough when you can farm out the bairns every other weekend.' He shrugs. 'And someone mentioned an *au pair?*'

'Trudi – but she lives with Muriel. Where the children went, she went.'

'What about when they stay with Mr Liddell?'

'Housework for Trudi, I should hope.'

Skelgill glances instinctively towards the scullery, from where strange noises continue to emanate.

'From what you tell me – and correct me if I'm wrong, madam – would there be something of the mid-life crisis about Mr Liddell's getting together with his second wife?'

A crease forms between Belinda Luker's carefully plucked eyebrows; it is an expression of scepticism.

'That would be somewhat premeditated, would it not, Inspector? Rather cynical.'

Skelgill's prominent cheekbones seem to redden – but maybe he is feeling the warmth of the kitchen – the *Aga* pumping out heat – and he has not been invited to divest himself of his jacket. And there is the hot tea. He makes a sound resembling a harrumph.

'I was thinking along the lines of it not quite working out for Scarlett Liddell. It must have seemed a glamorous option for her – being wooed by one of the country's richest men.' He notices Belinda Luker seems to flinch as he says this. 'But perhaps being pitched into the Liddell's domestic situation wasn't all high days and holidays.'

'That is possible, Inspector.' She tilts back her head and momentarily closes her eyes. 'Though I imagine plenty of women would trade places – despite the various downsides.'

'Are there others?'

Now she shrugs, as though she has inadvertently exaggerated when there is nothing much of importance.

'Oh – as I said, Will is known to be very demanding – I'm sure anyone who has worked with him will tell you that – and he applies the same principles to his private life. He likes things to run smoothly. A free spirit such as Scarlett might have met with certain frustrations.'

'Did she have friends of her own age?'

'One assumes so, Inspector – but I understand she moved up to Edinburgh from one of Will's companies in London – about a year before they were married. So I imagine one would need to look there for acquaintances.'

'What was your impression of her, madam – did you like her?'

Belinda Luker seems a little taken aback by this abrupt twist. But Skelgill notes that she does not appear willing to soften her stance.

'I had no particular reason to dislike her – it isn't really something one considers – at least, not when an established friend presents one with someone new – that is plainly going to be part of the furniture. It would not really be the best policy to look for negatives, would it, Inspector?'

'Aye – but if you don't mind me saying – you haven't exactly been gushing about her.'

The woman glances sharply at Skelgill, and then down at her hands, which she has folded on her lap. Her narrow lips are compressed into a flat line.

'It may be that there is a generational aspect – but when suddenly a good friend whom one has known for many years is supplanted by an outsider – an unknown quantity.' She looks up, perhaps appealing for understanding. 'It can take some adjustment. It entirely disrupts the social fabric. One can't very well say, "Wasn't it jolly two years ago in St Moritz?" when it was not Scarlett but Muriel who was there.'

Skelgill evidently considers that he is on something of a roll; again his question is blunt.

'Was she a bit of a flirt – Scarlett Liddell?'

If the suggestion catches her off guard, she is unequivocal in her reaction – as Skelgill reads it, yes: in mixed company, husbands present, drink flowing, an attractive younger woman at the epicentre – perhaps all the more irksome for one approaching *"The Big Four-O",* as Will Liddell had put it.

'Well, she certainly enjoyed the limelight, Inspector.'

'And how did Mr Liddell feel about that?'

Belinda Luker folds her arms; she reverts to her starched upright stance.

'You would need to ask Will – after all, most couples have their disagreements behind closed doors.'

Skelgill leans forward and presses his palms flat on the table. He has his head bowed but when he looks up it is with an ingenuous grin – as though to admit he has met his match.

'Madam – all I'm trying to do is understand Scarlett Liddell. Her medical history indicates nothing that would point to her committing suicide. So I'm left with trying to find out if there was something in her personal life that might satisfy the Coroner. If there's anything you can say that might help me along that road, I'd be much obliged. However, I appreciate you have a natural loyalty to your friend of longer standing, Mr Liddell.'

Judging by her expression, Skelgill's appeal seems to have elicited in Belinda Luker some notion of grave concern. Skelgill waits patiently for it to manifest itself in words. In due course she obliges.

'But, Inspector – aren't you rather overlooking something?'

'What would that be?'

'I can't be the only person – I mean, it doesn't require legal training to ask oneself the question – *did* Scarlett Liddell actually kill herself?'

Skelgill makes some odd shapes with his lips, revealing his front teeth.

'You might have a point there, madam.'

A more prolonged silence now ensues. Skelgill adds tea to his mug. Belinda Luker glances impatiently at a wall clock above the children's paintings. Skelgill stares reflectively at the surface of the pale brown liquid.

'I'm sure you're not the only person to think it, madam. But perhaps the only one bold enough to say it – and happen that is your legal training.' Now he looks at her pointedly. 'After all, it was just the eight of you staying in the castle.'

Belinda Luker is ready for this.

'But you don't know that, Inspector – there could have been an intruder – besides – there were the staff. Have you investigated their movements – run background checks?'

Skelgill chuckles. He can picture her across the table in her capacity as a solicitor – and he is happier too that the game of cat and mouse (in which he is not entirely certain of his role) has been replaced with a more frank exchange.

'I can assure you we're following all the expected protocols in a case such as this, madam.' With his two index fingers he taps out a little drumbeat on the surface of the table. 'But what I would remind you of – for it's no secret – it was more or less witnessed by you all – is that when Scarlett Liddell died, her external bedroom door was locked on the inside, and Mr Liddell was through in his adjoining suite the whole time.'

Skelgill conveys these facts very much as he might to a member of the legal profession – in his case it would be a Crown prosecutor – a tactic that might pander to the woman's analytical nature. However, he senses a tightening of her features, an emphasis of the fine lines at the corners of her eyes.

'Is this why you are asking me about Will? About where my loyalties lie?'

Skelgill grins sardonically.

'If you've worked at all with the police, madam – you know what our job is. Justice trumps sentiment.'

But Belinda Luker's evident alarm only intensifies.

'Look – if you're suggesting that Will was involved – I think you would be very wide of the mark. I would say he idolised Scarlett – even if that was a little misguided. And – yes – perhaps he could be possessive – and controlling, as you say – but the idea that he – well... it's inconceivable.'

Though Skelgill seems unmoved by her spirited defence, he is half-hearted in his rejoinder.

'Happen he's got a ruthless streak when it comes to business – making money.'

'I don't know from whom you might have heard that, Inspector. Mike – my husband, I mean – I'm certain would vouch for his integrity.'

Skelgill glances at his watch. It is more than a check on the time.

'I shan't ask you to put words in his mouth, madam – there's no need for that.'

It might now strike Belinda Luker – for certainly she must have known the fact, without necessarily realising the significance – that her husband is being interviewed contemporaneously. A crafty manoeuvre to pre-empt collusion? Not that the police would admit they anticipated any such subterfuge. The woman leans forward in her seat, her hands pressed upon her knees – it seems she is inclined to say something on her husband's behalf – but is having second thoughts. A lawyer would always advise upon silence in the event of any doubt. Her eyes, rapidly moving about with no obvious purpose, betray some inner turmoil. Perhaps it is simply that, having raised the possibility of a malevolent force in Scarlett Liddell's death, she is disturbed to have had this thrown back at her in the shape of Will Liddell.

10. RAVELSTON

FELICITY BELVEDERE

Tuesday, 2.00pm

S kelgill seems transfixed by the weir. Certainly it possesses
mildly hypnotic properties; constant movement and yet a
static form; a pervasive rush that seems to ebb and flow. A
heron wades in the downstream shallows, its movements
controlled, perhaps to ape passing clouds; it works – so far, five
strikes, five minnows. The waters must run cleaner than they
once were. Indeed, along the crest of the weir a skittering grey
wagtail tilts at hatching flies – olives, by the look of it. And in
the millpond calm of the upstream pool a trout is sporadically
sipping pupae from the sticky meniscus.

From his bankside bench Skelgill flicks spare crusts to ducks.
He was tempted by a poster in the chippy that advertised haggis
supper with a half deep-fried pizza thrown in. But it would make
a heavy lunch, even by his standards. In any event, now that he
has eaten them, the sandwiches have sufficed. For a few
moments longer, he basks in the spring sunshine. Down here in
the wooded sandstone gorge there is not a breath of wind. He
reflects vaguely upon his last visit; rain-soaked lung-bursting
exhaustion the overriding remnant feeling; there was no time to
enjoy the location – another of Edinburgh's extraordinary
metropolitan oases, where kingfishers and dippers and even
otters pass within a stone's throw of the city centre.

He wonders how DS Jones has fared this morning. Derek Duff at his office down river in smutty Leith, then Mike Luker in the more salubrious Charlotte Square. Next for her are Kevin Makepeace, and finally Will Liddell – at the same address in the Old Town. They – the two detectives – have agreed not to communicate piecemeal (except in the event of some stark revelation). Instead they have a 7pm rendezvous at an Indian restaurant near Haymarket station, recommended by Skelgill's old friend, DS Cameron Findlay – sadly absent on a fishing expedition in the north of Scotland. Skelgill's thoughts drift back via angling to his most recent foray upon Bass Lake – when Will Liddell's happily inebriated party disturbed his peace – his only and fleeting encounter with the redheaded Scarlett Liddell. He pictures the scene – recalls the lively group. Of the women, only Felicity Belvedere remains for him to see. A short walk from his present location, up into Ravelston via the steep path through the gallery of modern art. By elimination she must be the short-haired blonde.

*

'Cracking view you've got, madam. I didn't realise there was any high-rise in this part of town.'

She looks at him as if she is wondering if he has used a deliberately disparaging term – for the art deco apartment block is one of the capital's most sought-after addresses.

'Built into the sweep of the wooded hillside it tends not to stand out. When I see the Ravelston development from afar I always think of Sheffield.'

'Not a city I know, madam. Did you used to live there?'

'I studied at Hallam – for my architecture Masters.'

Skelgill turns from the window and takes the seat she has indicated. The apartment is furnished in keeping with its provenance – club chairs with curved arms upholstered in fawn suede and tan beading, a large figured walnut coffee table, and the Clarice Cliff tea service that was set out ready and waiting – it is like stepping onto the set of a *Poirot* movie. And, while Felicity

Belvedere is dressed (he guesses trendily) in flowing loon pants and a loose black top, her bob hairstyle would grace the bygone era. She is tall – almost Skelgill's height, though there may be high heels beneath the trousers – a slim slightly asexual figure that goes with her boyish looks, a retroussé nose and only the faintest hint of pale eyebrows; her posture is upright, and she moves with a certain careful stiffness suggestive of lower back problems. And she is indeed the blonde that Skelgill has anticipated. Though her tone of voice is cooperative, her expression suggests otherwise – but Skelgill begins to realise that the narrow lips and downturned mouth, and smooth stretched skin with little facial movement – giving the impression of a mask assumed for the purposes of concealment – simply represent the default position of her facial muscles. For there is life in her bright blue eyes – and her words come naturally – another accent that carries only a hint of Scots – more like a well-spoken southerner to his ear. One slight irritation: she has that kind of antipodean inflexion, the 'uptalk' that seems to pose a question with the completion of each answer.

'When did you first come to Edinburgh, madam?'

'Well I was –' She glances up from pouring tea. Now her eyes are quizzical – and she appears to adjust her reply. 'Kevin and I both worked in London until – it would be seven years ago. Then Kevin got the chance of a job up here – we thought it would be a better environment for Ella – our daughter?'

Her mask breaks as she flashes a smile – it is quite transforming – suddenly she acquires a new level of attractiveness. She has glanced at a framed photograph of a young girl in school uniform. Then her mouth drops back into its inverted u-shape.

'Your husband's job – your *ex*-husband, I should say – that was with Mr Liddell's organisation?' (She nods, rather glumly now by comparison.) 'So the children being at the same school – that was just a coincidence, was it?'

'Well – I suppose it was a coincidence. There aren't many options, however – even in Edinburgh – if you're looking for a real commitment to single-sex education?'

Again there is the uptalk – it makes her sound rather uncertain – while it draws Skelgill into what is not in fact a question.

'I can't say I'm qualified to have an opinion on that.'

'At this age, Inspector – Ella is thirteen – when you see them on social media – and they meet boys in town at the weekends – it is something of a blessing that at least for eight hours a day they can focus on their studies. And sport – of course – so many teenage girls drop out because they are embarrassed by comments from boys.'

'Aye – happen there's not enough sport being done – I'll give you that, madam.' Now he looks pointedly at the school photograph. 'And is your lass in the hockey team, as well?'

Felicity Belvedere seems surprised, and the fleeting smile somewhat forced.

'Yes – she is – though I wouldn't say it's her forte – but she's a trier – and she enjoys the camaraderie.'

'I was hearing that Mr Liddell's daughter is a bit of a player.'

She nods generously – perhaps now comprehending his interest.

'She's very good – she was selected for the district under-14s last year, when she was just twelve.'

'Happen she's got something of her father's talent.'

The woman looks keenly at Skelgill.

'Well – Muriel Liddell might beg to differ – she played for Scotland.'

'There you go – that's jumping to conclusions for you.'

Skelgill affects a look of sheepishness. She responds sympathetically.

'But I'm sure you'd be right in some respects – Will Liddell fought his way up from humble beginnings – he is a very determined man.'

Skelgill nods slow agreement.

'Is it his custom to pay for his friends to do things – like the past weekend?' He casts about in a mild way, as inoffensively as he can contrive. 'I mean – if you don't mind me saying, madam – you're all doing quite well by ordinary folk's standards.'

She looks unflustered by what might be interpreted as a criticism – an intrusive one at that – though behind the implacable mask Skelgill sees a change in her eyes – a flash of uncertainty – and she makes an uneasy movement, quickly drawing aside her hair – which is centre-parted and is beginning to encroach upon her eyes.

'I suppose – when something is presented to you as a fait accompli – it can be difficult to refuse.'

Skelgill looks puzzled.

'So, what – you're told the trip's been set up and there's nothing to pay?'

She gives a kind of nod-cum-shrug of acknowledgement – that he has it about right.

'And, then of course – if you knew Will – you'd know he'd be offended if you questioned it.'

Skelgill makes an ironic growl in his throat.

'I need to find a few friends like yours, madam.'

She smiles briefly. But he can see she only humours him.

'I shouldn't say it's an ideal situation – but –' She seems to run out of words. 'As the saying goes – it is what it is.'

Skelgill looks at her, his expression becoming graver.

'That's all changed now, madam.'

She nods pensively.

'Scarlett's death, yes.'

'Were you close to her, at all?'

She has bowed her head. Now she looks up and again has to draw back her hair with her fingertips.

'She wasn't easy to get to know.' Once more, the questioning intonation.

Skelgill responds in kind.

'Aye?'

He waits for her reply.

'She was rather self-absorbed – and what scope she had for empathy was focused upon Will.' Felicity Belvedere takes a deep breath, a reflective expression. 'Of course – I tended only to meet her in prescribed circumstances – everything is a little artificial – even at a dinner party – you arrive and exchange formal greetings with friends whose homes you've been popping round to for years – keep your uncomfortable shoes on – sit up straight at the table – there are barriers – you know?'

Skelgill is not entirely sure he does know – the dinner party not featuring in his social calendar – but he nods encouragingly – and her words do prompt an idea.

'Are there any photographs that were taken on Saturday?'

That she glances instinctively at her mobile phone that is lying on the coffee table between them tells him there probably are.

'I took a selfie – when we met for cocktails – I think I kept it.'

She regales him with a strained look – but he understands her to refer to the unfortunate timing.

'Mind if I see it?'

'Sure – I mean – not at all.'

She manipulates the device and turns it and holds it at eye level – he notices she keeps a firm grip. He leans forward, squinting – and now he affects a certain professional aloofness – but inwardly he wrestles with a more base reaction. The picture is a head-and-shoulders shot of the three women – Suzy Duff, Belinda Luker and Felicity Belvedere – in close embrace raising their martini glasses and pouting to the raised camera. Their make-up and hairdos reflect the spirit of the 1920s – Belinda Luker wears a diamante flapper headband, and Felicity Belvedere has a drastic side-parting swept across her forehead and pinned above one ear. But it is the outfits that particularly draw his eye – the contrast – for both the aforementioned females wear dresses with modesty-preserving opaque illusion necklines – whereas Suzy Duff – her eyes sparkling alluringly has on a plunging crimson showgirl outfit that leaves little to the imagination. Skelgill inadvertently swallows – and then makes a bowing motion with his head to indicate he has seen enough. She withdraws the handset – then she intones into the silence that he leaves.

'I only took that one – it was obviously not long before – you know – Scarlett was found?'

'What about during the day – do you have anything from earlier on?'

She shakes her head.

'We were advised not to take mobiles on the adventure course – there was mud and puddles and lots of bashing about. And Will had been saying he didn't want us with our heads buried in our phones – that it was a chance to get away from all that – escape to the 1920s. Besides, there was no mobile signal inside the castle – and pedestrian wireless in odd spots.'

Skelgill nods. 'Aye – you're describing Cumbria in general.' He makes a scoffing sound. 'Suits me down to a T, if I'm honest with you, madam.'

She seems surprised by his candid overture.

'Is it not essential for your job?'

'In my book it more hinders than helps. Being dragged in seven directions at once. But there's folk more important than me says otherwise.'

She listens to him reflectively.

'For me – I suppose – it is both boon and bane. Technology means I can work flexibly from home – especially as a single mother – but when you're self-employed it's easy to let your job fill up all your spare moments. That can be frustrating for Ella – like when she wants a lift home from her father's – and he's had a beer watching the football – and I tell her I have a technical drawing to finish.'

Again she plies him with the smile – her white teeth are small and even and contribute to a youthful countenance that belies her age. And though the warmth just as quickly fades, Skelgill does not sense his presence is resented in the same way as with Belinda Luker – but maybe she had somewhere to go. He pokes awkwardly at his teacup by way of moving on to his next point.

'Madam – this is me just being a bit nosey – how come yourself and Mr Makepeace went along on this jaunt to Greenmire Castle – as a couple, I mean?'

Now she tilts her head to one side and looks at him rather quizzically through what must be her dominant left eye. Her hair spills across and she flicks at it ineffectually.

'Inspector – believe it or not there are couples that separate and remain on perfectly amicable terms.' (Skelgill looks like he might *not* believe it – but she continues.) 'In any event we didn't go as partners in the conventional sense – you obviously know the arrangement of the castle – Will had explained in advance that, in effect, everyone had their own room – he'd made sure of that – that we could lock ourselves in, if necessary.' Now she breaks off, as if a momentary thought has distracted her. She gives a small shake of her head. 'Besides – there's nothing so undignified as a party arriving and people pretending they are not scrabbling to secure the best rooms.'

'Happen there's not a lot to choose between them – at Greenmire.'

She regards him with a slightly superior grin – to her trained architect's eye there is perhaps a great deal between the various suites.

'The boys got the sunrise, the girls the sunset.'

Skelgill wonders for a moment if there is some cryptic meaning – but he cannot fathom it – other than she shows an awareness of a phenomenon that would pass most people by – but then light and architecture must go together like bangers and mash.

'You would have been mainly friendly with the first Mrs Liddell – and Mr Makepeace more with Mr Liddell – would I be right?'

Though she evidently ponders, there is little in her expression to suggest this question troubles her.

'Well – yes – I see your point – I suppose you are thinking what happens if one of us gets a new partner – that Kevin would probably take precedence in the group?'

In fact the future dynamics of their social circle have not particularly occurred to him – though it does prompt the realisation that there is now a gaping hole. However, he responds in accordance with her suggestion.

'Aye – I was just thinking – what with your ex-husband working for Mr Liddell – he's more likely to be keeping in regular touch with him.'

'Provided Will doesn't decide that Kevin has served his purpose.'

Skelgill wonders if he sees a glint of irony in her eyes. It seems a curious remark.

'Did your ex-husband come to work directly for Mr Liddell's company – or was that another job?'

'In London – he was already employed by a subsidiary. So it was closer to an internal transfer – albeit a different sector. Down south Kevin was in fragrances – now it's spirits – Scotch whisky.'

Skelgill is nodding slowly.

'So – Mr Makepeace – he would quite likely have come into contact with Scarlett Liddell – she worked here in Edinburgh for a year before she married Mr Liddell?'

For a moment she exhibits no visible response whatsoever; but when her reply comes her voice is relaxed.

'Well – I don't recall that Kevin ever mentioned her, as such – except to say there were rumours that Will was in a relationship with a member of staff – but it quite quickly became public knowledge – and Scarlett left the firm.'

'What – a scandal, like?'

She shakes her head calmly.

'No – I gather it was Will invoking his own long-standing company policy. Relationships between staff are forbidden – or at least frowned upon.'

Skelgill glowers.

'That sounds illegal to me, madam.'

'Well – I don't suppose it is explicitly stated in contracts of employment.' She lifts her head and gazes beyond Skelgill – at the brightness of the window – and her pupils noticeably constrict, causing the rich blue of her eyes to intensify. 'But as Kevin put it – when you have a junior member of staff sleeping with the chief executive – it's difficult to tell them what to do. And I imagine Scarlett was enough of a renegade, without acquiring extra powers.'

'I thought she was employed on merit – she was good at French or something like that?'

Felicity Belvedere refocuses upon Skelgill. She nods faintly.

'Yes – something like that.'

But if a troubling sentiment underlies her strained response Skelgill appears to miss it – for he too seems preoccupied with some thought. When he speaks it is to revert to the subject that led to this diversion in the first place.

'Then again, madam – I suppose your daughters are in the same year at school – while they're still friends you've always got something in common.'

'That is true, of course.'

Skelgill glances again at the photograph.

'How have they handled this tragedy – leastways, your young lass?'

'Well – for one thing – in this age of uncensored news we decided – we, the adults, that is – to be frank and open about what has happened – to the extent that we can be?'

She regards him interrogatively – as if seeking his consent.

'I was more thinking about the shock of it – of someone dying – on a celebration weekend.'

'Well – I don't know if you can shock this generation – sadly it is weekly fare on social media – a high-flying young woman commits suicide when it seems she has everything to live for.'

Skelgill looks doubtful.

'I reckon you'd know more about that than me, madam.'

'And at a personal level – apart from Will's children – the others barely knew Scarlett – so I don't believe they will suffer personal grief. The school held a special assembly on Monday morning – they have very good pastoral care. But you'd need to ask Muriel – about how the Liddell children have been affected?'

Again she poses this as a question – and Skelgill finds himself nodding – and now he senses she is watching him minutely. Could it be to glean from his reaction whether he will be seeing the first Mrs Liddell? Or perhaps her suggestion tells him that she already knows the answer.

11. ST SALVATOR'S

MURIEL LIDDELL

Tuesday, 4.00pm

'Can 'ah I help you, sir?'

Skelgill realises he is being eyed with some suspicion. The official – boiler-suited and short and squat and shaven-headed and wearing a yellow reflective vest – has broken off from directing traffic to intercept him. Skelgill realises he must stand out as a stranger. He has followed signs into the school grounds, wading against a steady tide of small teenage girls in smart navy blue uniforms, laden with backpacks, and kitbags with lacrosse sticks poking out of them; some dwarfed by oversized musical instrument cases; and yet others clad in freshly laundered military fatigues and polished combat boots. He has been struck by their neat appearance; hair tied back, garments tucked in where they ought to be – and a collectively happy, unselfconscious demeanour. They indulge in restrained chatter and politely ogle news from each other's expensive-looking mobile phones. It is not a school coming-out that he recognises; the headlong rush, a rag-tag exodus, yells and shrieks, boys speculatively punching, shirt tails flapping, shoes scuffed beyond redemption; girls chewing scornfully, skirts hitched provocatively.

Older, taller girls, however, wear short kilts and less formal tops, their hair swept casually free; with their long slender necks they move like young swans among the more ubiquitous flock; serene, poised, soon to be young women – sixth formers, maybe?

He notes several eye him with curiosity, and coyly exchange comments with their confidantes.

The narrow entry road is tree lined, with a single footway; it jerks left and right to pass into a well-maintained grassy quadrangle with neat beds and criss-crossing paths. At one side stands the main school building – an imposing sandstone edifice, four storeys, and the square tower pointed out from afar by David Balfour. Around is a collection of more modern constructions that look like they might be sports and art and technological facilities. From somewhere there drifts the smell of baking and coffee. He can see a car park across the far side, and beyond that but out of sight below a grassy ha-ha what must be the sports pitches – for a rank of zinc floodlight posts guards new-looking green mesh enclosures.

'I'm meeting Mrs Liddell – a parent? She's expecting me.'

The man lifts his head then tilts it to one side.

'Aye – that's her car.'

He indicates a white Range Rover parked on the hatched tarmac in front of some delivery doors – there is a large sign stating, "Keep Clear". Skelgill notes that the registration contains the combination *L1D*.

'Is she allowed to park there?'

'Pal – parents cannae drive intae the school until half past four. Look at this wan the noo!'

He breaks off to jump into the roadway and remonstrate with the female driver of a monstrous road-hogging 4x4 – but she feigns not to see him and the car surges forward with a great roar of its superfluous cylinders. More oversized vehicles follow. He retreats for his own safety.

'What can I dae? They pay my wages – and they ken it.'

The man utters short staccato bursts that Skelgill can just grasp. He wonders why he was expecting an ordinary worker to have a more refined accent. He notices the letters *H-I-B-S*, a faded amateur biro tattoo on the knuckles of one hand. But the man seems to have decided that Skelgill – perhaps by dint of his disavowal of his quarry (over her unreasonable parking) – is in his camp. Certainly Skelgill has noted his appellation was swiftly downgraded from "sir" to "pal".

'You should get the police along.'

'Aye – we dae that. By the main entrance, ken? It works while the polis is there – next day, they're back up tae their tricks. Stop on the yellow zigzags – come in tae the school during restricted hours. The new Head's been sending out polite requests. They take nae notice. Cannae be bothered tae walk a couple o' hunner yards. I cannae manage it ma sel – I'm the janny – no' a traffic warden.'

Skelgill grimaces sympathetically (despite some deleted expletives). The man obviously does not often find such an understanding ear. More large vehicles rumble past. Now the janitor vents additional spleen – that these idle mothers treat the school run as a daily fashion show – they get "dolled up" and totter about on preposterous heels. Skelgill manages to steer the conversation around to hockey – that, whatever unsuitable outfit she may be wearing, he is due to rendezvous with Mrs Liddell pitchside. He learns that it is half time – however, from beyond the ha-ha emanates a clue that the restart is imminent: a high-pitched war cry to the beat of a familiar rugby chant: "Sally, Sally, Sally – Oi, Oi, Oi!"

*

'Go, Sallies!'

Skelgill holds his breath. It has never occurred to him that hockey might be exciting. For five minutes he has been gripped and delayed in his mission. He has divined that the score is 1-0 to St Salvator's. Now their tenuous lead is threatened. The visiting side has a penalty corner. The home defence is crowded onto the goal line. Masked, they look ominous. As one they rap the crossbar three times with their sticks. They crouch like sprinters, coiled for action. The whistle shrieks. As the ball skims across the smooth green astroturf one girl streaks from the goal as her teammates fan out behind her. The ball reaches the first attacker – but incredibly, so does the spearhead. In the instant that the former traps for her strike partner to sweep, the defender smashes the pair of them. There is a clatter of sticks – one spins through the air. From the conflagration, without breaking stride the flying defender emerges with the ball – and she is away down the pitch. With a feint she easily beats the onrushing midfield and backstick chops a defence-splitting pass out to the flank. A teammate gathers – she hares for the byline – crosses – and the erstwhile defender swoops to lash the ball into the net. Ten seconds, end to end. Two-nil, Sallies. Skelgill realises he is clapping.

'Attagirl, Lulu!'

It is the same woman that utters these words as the earlier exhortation, "Go, Sallies!" – but now with a degree of reserve – indeed perhaps even through gritted teeth, holding back the emotion – for Skelgill detects a sparkle in her proud maternal eye. He has established the woman's identity by inquiring among spectators – and has moved in slowly, engrossed by the contest. Now, at close quarters, he senses she is aware of his approach – but he hesitates to make an introduction. As per the janitor's assertion, she – like all of the women around – is finely attired – but there the similarity ends. If there is some insidious fashion parade, then the 'models' fit the bill – these are 'yummy mummies', as the saying goes. But, Muriel Liddell is decidedly plain looking. In profile – as Skelgill sees her – her nose is rather too large, and hooked, and her chin and brows heavy and protruding, her mousy hair cut short and straight. He stops a yard shy, and swivels on his heel so that they both face out onto the pitch. Meanwhile the teams form up for the restart. The winger that provided the assist comes alongside, breathing heavily.

'Nice cross, Poppy!'

The girl flashes a steely glance through pale blue eyes – then grins briefly, and sprints away.

'You're the Detective Inspector.'

But Skelgill is plainly distracted; he is watching the winger. It takes him a moment to respond.

'Poppy – isn't that the Duffs' lass?'

Muriel Liddell turns her head to look at him curiously.

'Don't be surprised – her father was a professional footballer.' When Skelgill continues to frown, she elaborates. 'Derek Duff? Heart of Midlothian? He was forced to retire through injury in at twenty – he had just been called up for Scotland.'

Skelgill makes a face of vague acknowledgement.

'And you actually played for Scotland, madam.'

She smirks, it seems rather sardonically.

'Look – I don't wish to sound resentful, Inspector. But spend two minutes at a parents' social evening and you'll find surgeons – *plastic* surgeons – chief executives, entrepreneurs, political leaders – and, some, mere athletes.'

Skelgill hunches, and glances about – as though he should feel in awe of such august company, the *who's who* of Scotland's capital – though he does wonder if these are mainly the wives of those to whom she refers. But all he can glean is that his approach to Muriel Liddell has elicited some attention. She perceives his concern.

'Would you prefer to go over to the *Hub* – there's a self-service cafeteria and we can sit more comfortably in a booth?'

Skelgill bites his cheek.

'I'm happy watching, madam – I shouldn't like to tear you away – I get the feeling this is a bit of a grudge match.'

The woman grins.

'Sallies v Muirhouse – it's the oldest rivalry in Scottish women's sport.'

Indeed the girls fight like tigers – limbs and sticks flailing, red faced, gasping, bright gumshields flashing sinister snarls – it is a battlefield where the point of combat moves with alarming speed from one locus to another as girls successively try to beat the hell out of their opponent, the ball a mere excuse.

'If these are thirteen-year-olds I shouldn't like to face the full size version.'

Muriel Liddell seems to appreciate his comment. She smiles softly. Her eyes track the play hawkishly.

'I would ask how may I help you, Inspector – but of course you want to know about Will.'

Skelgill's candid answer would be that he doesn't yet know *what* he wants to know – but more likely about Scarlett Liddell.

'Have you spoken to him, madam?'

'He telephoned on Sunday morning – with the children in mind.'

Skelgill notes she is quick with the rider.

'I gather you've been up front with the youngsters.'

'The bare bones – if that is not an unfortunate turn of phrase.'

Skelgill gives the hint of a shrug.

'I wouldn't call it gruesome.'

Though her gaze continues to follow the action, he senses her concentration has shifted.

'There is something particularly disturbing about suicide, Inspector.'

Skelgill's face is grim. To his mind – yes, when it is in doubt. But, if he is honest, there are times when to find no foul play comes as a relief.

'Were you surprised, madam?'

'Not especially.'

'What makes you say that?'

She is pensive; her gaze becomes fixed.

'I suppose when you accumulate a certain number of traumas of magnitude – a critical mass, if you like – thereafter, their occurrence becomes the norm. You understand that is the nature of life.'

It is a philosophical answer, not what he was expecting.

'I was thinking more along the lines that you would have known her – known their circumstances –'

Skelgill tails off but she is quick to fill the void.

'I knew little of either, Inspector.' Now she pauses – quite deliberately it seems – before resuming in a controlled monotone. 'But objectively it would seem to be curious timing – when Will has only recently doubled his fortune.'

Skelgill's features become strained – an outward sign that he resists a little flood of otherwise intoxicating possibilities.

'You mean – it would be a good time to be married to him?'

'If super yachts are your thing, I should say so.'

Skelgill opts for a pragmatic question.

'What was the source of the financial success?'

She casts him a sharp sideways glance – as if she distrusts his naivety.

'A website – for the exchange of reputable trades services – plumbers, plasterers... *prostitutes.*' She allows the final word to sink in. 'I imagined you would be aware of it – there was an exposé by a tabloid newspaper a couple of years ago.'

Skelgill glances around, as though concerned on her behalf.

'Oh, don't worry, Inspector – I am not tarred with that brush.'

She turns slightly and bends back her wrist over her shoulder, indicating with one finger. It is an act of reluctant acknowledgement. Skelgill follows the direction and squints through the wire fencing – beyond grass hockey pitches stands a modern clubhouse. 'Besides – when Will sold it to the Americans he paid off the school's mortgage on the new sports pavilion.'

Skelgill contorts his features. It is one way to suppress dissent. But again he notices they are being observed; a couple of striking blondes further along the touchline have them under surveillance. It must be pretty obvious what they are talking about. He turns back to the pitch, and pointedly follows the play for a couple of minutes. Muriel Liddell sporadically shouts encouragement – of a sufficiently technical nature to convince Skelgill that she knows what she is talking about. He joins in each time she claps.

'Madam – just coming back to what you were saying – that Scarlett –' (here he hesitates – but manages to refrain from using the surname – or 'Mrs' – it seems a sensitive expedient) 'that Scarlett was motivated by – well – plain and simple, money?'

She flashes him an old-fashioned look.

'What attracted the nubile nymphet to the dour middle-aged businessman?'

'He's only just turned forty. That's no age at all, madam.'

Muriel Liddell is clearly amused by his reaction – as if she recognises the intervention of his ego – but she makes a little curtsey, implying he has by default aimed a compliment at her.

'Unfortunately, Inspector, there comes a day when one begins to develop religious feelings for the claims of anti-ageing creams.'

Skelgill averts his gaze – a clumsy act of chivalry, and not his forte. He folds his arms, a subconscious gesture of solidarity – but his mind replays her words – for she has juxtaposed a succession of insinuations. And her tone – can he synthesise some sentiment from its echo before it fades – is it bitterness – or resignation – or is it *relief* that he detects? Whichever, her next line jolts him from his musings.

'At least I cannot be a suspect – unless you think I am some kind of Svengali?'

'Madam – you said yourself – it's a suicide we're investigating.'

'You are going to some considerable lengths, Inspector.'

Skelgill shifts position, a little awkwardly. He digs his hands into his trouser pockets and sways forward, as if he might topple over the touchline.

'Look – we'd be investigating whatever the circumstances – it's an unexplained death – it's the law – you can't just have folk popping their clogs – then sign it off as though it were nothing unusual.'

His colloquial turn of phrase entertains her; there is a gentle smile on her lips.

'But it is evident that you believe there is something more sinister afoot. Isn't the expression, *driven to suicide?*'

She says no more – and Skelgill stumbles over his eventual rejoinder.

'Happen – that's just me, madam.' He casts about – almost helplessly – as if to demonstrate such exalted surroundings find him outwith his comfort zone – and are the root of the misapprehension. 'I'm probably too ham-fisted for this sort of thing.'

'Oh, I don't know – a certain guilelessness probably helps to pierce the veneer of artificial respectability.'

It is a frank acknowledgement, if perhaps inadvertently a little patronising. But it reinforces Skelgill's impression of Muriel Liddell continually sailing up close to the wind. And it invites a more precarious tack on his part.

'Madam – you must know Mr Liddell better than anyone.' Though he watches the game, he can sense that she is nodding. 'Would he harm his new wife?'

She makes an immediate movement – a little jerk backwards of the head and shoulders – as if this is an impossible statement. It is a good five seconds or more before she replies.

'Do you have a dog, Inspector?'

'Aye – I do, as a matter of fact – Bullboxer.'

Now he detects a little raising of her head – as if she understands the character of the powerful breed.

'Is it well behaved?'

'It's daft as a brush.'

'What about when you are not home?'

'It gets bullied by the cat, I reckon.'

She suppresses a little chuckle.

'Your cat is obviously expendable, Inspector.'

Skelgill begins to protest that she doesn't know his Scottish cat – but she interrupts.

'Would you leave your dog with a baby?'

'No one in their right mind would do that.'

She falls silent – and Skelgill realises she rests her case. Much as it is a curious analogy, he feels license to probe further.

'Was he ever threatening towards you – violent?'

She shakes her head. But there is something unconvincing in her demeanour as she stares out across the pitch. Just then a great cry goes up – suddenly they are both drawn to the action. Skelgill saw it – a Sallies attacker bearing down on goal was blatantly tripped – hooked around the ankle – but the umpire at that end – one of the visiting coaches – has called play-on, much to the displeasure of the home contingent. And now from the dugout on the far side the Sallies coach races onto the field of play – to Skelgill it seems to remonstrate with the umpire. It is perhaps just as well that the injured girl lies in her path – for she recalibrates her urge in the nick of time – she skids to a halt and stoops to tend her charge. But even at a distance Skelgill can see the fire in green eyes that burn beneath a flaming mane of red hair. Familiar eyes – familiar hair – for she is the runner who swept past him early this morning.

'Who's that?'

'Miss Brodie – Head of Sport – she coaches this year-group and above. She likes to win.'

'She looks like my kind of coach.'

Muriel Liddell glances interrogatively at Skelgill.

'Her temperament matches her hair.'

Skelgill wonders if he detects some irony in her tone – a deliberate allusion to Scarlett Liddell, perhaps. He opts to remain neutral, and silent. Meanwhile the incendiary incident seems to have defused itself – the fallen girl has climbed to her feet and declared herself fit to continue. The coach stalks away. Presently the umpire awards a series of soft decisions in favour of St Salvator's – perhaps trying to atone for her error; the home team keep their opponents pinned in their defensive half – and soon there is a long blast of the whistle. The girls in navy blue raise their sticks two-handed above their heads in celebration. Skelgill notices the redheaded coach turn away into the dugout and pump her fist. The teams line up to exchange three cheers – Sallies led by the Liddell girl – and then snake past one another sportingly shaking hands. They trot to their coach for what is a short debrief. Skelgill watches as the girls break out into little knots, and begin to drift away, still congratulating themselves. A lone wolf himself, he feels a certain pang of longing for such camaraderie.

Muriel Liddell clears her throat; she has begun to back off.

'I must take Lulu – she has training at her club in thirty minutes.'

'More hockey?'

'She plays in her sleep.'

'Aye – I do that with fishing.'

The woman grins. 'So – was there anything else you wanted to ask me? The rush-hour traffic – you know?' She indicates vaguely with a wave of a hand. Skelgill seems partially distracted.

'Are you about tomorrow?'

'I have a couple of engagements – but I could work around them.'

Skelgill nods perfunctorily.

'I'll let you know madam.'

'Nice to meet you, Inspector.'

Skelgill watches for a few moments as she walks away, making a beeline that will intercept her daughter, who is heading with several of her cohort towards a gate in the high fence. Then he turns to see that the coach is packing items of gear into a wheeled kitbag. There is a ball close by that has rolled against the sideboards. He picks it up and then ambles across towards the dugout. The woman is crouching to zip the bag. Now he sees that her lilac and black outfit must be the school coaches' colours – there are other staff around in the same strip.

'It looked a clear foul, to me.'

She rises – and stands her ground, the green eyes unblinking, guarded.

'And you are?'

It flashes through Skelgill's mind that he could be a prospective parent about to donate a million pounds to the school. And there is no sign that she recognises him from their fleeting encounter before breakfast. Yet in her recalcitrance Skelgill feels some affinity – she is still emotionally in the heat of the battle – and he takes no offence. As he passes her the ball with one hand, with the other he slips his warrant card from his hip pocket and displays it casually. Her eyes rest on it for a moment.

'I'm investigating the death of Mrs Scarlett Liddell.'

Now she looks at him – her features are benign but her gaze is penetrating – and she calmly waits for him to speak. He finds her silence a little unsettling.

'I wouldn't mind a word.'

'In what way can I help?'

Skelgill realises he is acting upon impulse – and has no ready answer. He casts about as if he is afraid of eavesdroppers – and although no one is near he turns back to her and jerks a thumb over his shoulder. 'What about this *Hub* café you've got?'

'That's fine, Inspector – provided you don't mind trending on social media before you've put a cup to your lips.'

He makes a rueful face. He gets her point – manna from heaven for the schoolgirls' gossip grapevine. He swallows.

'I noticed there's a new wine bar in that row of shops – down at Roseburn?'

Uptalk – now he's doing it! He mentally chastises himself. Meanwhile the woman still has the look of one fending off a chancer hoping for a date – a mixture of disbelief that he would have the audacity to ask, and revulsion at the prospect.

'I have to post the match report on the school website.'

Skelgill wrestles with his features – he does not want to show he is rattled – but suddenly the woman flicks the ball at him – instinctively he catches it left-handed in front of his heart. She smiles.

'It *was* a foul. Maybe you can help me with the wording – since I was seeing red at the time. There's free Wi-Fi in that bar.'

12. LALDHI MAHAL

Tuesday, 7.30pm

'**S**orry I'm late, Guv.'
Skelgill is looking at pictures on a menu, angling it as though a different perspective will illuminate the subject. And he makes curious facial contortions – as if straining to get his tongue around his back teeth. There is a plate in front of him on which lie a few crumbs of poppadum, perhaps the explanation. To one side is a half-drunk bottle of Indian lager – rare for him, but of course there is no cask ale on offer. For her part, DS Jones seems a little red-faced, there are rosy patches on her prominent cheekbones, she looks hot as if she has hurried, and has her jacket over her arm. A waiter comes up and takes it and helps her into the seat opposite her superior. Skelgill regards her questioningly.

'I went for a drink with Will Liddell.'

That she blurts this out rather confessionally perhaps elicits an unreasonably accusing tone from Skelgill.

'*A drink?*'

'Oh – I just had water. They've got renovations in progress – the builders come in at 5.30pm and work through the night – so as not to disturb the employees. Someone started drilling into a wall – Will Liddell suggested we went down to a bar on the street below.' She glances at Skelgill to see that he is glowering. 'After Greenmire Castle – I thought he might become a bit more talkative?'

'And was he?'

'A little – *ha-hah.*' Her laugh is of the nervous variety.

'What?'

'*Little* – and Liddell. You know what his firm is called – the holding company?' (Skelgill shakes his head – he does not look particularly enamoured of the subject.) *'Liddell Acorns Incorporated.'*

'Is that meant to be funny?'

'Well – I suppose it's quite clever – they invest in small businesses and help them grow into much bigger organisations.'

Skelgill's retort is rather acerbic.

'His ex told me that he's just made a packet out of some website that was a front for escorts. Flogged it to an American crowd.'

DS Jones looks a little disconcerted.

'Hmm – well – that never came up. They seem to be very ethical in what they're trying to do. They identify craft operations where the founders have the technical skills – but not the capital or marketing expertise needed to expand.'

'Jones – you sound like their PR girl.'

His sergeant grins bashfully.

'Guv – like I say – I thought I was doing well getting him talking. He seemed quite keen to tell me about the company – it's obviously going places. He said he got back on 10ᵗʰ of March from a month in Shanghai – he's just established an investment office there.'

Skelgill is looking sceptical.

'Sure it weren't a smokescreen? I don't mean China – I mean giving you all this corporate flimflam.'

A waiter ghosts up and pours water from a jug and asks DS Jones if she wants something else to drink, but she declines. Skelgill taps the menu.

'We'll go for this banquet – the *Six Chillies.*'

DS Jones waits for the man to retreat before she answers.

'I don't think so, Guv – I wouldn't say he ducked any questions. He's just economical with his replies. You saw that.'

'I'm more interested in what he asked you.'

Skelgill's gaze is penetrating – as if he knows something. It is at this juncture that DS Jones decides not to mention the very last thing that Will Liddell *did* ask her – whether she would care to dine with him, and quite persuasively so – and that he had just momentarily put his hand at the small of her back as he courteously chaperoned into the elevator. As such, her response is slow in coming.

'I decided not to raise the subject of the pregnancy – and he didn't allude to it – if that's what you mean, Guv?'

Now Skelgill seems oddly indifferent to the answer. He casts about the restaurant, cursorily eyeing the other diners, and optimistically eyeing the kitchen.

'Aye – that – whatever.'

DS Jones places her hands together and rests her chin upon her fingertips.

'Has anyone asked you, Guv – if we're suspicious?'

'Aye – more or less. I reckon the women have definitely discussed it. I'd go so far as to say they've even worked out who we're most likely to suspect. It's hardly rocket science.'

DS Jones nods in agreement.

'Circumstantially, Guv – it's understandable. Assuming she did commit suicide – then everyone else most likely went about their innocent business – and in doing so, Will Liddell would apparently have been in her vicinity at the time it happened.'

But Skelgill is looking doubtful – distressed, even – as he has each time this analysis has been attempted.

'We don't know the exact time she died – if someone went in or out – invited or otherwise – crept away while Will Liddell was asleep – hid themselves when he called her. We don't know whose story's accurate and whose isn't.'

DS Jones's face carries a look of resignation – that to make headway they have to find another route – their reason for coming to Edinburgh. She grins mirthlessly.

'We needed a cracked wristwatch, Guv – on the bathroom floor – stopped at the time of the incident. Like there would be on a Murder Mystery night.' She pauses – as a notion strikes her. 'Imagine if there had been clues laid down and one of them fooled us.'

Skelgill glances away broodingly. It is a while before he picks up his original thread.

'What else – about Will Liddell?'

DS Jones inhales to reply – but she is trumped by the arrival of the first course – a salver heaped with an assortment of appetisers – and Skelgill's attention is diverted.

'I was warned about the portions here, Guv.'

Skelgill eyes her apprehensively – wondering what conversation she has had and with whom – but he already has his teeth into a pastry. DS Jones leans to one side and extracts her notebook from her shoulder bag.

'Maybe I should work through it in chronological order, Guv – some of the points will make more sense that way?'

Skelgill scowls, as if he suspects she is skirting around the subject of Will Liddell – but it may simply be the unfamiliar selection of food that vexes him. He makes an indeterminate growl in his throat that DS Jones takes as a sign of agreement.

'Okay – Derek Duff, first of all.' She thumbs through the pages to the beginning of her notes. There is a numerical reference at the top that sparks some recall. 'By the way, Guv – the number 12 bus from the hotel was great – it stopped literally outside his office.'

'What sort of place is it?'

DS Jones takes a sip of water. She appears to have recovered her composure after a somewhat disjointed opening.

'Well, Leith seems half trendy and half run down – the office falls into the latter category. A Victorian building – quite grand but stained with soot and the paintwork on the windows flaking. A shared entrance and an untidy hallway – poorly lit and a damp feeling – smelly carpets – you know?'

Skelgill nods. She could be describing one of his favourite pubs. He chews pensively as she continues.

'Coming full circle for a moment – I couldn't help drawing the comparison when I went to *Liddell Acorns'* HQ – that Derek Duff is like a poor man's version of Will Liddell.'

'His missus is mithered about how they'll pay the school fees. They've got three more bairns coming down the tracks.'

DS Jones frowns reflectively.

'Strangely enough, Guv – he was quite happy-go-lucky. That was another contrast with Will Liddell – and yet *he* must be financially secure – if he never lifted another finger.'

'What does Derek Duff do, jobwise?'

She glances at her notes, written in shorthand; she grins.

'It's a marketing business. He called it "freebies and fantasies" – you know – when you find a plastic shark swimming in your cornflakes – or you can win a trip to Barbados with your sunblock?'

Skelgill's countenance darkens.

'It's all gimmicks as far as I can see.'

'I'm not even sure Derek Duff believes it works – but he seems to be scraping by on it.'

'Does he employ any staff?'

'He apologised for having to let me in himself – he said his assistant is on maternity leave. He kept using the term "we" – I didn't press him on it, Guv – but I suspect he's a one-man band.' She breaks off, and her gaze drifts away in the manner of one musing over some deeper feeling. 'But, you know – he was consistently effusive about Will Liddell.'

Skelgill does not respond immediately, and so DS Jones takes the opportunity delicately to spear a vegetable pakora.

'Happen Will Liddell feels sorry for him.'

DS Jones's fork hovers over the chilli dip.

'In what way, Guv?'

'They knocked about at uni – still regular drinking partners according to Suzy Duff.' He waves an onion bhaji in the air between them. 'If it was obvious to you in five minutes that Derek Duff's on his uppers – it must be plain as day to Will Liddell. So he helps him out.'

'You mean – like paying for the trip to Greenmire Castle?'

Skelgill shrugs.

'Aye – and he subs folk who obviously don't need it. Pay for the lot of them – saves Derek Duff feeling bad. Not like free school dinners – they make the poor kids pay with tokens so all their rest know their parents are skint.'

DS Jones is intrigued that her boss has seen it this way – that he has homed in on this charitable motive. Then it occurs to her that he might be speaking from experience.

'Did you know Derek Duff was a professional footballer, Guv?'

'Aye – I heard that – from Muriel Liddell. Career cut short by injury.'

'There's a framed shirt on the wall of his office, and some faded press cuttings. He said he left university halfway through – got injured in his second season – never finished his studies. Will Liddell went on to get a First and a Masters in Business.'

Skelgill contrives a wry smile.

'Happen the boot was on the other foot.'

'What do you mean, Guv?'

'Now it's Will Liddell who's cock of the walk. But back in the day Derek Duff would have been the big cheese – footballer's pay packet, flash car, pulling the birds – his best mate's a student, hard up – so maybe he was the generous one.'

DS Jones is nodding.

'He strikes me as that sort, Guv – and a bit of a dreamer. He probably would splash cash on his mates. And he has obviously remained good friends with Will Liddell.'

'What about the affair with Scarlett Liddell – reckon he took Derek Duff into his confidence?'

Now DS Jones's expression becomes uncertain. She flicks back over several pages of her notes.

'That whole aspect, Guv – he's got a good line in charming flannel – he was convincingly vague.'

'Such as?'

'I asked him if it was a surprise when Will Liddell split up with his first wife. His answer was along the lines of, Will looks a plain ordinary guy – but if you see him on his phone in a café – you think he's booking a taxi – he's probably buying a company. I guess it was a roundabout way of saying that Will Liddell is a dark horse – and that he admires him for it. When I pushed him, he just said Will Liddell was very good at compartmentalising – he wouldn't burden someone with his problems.'

'Sounds like a maybe. Besides, Suzy Duff reckons Derek Duff had wind of something – that Will Liddell was getting divorced and had a younger girlfriend.'

DS Jones nods reluctantly. She might have cause for feeling that Skelgill was unreasonably holding back this information. She contrives a defence of her powers of interrogation.

'Having met them both, Guv – I can completely see why one is successful and the other isn't. I don't for a minute think Will Liddell would tell Derek Duff – or anybody, come to that – something that might jeopardise his position – however insignificant a point it was – or however much he trusted the person. I have to admit – he's quite an impressive character.'

Skelgill looks up sharply from his plate. Spontaneously, it seems, DS Jones stretches, raising her arms and bending them so that her thumbs brush her shoulders. Her silky white blouse reveals something more of her figure. Skelgill's eyes flicker. She looks like she is expecting him to say something – but when he does not she resettles herself in her chair and regards him questioningly. Now her silence prompts Skelgill to speak.

'You not having more of these veggie things?'

DS Jones smiles sweetly.

'I'm pacing myself, Guv – you know what these banquets are like – the courses just keep coming. You finish them.'

Skelgill makes a pained face, but does not demur in deed.

'What about the relationship between Scarlett and Will Liddell?'

'Derek Duff said Will Liddell was happier than he'd known him for years – even if he didn't expressly show it.'

'What did you make of that?'

'Well – again – having just spent time with Will Liddell – I kind of understand what Derek Duff means.' She pauses to brush at her hair on one side with her fingertips. 'He is very measured – but I imagine if you know him well – perhaps know him of old – then you could probably read the more subtle signs.'

Skelgill swallows and then takes a swig from his bottle of lager, and makes a face that suggests he does not enjoy the taste.

'So – what – nothing from Derek Duff to set the heather on fire?'

DS Jones looks somewhat crestfallen. She bows her head and reviews her notes.

'I asked him again about Friday and Saturday. He admitted to overindulging in alcohol and that he didn't really have his wits about him, a good part of the time. He repeated his previous statement – that Scarlett Liddell had appeared fine to him – and that on Saturday he was in his suite between afternoon tea and when Mike Luker gave him a knock at about five past seven. I asked whether his wife had left her room – or had specifically been to speak with Scarlett Liddell – he said he was fairly sure she hadn't – but that he might have had forty winks.'

At this juncture there materialises a flurry of waiting staff in smart white outfits – and like stage conjurors they whip away used plates and replace them with new ones, and begin to lay down a fresh selection of food. Skelgill's gaze darts about like a wolf straining to pick out the straggler from a herd. DS Jones watches him with a glint of amusement in her eyes – but he seems to detect her attention.

'I'm listening.'

She grins.

'Mike Luker, then, Guv?'

Skelgill nods, having resumed his demolition of the food.

'He seemed uneasy.'

'Aye?'

'You know what you always say about skeletons in closets – even when it's nothing to do with the case?'

'He is a financial advisor, Jones.'

'Well – that was the explanation I assumed. I guess when you specialise in tax avoidance you're never going to be comfortable sitting across a desk from a police officer. I asked him how he got to know Will Liddell. He said it was through the wives and the girls being at the same school – parents' evenings, dinner parties – they inevitably talked about business – and at some point Will Liddell started to use him formally for financial advice

– effectively became one of his clients. He said that was just over five years ago.'

'They say you should never mix business with pleasure.'

DS Jones ponders this aphorism. Is it a necessary evil?

'I rather suspect Mike Luker saw an opportunity at an early stage – he affects indifference – but there's an underlying hunger in his manner. Will Liddell must have seemed a golden goose – business expanding rapidly and cash pouring in.'

'Will Liddell's no pushover – you just said it yourself.'

DS Jones taps her notebook musingly.

'But probably too busy to spend much time on small print.'

'What about Scarlett Liddell – did Luker have any involvement with her?'

She shakes her head.

'He said he deals exclusively with Will Liddell – and always has done. He said he's as much a personal advisor as a business consultant – that when you run *and* own the firm, decisions about tax efficiency are often one and the same.'

'And what about when Scarlett Liddell came on the domestic scene?'

'I got the feeling he disapproved, without exactly putting it into words.'

'Happen it messed up their cosy group.'

Skelgill intones this as a statement – but DS Jones seems unconvinced.

'I'm not sure if it was that, Guv. He said something like, it's not for him to tell Will Liddell how to behave.'

'So he was jealous.'

DS Jones shoots a probing glance at Skelgill.

'That's possible, Guv.' She seems to give a little shake of her head. Was it a note of piety that she had detected? 'But they had an affair, after all – and there are plenty of people who disapprove of that.'

Skelgill rests his forearms on the table and with the fingers of his left hand flicks at the bottle of lager. Certainly of the females he has seen today, Belinda Luker struck him as the most 'straight-laced', as the expression goes – and it might hold therefore that her husband is of a similar ilk. But he is troubled by his own intuitive reaction – and the corollary that Will Liddell, by parachuting an attractive young woman into their midst, had not just stirred up feelings of envy among the females, but among the males, too – despite what they might generously have said about him 'falling on his feet'. It brings his thoughts back to the impressions he has formed of Saturday night, when the group were assembled, awaiting the 'grand entrance' of Scarlett Liddell.

'Owt else from the castle?'

DS Jones shakes her head.

'Not from Mike Luker. He was very precise in repeating his original statement. That he and his wife were in their rooms between teatime and when he went to knock on Derek Duff's door.'

Skelgill nods pensively. Now the servers bring the next course – a main course it seems, judging by the volume. He gestures with a fork.

'You'd better eat something – I'll shut up asking you questions a while.'

DS Jones grins good-naturedly.

*

'Kevin Makepeace – one of the first things he told me, unprompted – was that when they married he agreed with Felicity Belvedere that she'd keep her maiden name – and subsequently they would use it for any offspring.'

Skelgill's retort is somewhat left of field.

'Saved the bairn from a name that's part of a sentence.'

DS Jones looks like she is unsure whether to take seriously her superior's remark.

'He said it was because the Belvederes are a prominent Edinburgh family – and Felicity is the last of the line – her daughter excepted.'

Skelgill persists with his rather sceptical take on the matter.

'Turned out to be a good decision – given they split up.'

DS Jones considers this proposition.

'Yet Muriel Liddell didn't revert to her maiden name, Guv.'

Having met Muriel Liddell, however, Skelgill is well placed to appreciate why she might have retained her husband's name – although DS Jones now supplies him with a less Machiavellian motive.

'I suppose when the children have an established surname at school – it's not so unsettling – especially as they mainly live with their mother.'

'True.'

'But on your literal point, Guv – about Makepeace – I was kind of expecting a character to match.'

'And he weren't.'

'He was quietly indignant. Actually the only one who behaved like he was being treated as a suspect.'

Skelgill harrumphs sarcastically.

'Happen he were the only one being straight with you – they all must know we've got an open mind about Scarlett Liddell's death.'

But DS Jones is perturbed.

'Ordinarily, I'd agree, Guv – but I felt the belligerence was a bit of a put-on. And I wonder why.'

'It's the way some folk defend themselves – go on the attack.'

Perhaps she replays elements of her visit, for her soft hazel eyes seem to glaze over for a moment. 'Yes – you're probably right – telling me about the surname – it must bother him.'

'His ex said Will Liddell might decide he's surplus to requirements.'

DS Jones looks at Skelgill with interest.

'Really? Remember what Will Liddell told us about Saturday night – that Kevin Makepeace had arrived at the library early so he could talk to him about some work issue? He must have been worried to bring it up on Will Liddell's birthday weekend.'

Skelgill's mind drifts to consider a parallel – the inadvisable idea of approaching the Chief at some official function – being the bearer of bad news – her eyes like lasers – the messenger about to be exterminated. He shudders involuntarily, and promptly resurrects their discourse.

'What does he do?'

'He's in charge of the marketing department for a subsidiary that exports malt whiskies. They buy the product from obscure Scottish distilleries and package it for different countries. He says India has been a big growth area, and now they're moving into Hong Kong and mainland China.'

Skelgill looks unimpressed at the mention of these far-flung empires.

'What about London?'

DS Jones is quick to follow his train of thought.

'You're thinking of Scarlett Liddell?' (Skelgill gives a small nod of confirmation.) 'Of course – Kevin Makepeace moved to Edinburgh long before she joined the company in London – but, yes – he said his advertising and PR agencies are based in Soho – close to Will Liddell's Covent Garden offices – they handle all of the company's brands. So he travels down for regular meetings – and has done since he took the Edinburgh job.'

'Did he have contact with her?'

DS Jones's demeanour seems to sharpen – she leans closer to Skelgill. However, her manner is businesslike, and her tone matter-of-fact.

'He said that he didn't know her beforehand, or interview her – but that she was the recommended candidate for the Edinburgh vacancy – and after that he got good reports of her work. She was competent and industrious. But that only lasted for about nine months. She was internally headhunted for the French acquisition project, in Will Liddell's corporate team.'

'So what about the affair?'

'He was pretty tight-lipped about that, Guv – which is understandable – I mean, given his position in relation to Will Liddell.'

Skelgill frowns – but she is right. If Kevin Makepeace's hold on his job is tenuous, to expect him to be forthcoming about his employer is optimistic.

'So what *Liddell* did he say?'

DS Jones grins at her superior's take on her earlier play on words.

'As far as he was concerned it was a private matter. That people are entitled to have relationships.'

'Not in that company.' Skelgill's tone is scathing. 'Not according to Kevin Makepeace's ex-wife. That's why Scarlett Liddell was out of the door so quickly.'

Skelgill now relates what Felicity Belvedere told him about Will Liddell's policy on what an HR department might describe as 'intra-company interpersonal relationships'. DS Jones regards Skelgill through the fluttering veils of her long lashes. She is obliged to recalibrate her impressions of her meeting with Will Liddell in the light of this altered perspective.

'I guess – provided it's made clear when you join – at least you'd know where you stood.'

But Skelgill remains cynical.

'Just means folk'll keep it secret. Hang on to their jobs. Or in some cases put their jobs first. Then there's trouble both ways.'

DS Jones looks momentarily discomfited by Skelgill's fatalistic attitude. She purses her lips a little dejectedly, and takes a couple of slow silent breaths through her nostrils.

'Anyway – it appears to have been handled pretty efficiently, Guv. I imagine if Scarlett Liddell was happy about the outcome, then leaving her job was no great skin off her nose. Maybe she wasn't particularly career-minded.'

Now it seems to be Skelgill that is wrong-footed. He pushes himself back in his chair and casts about, and for a second looks like he might get up. Had they been in his office DS Jones would expect him to rise and stalk to the window to stare out, or turn broodingly to his map of the Lake District on the wall behind his desk. But after a short hiatus he reverts with a new question.

'What's he like – Kevin Makepeace?'

DS Jones appears torn over how she should couch her response.

118

'Well – trendy haircut, tailored suit, polished shoes, expensive wristwatch – on the face of it, you might say good-looking.'

Skelgill scoffs.

'You'll be telling me next he invited you for dinner.'

DS Jones gives a small nervous laugh.

'He is rather preening, Guv – he's got professional photographs on his office wall – it looked like from an *Iron Man* event. And various action shots – abseiling, skiing, scuba-diving.'

Skelgill looks unimpressed by this act of vanity – but his response perhaps reveals some self-referencing on his part.

'What *should* he have on his wall?'

DS Jones seems puzzled by her superior's question.

'Well – I suppose – true enough – Mike Luker had certificates of his qualifications – although in his field there's a case for demonstrating professional competence to your clients. But – by contrast – in Will Liddell's office it wasn't about him – there were modern artworks – you know the Scottish painter, Bellany? Quite a collection.'

'So – he can afford it – that's what it tells you.'

DS Jones opens her palms in a gesture of mitigation.

'At least it was in good taste – and the photographs on *his* desk were of his children.'

Skelgill has a swift rejoinder.

'Don't suppose his wife was in them?'

She shakes her head musingly.

'I guess it wouldn't have been particularly diplomatic – to display a picture of either Muriel or Scarlett Liddell.'

'A rock and a hard place.' Skelgill speaks rather bleakly – then he pauses. He is thinking of something Muriel Liddell said. 'I reckon Muriel had Scarlett Liddell down as a gold-digger.'

DS Jones seems unwilling to agree.

'I'm not sure Will Liddell would fall for something like that.'

Skelgill makes an admonishing growl.

'That's not what he'd be falling for – is it?'

'Well – not exactly, but –'

Now Skelgill interrupts.

'Attractive lass – spending time working together – the south of France – and Derek Duff's more or less told you Will Liddell was unhappy in his marriage – we all know what that means. Chuck in the mid-life crisis. Bob's your uncle.'

Skelgill puts down his cutlery and folds his arms, and looks away with apparent dissatisfaction. For her part, DS Jones seems conflicted, her expression pained yet sympathetic. She lowers her eyes – almost closing them, as if to access deeper sentiments.

'Sure – I understand all that, Guv – but I think – I think that there was more to it – on *both* sides – Scarlett *and* Will Liddell – otherwise it would have just been an affair – a fling – and it would have fizzled out. He must have wanted it – and so must she.'

She looks up to see that Skelgill is regarding her minutely. She seems unnerved by his scrutiny and rather uncharacteristically turns in her seat to look for a waiter – and with a jerkily raised palm summons an alert young man.

'I think I shall have that drink – what about you, Guv – another?'

Skelgill inhales with a hiss, preparatory to voicing an objection – his lager is not his first alcohol of the evening – but the determination in DS Jones's voice tips the balance, and he yields.

'Aye – go on, then – another bottle of Hobson's.'

DS Jones squints at his empty bottle – which is certainly not labelled "Hobson's" – but she realises he is making a joke about the limited choice of beer; she instructs the waiter accordingly. Alcohol is obviously a profitable line for the establishment, for no time is wasted in procuring a fresh lager, and a large glass of chardonnay for DS Jones. It seems with mutual relief that they clink their respective receptacles and each takes a drink, and they both settle back in their seats. When DS Jones resumes, she comes full circle to address what was Skelgill's opening inquiry.

'You said, what did Will Liddell ask me? And the answer is, not a great deal.' She holds up her glass and swirls the pale liquid reflectively. 'As far as the death of Scarlett Liddell is concerned, his attitude was that I was there to give him an update. He had no agenda of his own that I could detect.'

'Reckon he's got wind that we're sniffing around his contacts?'

'Oh, yes – he's clearly aware of that. But I don't think he's expecting us to unearth anything practical as far as the weekend is concerned. I'd say his perspective is that he knows them all well enough – that he knows what happened in his and Scarlett Liddell's suites – and therefore there can be nothing more to it.'

Skelgill nods reluctantly.

'He must have asked about something.'

'Well – yes – in relation to making funeral arrangements.'

'What did you tell him?'

'As we'd agreed, Guv – that the Coroner is waiting for the results of some final tests – but we're hoping a death certificate can be issued by the end of the week. He seemed to accept that.'

Skelgill nods slowly.

'The sixty-four thousand dollar question, then – does he know she was pregnant?'

'I feel certain he doesn't know, Guv.'

Skelgill rather distractedly rubs the stubble on his chin, as if he has an itch on his palm.

'He couldn't very well come out with it now – after not mentioning it before. What about his famous compartmentalising?'

DS Jones shakes her head ruefully – it is an admission that she cannot truly be certain.

'He did inquire whether we found anything helpful on her mobile phone – that was the only thing that made me wonder if he was thinking along those lines. But then he said although she had some contacts from her time in London – he wasn't aware of any close friends. I told him we have someone looking into it – but there is nothing to report as yet.'

Skelgill stretches and suppresses a yawn. He glances at his wristwatch and then his eyes survey the dishes that they (mainly he) have emptied. He shifts restlessly in his seat. When he does not speak immediately, DS Jones leans back and folds her hands upon her lap. She tilts her head inquiringly.

'What about you, Guv – how did you get on?'

Skelgill looks suddenly wide-eyed, as though he has just woken and is startled by the light. It takes him a moment to contrive a response.

'I never realised posh bairns were so tough.'

DS Jones seems amused by his unorthodox answer.

'What makes you say that?'

Skelgill shrugs.

'I met Muriel Liddell at the school, right?' (DS Jones nods; she is aware of his itinerary – most of it, at least.) 'These girls all coming out at home time – smart, well behaved – wouldn't say boo to a goose. Next minute they're beating the living daylights out of each other on the hockey pitch. Taking no prisoners.'

He looks at her as if he has supplied a significant insight. DS Jones waits a moment before she replies.

'It's in the genes, Guv.'

'What?'

'I've been thinking myself – these parents – and Will Liddell is probably the best example – quite often come from ordinary backgrounds. But they've all got something about them. Maybe a special natural aptitude – like Derek Duff had for football – maybe just ambition and the ability to work really hard. Whatever it is – they've fought their way up into senior roles – good salaries – so they can afford to send their kids to private school. We shouldn't be surprised if the next generation inherits the same drive and tenacity.'

Skelgill is listening to his sergeant somewhat quizzically – yet she simply reiterates what Muriel Liddell told him quite bluntly a few hours earlier. In his mind's eye he replays the devastating counter-attack – the Liddell girl and her teammate combining with ruthless efficiency to rip through the opposition. And – moments later – the penetrating pale blue eyes of the Duff girl when Muriel Liddell called to her – before she fleetingly lowered her guard and grinned self-consciously.

'They're no pushover, Guv.'

122

'Come again?' Her assertion stirs him from his reflections.

'The group we're dealing with – they're a smart crowd.'

Skelgill now makes a contrary face.

'Is Derek Duff smart? I thought brains didn't go with being a footballer. They get in the way of instinct.'

DS Jones gives a light shrug of her shoulders.

'Streetwise – certainly, Guv. He hides it behind a boyish innocence. And he did get to uni in the first place – even if he never went back.'

Skelgill remains disconcerted. Was he, in fact, out of his depth with the women he has interviewed today? Were they looking down their noses at him? Not Suzy Duff – surely – but the others – well, perhaps. Suddenly he surprises himself with a little outburst.

'I had a chat with the Head of Sport.'

'Oh, yes?'

'Apparently Will Liddell was a regular spectator. He'd get there early and stay in his car – the school's parking area overlooks the hockey pitches. He'd be doing some work on his laptop. There's a group of dads that stand together. He didn't mix with them.'

'What about Muriel Liddell – she obviously goes, too?'

'It sounds like they kept their distance. That's probably why he'd wait in his car until the match started – get the lie of the land. Catriona said sometimes she'd see him talking with one of the other mums.'

'*Catriona*, Guv?'

'What?'

'You said Catriona.'

Skelgill looks momentarily nonplussed.

'Aye – the coach – Miss Brodie's her name.'

DS Jones grins benignly. She notices little patches of blush on Skelgill's cheekbones – and her expression becomes just a hint interrogative. He reaches for his lager – there is not much left and he tilts the bottle to drain it. He wipes his lips, and then his brow.

'That chilli's getting to me.'

DS Jones nods accommodatingly.

'I think I avoided the worst of it.'

Skelgill remains agitated. He shifts in his seat and puts his palms upon his midriff.

'Tell you what, Jones – I'm stuffed. Why don't we skip the pudding and get a proper drink?'

'Sure. I noticed from the bus there's a new wine bar near that pub DS Findlay took us to – at Roseburn? That's on our way back – we could even walk from here.'

For a moment Skelgill's unease turns to alarm.

'Maybe the pub, eh, lass?'

13. LOGANLEA

Wednesday, 6.30am

'Whose idea was it to have a "proper" drink?'

'Er – yours, Guv?'

Skelgill makes a resigned growl.

'I blame Cammy for putting me on to that IPA – it's the best bitter this side of Cockermouth.'

'Apart from the hangover.'

'I reckon that was the Hobson's.' On top of the wine that he has not mentioned.

They sit in silence for a few moments while Skelgill concentrates. He is tying a fly onto what seems to DS Jones's eye an invisible length of line. It is barely after dawn, and a smooth blanket of grey stratus affords only flat early morning light; objects near and far lack resolution, with neither shadows nor highlights. The little loch on which they float is hemmed in by dark heather-clad banks that rise steeply into hills – the Pentlands, the range that guards Edinburgh's southern reaches. To all intents and purposes they might be somewhere in the Highlands, so wild and secluded is the scene – yet hardly half an hour ago Skelgill was waking his sergeant with a proposal that, bleary-eyed and somewhat befuddled she found herself accepting. Skelgill seemed to know the way, hammering round the deserted city bypass and taking a couple of obscure turns that found them on a single-track lane, winding its way up first through a wooded glen and then into more open country, over rattling cattle grids and past staring sheep and rusted signs prohibiting unauthorised vehicles. His manner had seemed spontaneous; and yet a certain note of preordained mischief that DS Jones had detected was borne out when they arrived at a planked landing stage to 'discover' that one of half-a-dozen rowing boats – apparently chained – had been left cleverly unlocked, its oars shipped ready for use. Skelgill had dragged a crate of tackle from the back of his shooting brake, and selected a rod from an assortment strung up on a DIY rack that incorporates the interior grab-loops. Now he bites on the line and spits the loose end. He is ready to fish. But he has one more act. He rummages in the crate.

'Here – put this on.'

Waiting patiently, DS Jones has become mesmerised by their surroundings. Blinking, she accepts the little bundle that he thrusts at her.

'What is it, Guv?'

'Midge hat – the visor'll protect your eyes.'

'Isn't March early for midges?'

Skelgill glances at her sternly. He lifts the rod and gives it a sharp flick. There is a whip crack and the loose line shoots out and settles upon the water in front of them.

'Do you know how fast a fly travels?'

She realises he means the artificial variety – that which has for its undercarriage not six legs but a glinting hook. She does not need to know the answer; his demonstration is sufficient. She nods compliantly and attends to what is a faded green bush hat with a beekeeper-style veil that has a clear plastic panel for the eyes. She works out that she does not need to wear the full veil, and tucks most of the mesh up inside the crown of the hat. She puts it on and turns to Skelgill for approval.

'That's the ticket.'

'What about you, Guv?'

Skelgill scowls and begins to cast, yanking out line with squeals of protest from the reel, and simultaneously increasing the airborne load until he finally lets it go with a forward sweep of his left arm.

'With my looks – why worry?'

He stares out as the leader unfurls in a neat loop and drops the fly gently upon the meniscus. He is using sinking line and the crease it makes on the surface seems progressively to be ironed out by an invisible hand that runs away from them and finally drags the lure under.

DS Jones must be tempted to quip that he is surely fishing for a compliment.

'Well, I'm up to date with my first aid, Guv – but I can't promise cosmetic repairs.'

Skelgill grins ruefully – and then abruptly he hands her the rod.

'What – me? What do I do?'

Skelgill positions her hands, one at a time.

'Trap the line there against the rod with your index finger – lock it if you feel a pull – lift into the fish. Otherwise retrieve with short tugs of your left hand.'

She begins doing as he instructs.

'Guv –'

There is sudden urgency in her voice and with a lunge Skelgill assists her to strike. He is ebullient.

'Wha-hey! They're hungry – I bet they've not been fed all winter!'

The fish – a decent rainbow trout – is leaping out of the water, tail dancing and turning somersaults. It disappears and the rod bends alarmingly.

'Let it run – just keep it tight – when you feel it turn and come back, strip in the line as fast as you can.'

The reel shrieks as the trout takes line, but DS Jones seems to have the idea of braking its progress – and then strips in more or less correctly. A couple of runs and it begins to tire. Skelgill directs her to lift the rod tip to bring the fish alongside. He leans over and has it in two hands.

'Wow – what a beautiful creature, Guv.'

Skelgill flashes her an inquiring glance.

'Want it for your tea – your Ma?'

DS Jones frowns reproachfully.

He picks out the hook and sets the leader aside.

'Nice job – you had it in the scissors – didn't even make a mark.'

The fish appears to be panting, but Skelgill seems relaxed. He holds it up to inspect it – and then presents it to his colleague.

'Get a photo – that'll impress Leyton. Wet your hands.'

DS Jones looks askance for a second time. But she dunks her hands into the water and gamely accepts the fish.

'Get a good grip.'

Skelgill pulls out his mobile phone.

'Oh, Guv – I'm going to stink!'

However, she obliges for the snapshot.

'Now put it back – lean over and submerge it – hold it gently until it swims away.'

He shifts to the opposite side of the boat for counterbalance. DS Jones lowers the fish into the water – it becomes buoyant and she relaxes her grip, cradling it in outspread fingers. Its gill flaps start working, its fins begin gently to cycle, it waggles its body – and then with a sudden spurt it darts away, making a little bow wave with its dorsal fin before diving from sight. Skelgill is observing DS Jones; her eyes are alight.

'How do you feel?'

'That was amazing – my heart's pounding! How much do you think it weighed?'

'Three-pound-seven – maybe eight. Call it a four pounder in the pub.'

She grins.

'I can't believe how strong it was.'

Skelgill seems pleased with her assessment.

'A fish is a muscle with fins and a mouth.' He is admiring the photo. 'You know what I like about fishing here?'

He turns the screen for DS Jones to see. She squints – the reflection of the sky may be interfering – but he suspects she is as intrigued by her own image as her catch. She looks up at him with insouciance.

'The company?'

Skelgill grunts sarcastically.

'Look again.'

She does.

'The scenery?'

He shakes his head.

'It's connected with that.'

She purses her lips.

'I give up, Guv.'

Rather jauntily, Skelgill pockets his phone.

'No signal.'

DS Jones chuckles. Now she slides her wrists over the gunwale and dangles her hands in the water. As she rubs them together, there is a sparkle as scales tumble free.

'I can feel the slime, Guv – it doesn't want to come off.'

'It's doing what it's designed for.' He swivels at the waist and delves into the crate of fishing tackle and related paraphernalia. He retrieves a frayed and rather disreputable-looking hand towel. 'Here – this'll do the trick.'

DS Jones accepts the rag with a small amount of trepidation. Skelgill watches her closely. He suspects she has perhaps had her fill. And all of a sudden he is feeling hungry – and for once he lacks the wherewithal – rainbow trout excepted. DS Jones perhaps detects something of his ambivalence.

'How long do you think we should stay, Guv?'

Skelgill makes a face, his features screwed up, his front teeth revealed. An image of the hotel's well-stocked breakfast buffet is erupting Vesuvius-like in his mind's eye.

'Half an hour. Hour max. Cammy reckons the chap that keeps the place opens up at seven. I wouldn't mind seeing him. Let him know we've been and that Cammy's regular tub's still in one piece.' He raps a knuckle twice against the strakes of the hull.

Now something of a silence descends between them. Skelgill seems in no hurry to re-cast. They inhale the still, fresh, dewy air – it is cool, cold almost – but they are well wrapped up. Sound is resonant across the water. Early birds are beginning to make their presence known – a pair of ravens sail over high, croaking to one another like a cantankerous old couple – a distant red grouse prevails upon some rival to 'go-back' – repeating its entreaty a dozen times in a quacking diminuendo – and nearby a parachuting meadow pipit proclaims precedence over its little patch of heather.

It is DS Jones that finally breaks the spell.

'I made a list, Guv.'

'Not of suspects.'

Skelgill's tone conveys that to do so would surely be stating the obvious.

'Not exactly, Guv – after our conversation last night – not so much the who, as the why.' She has her shoulder bag with her, stowed in the bows behind the thwart on which she sits. She reaches around and extracts her notebook. 'I thought – now that we've seen everyone – closer at hand – back in their comfort zones – found out a bit more about them.' She removes the midge hat and lays it on the thwart and shakes out her hair. 'If Scarlett Liddell *were* killed. Why that might be – looking at it from the perspective of possible motives.'

The notebook falls open at a marked page. She rotates it and hands it to Skelgill. He squints suspiciously, and is reluctant to accept – but then is perhaps relieved to see she has in fact drawn a diagram, a sketch. It might almost be for his benefit. There is the outline of Greenmire Castle, with roughly drawn crenulations, its two towers and their staircases, and five storeys, with the guests' names in positions corresponding to their rooms on descending floors:

4th – Scarlett Liddell – Will Liddell
3rd – Felicity Belvedere – Kevin Makepeace
2nd – Belinda Luker – Mike Luker
1st – Suzy Duff – Derek Duff
Lavinia Montagu-Browne – Thomas Montagu-Browne

The Montagu-Brownes are marked on the ground floor – and set apart, away from the building, a stick figure, beside the name, Muriel Liddell. Above the castle float a series of overlapping clouds, a kind of Venn diagram – and inside each of these is written a single word:

Jealousy
Revenge
Greed
Threat

Skelgill scrutinises the page. He is frowning.

'There's at least one missing.'

'A person?'

He shakes his head.

'Control.'

DS Jones appears perplexed.

'How do you mean, Guv?'

Skelgill immediately looks unhappy. There will be a place – and a time – for this kind of speculation, but his gut knows this is neither – and not because they bob at dawn upon an obscure Scottish loch. His pained expression tells that he regrets raising the point. Unwillingly, he elaborates.

'Say it were Will Liddell – killed his wife.' He glances up from the page to see that DS Jones seems uncomfortable with the suggestion. 'If I heard one thing about him yesterday, I heard it half-a-dozen times dressed up in different ways. He likes to be in charge. Scarlett Liddell was a bit of a rebel, a redhead – a hothead. Put the two together and what have you got? He goes in to her bathroom – doesn't like the way she's dressed – or *not* dressed – she tells him where to go. He loses his rag and –'

Skelgill glowers – in fact not so much at what might have happened next – but that he is being drawn down this route – much as it is a perfectly logical train of thought. There is silence for few moments before DS Jones responds.

'I suppose I would have put that down as jealousy, Guv. You know – the idea that she intended to go without underwear – it might have sent the wrong signal.' She regards Skelgill rather tentatively. 'But isn't it more likely she did it for his titillation?'

Skelgill is staring out across the water – he gives the impression that he is looking for promising rises at which to aim his fly – except that his gaze is fixed, his features stern, and perhaps the only fish he imagines making a leap is a red herring. When he does not speak DS Jones adds a rider.

'Besides, Guv – what you say about 'control' – that might be the way he likes things to be – but it's exactly his nature. Have you ever met anyone so in control of their emotions? I just can't imagine him flying off the handle.'

Skelgill grimaces. There ensues another long pause.

'What kind of dog would he be?'

Now DS Jones does a little double take.

'Sorry, Guv?'

Skelgill looks at her as if this is a perfectly regular question.

'If he were a dog – what breed would you say he were?'

DS Jones remains puzzled. Her tone is uneasy.

'I really don't know.'

'Start with one of the others, then.'

Eventually DS Jones comes up with a suggestion.

'Well – Kevin Makepeace – maybe – maybe a Dalmatian?' She pulls a face as if to suggest she is not convinced. 'He's quite showy.'

Skelgill shrugs in a way that indicates he grudgingly accepts her first attempt.

'Derek Duff.'

'Labrador.' Her answer here is unequivocal. 'A friendly one, trying to please.'

Now Skelgill grins fleetingly.

'There you go – it's easier than you thought. Mike Luker, then?'

'Hmm. Something of the Bloodhound, I think, Guv. He looks a bit hangdog and disinterested – but you probably wouldn't want him on your case. He'd be determined to sell you an investment.'

Skelgill waits and watches. DS Jones knows she has to come up with a proposal for Will Liddell. Still she finds this most difficult.

'I think – it's hard to say –' Now she closes her eyes. 'I kind of see a – a *Husky*.'

'Husky? He's nothing like it.'

DS Jones shrugs rather helplessly.

'Well I know, Guv – not to look at – but maybe it's because of his eyes – they're a really icy blue – and that's what I associate with Huskies.'

Skelgill ponders this assertion. His silence suggests he buys into her logic.

'Er, Guv?'

'Aye?'

'Why do you ask?'

Still holding the notebook he stretches, reaching his arms above his head and bringing them down and flexing his biceps like a strongman.

'Muriel Liddell – I don't know if she was trying to tell me something – like Will Liddell's not what he seems.'

Now Skelgill looks again at the page. Whether to see if some connection has emerged following his unorthodox intervention – or just long enough to pay lip service to his sergeant's efforts, it is hard to say. But he hands it back with a wry grin.

'You need a list of weapons – like, what's it called? – *Cluedo*.'

DS Jones looks momentarily downcast – that his allusion reduces her method to that of a parlour game.

'Except we know it was a feather boa, Guv.'

Skelgill grimaces.

'We just don't know if it was a *murder* weapon.'

*

'Feeling better, Guv?'

Skelgill has cast down his cutlery and now he settles back in his seat. They have the same breakfast table as yesterday morning, overlooking the Glasgow road, silent through the thick plate glass. He nods, experimentally almost – as if he is testing for a sore head. The good old 'Full English' – although in this case he has to remind himself it is a 'Full Scottish', bacon, egg and beans, augmented by potato scone and haggis pudding, and the sausage a square of Lorne. It has no basis in biochemistry, but saturated fat and salt, washed down by sugary tea, seems to cure hangovers where paracetamol fails.

'There's sommat not right.'

DS Jones looks at Skelgill with apprehension – she realises he doesn't mean with himself – he might be recalcitrant but her boss is no hypochondriac.

'In what respect, Guv?'

Skelgill looks out on the commuter flow.

'On that loch – there was an unusual sound?' Skelgill is straining his features, an effort it seems to conjure up the memory. 'Like a – what would you call it – like a traffic noise. Distant traffic – reminded me of what the A66 sounds like when you're on Bass Lake – it's this constant sort of – I dunno – somewhere between a hum and a hiss.' Absently he digs at a tooth with a fingernail. 'Except – up in those hills there's no way we could have heard traffic.'

'I don't think I noticed, Guv.'

'That loch is actually an artificial reservoir. I looked more closely when we left. There's a dam and a concrete spillway – it was the sound of the water rippling over the corrugations. But in that tight little glen the sound waves had nowhere to go – they were echoing about and filling the air – so you couldn't locate the source.'

While in these circumstances, were DS Leyton present, he would simply ask, "So what, Guv?" – but DS Jones surfs the wave of her superior's obscure logic. She takes a shot at his meaning.

'There's something pervading this investigation, some context that we don't properly perceive?'

Skelgill frowns, albeit benignly.

'Say that again for someone who's not got an English degree.'

DS Jones grins sheepishly.

'Okay – it's like – like when you see a little kid with their parent – you wonder why they're walking strangely, pulling the adult about – then you realise they're trying not to tread on any cracks, in case the bears get them.'

The graphic image appeals to Skelgill's mind, and DS Jones probably knows it.

'Aye – that is what I'm saying. There's something about this crowd that we don't know about. Cracks – bears – whatever.'

DS Jones would be forgiven for wondering if her superior is simply not struggling with some cultural barrier. The sphere in which they are operating – if not exactly representing Edinburgh's titled upper classes, is not far beneath – an echelon of society that has famously been painted as *the crème de la crème*. Moreover, he may be disappointed that she does not enthusiastically share his discord. While she has made intuitive observations that raise questions about each of Derek Duff, Mike Luker and Kevin Makepeace – her assessment of Will Liddell has been neutral, if not mildly positive – when twenty-four hours ago it was plain Skelgill felt uneasy in despatching her alone to deal with him. Thus she might also appraise her own performance – has she done well – or in some perverse way have Skelgill's indeterminate fears been borne out?

Such deliberations on DS Jones's part are halted by a jaunty musical interjection – *The Lambeth Walk*. It is Skelgill's ringtone for DS Leyton. His handset lies on the table and he jabs twice with an index finger to accept the call and activate the speaker.

'Get the photo, Leyton?'

'You're winding me up, Guv – it says it was taken at six-thirty this morning.'

'Early worm catches the trout, Leyton.'

'*Ha-hah* – very good, Guv. Just as well it's DS Jones with you – you wouldn't get me in a boat to save myself from flippin' drowning.'

'You're on speaker, Leyton.'

'Oh – righto – morning, Emma – nice one, girl.'

DS Jones chuckles – and exchanges further pleasantries with her colleague – and jokes that at least their superior did not make her eat her catch for breakfast. Skelgill listens with a certain mildly affronted diffidence. However, DS Leyton has a purpose for calling – and despite his engagement with the casual banter, he is about to drop a little bombshell.

'Guv – thought I'd better let you know. Lab report came in early doors. They found traces of alien skin under Scarlett Liddell's nails – they've run a DNA test – *it belongs to Will Liddell.*'

14. CATRIONA

Wednesday, 6pm

'Mr Liddell – we have the doctor's report of the examination you voluntarily submitted to.' DS Leyton pats the clip of notes on the desk. He does so ostentatiously, and speaks slowly and perhaps with more careful enunciation than is his custom. Having journeyed up to Scotland, it is as if he believes the recording equipment – belonging to the local constabulary – might struggle with his rogue accent. 'The report states there are scratches on your left forearm that are consistent with the fingernails of an adult. The extent of healing corresponds to the marks having been made around four days ago. That would be Saturday. Could you provide an explanation for how you got them?'

Will Liddell sits implacably, his arms folded. He wears a somewhat creased pink open-necked shirt with the cuffs buttoned down. That he has cooperated with what could be described as a police 'swoop' upon his office premises, ostensibly taking him into custody in the – if not full glare – then certainly semi-public view of some members of staff, can perhaps be credited in his favour. Likewise that he has not objected to attending the local headquarters for the purposes of 'helping police with their inquiries'. On the other hand, his taciturn manner might be considered an obstructive tactic – were it not something of which Skelgill has recent experience. That events have taken this sudden turn may be traced back to a quirk of fate of almost two decades earlier. In his final year at St Andrews University – through a piece of what Skelgill, upon hearing the details of the report, considered was probably bad luck – Will Liddell had managed to get himself on the national DNA database. Playing beach football one afternoon in summer term,

Will Liddell's group had found themselves embroiled in some altercation with local hoodlums. Police had been called to intervene, though the fracas proved to be much ado about nothing. However, a search of persons and effects had found 2 ounces of marijuana in Will Liddell's sweatshirt pocket. The offending garment had been pressed into service in the time-honoured manner of 'jumpers for goalposts'. That the pocket also contained tobacco, cigarette papers and a lighter – Will Liddell a non-smoker – and moreover a state-of-the-art mobile phone and a fat wallet (neither of which being common student possessions back in the day) – began to cloud the issue. And, when none other than the mercurial Hearts playmaker Derek Duff claimed the mobile phone and wallet, further doubt was cast upon Will Liddell's guilt. Indeed his defence was that, clearly, his sweatshirt had been treated as a safe repository for 'valuables'. Regardless, the lack of enthusiasm on the part of the real owner to come forward, and a general unwillingness amongst the group to point a finger, left the police with no option but to charge Will Liddell with the possession of a controlled substance. However, official resources being stretched, the case gathered dust, an accumulation that ultimately buried it out of sight, and finally out of mind. But, while the matter faded from the memory – what did not was the DNA sample that Will Liddell had been required to provide as part of the charging procedure. In due course he would have been within his rights to request that this be deleted – but, unaware that it had survived, he did no such thing. And thus, a minor transgression of presumably none other than Derek Duff's led two decades later to the identification of his long-standing friend Will Liddell as a suspect of greater import in the unexplained death of his second wife.

'It must have been at Greystoke – the assault course.'

At this rejoinder of Will Liddell's DS Leyton's tone loses something of its authority.

'Can – can you remember that occurring, sir?'

'Not especially. It was a rough-and-tumble. The competitive spirit took over – you didn't pay particular attention to what damage you were doing to yourself – nor probably to others in the process.'

This much may be true – since also mentioned in the medic's report are minor grazes and bruises to the knees and elbows, and the semblance of rope burns to the palms of the hands and around the shins. DS Leyton casts a shifty sideways glance at Skelgill. His superior pinches his nose between the thumb and forefinger of his left hand. DS Leyton seems to regain his composure, as if it were a prearranged signal.

'The thing is, you see, sir – the forensic information indicates that these scratches on your arm were made by your wife.'

Skelgill observes from behind the cover of his nose. But Will Liddell remains unperturbed.

'Then I have no reason to doubt that they were, Sergeant.'

DS Leyton makes a grumbling sound in his throat.

'Did you notice the scratches – when you got back to your room on Saturday evening, sir?'

'I didn't take time to examine myself. Like I say – bumps and bruises were par for the course. I submerged in a foam bath.'

DS Leyton flicks agitatedly through his notes and glances again at Skelgill, but his superior appears to have cast him adrift, and sits motionless. They had recognised the importance of an urgent examination of Will Liddell – something that had appeared to bear fruit. Had the scratches, apparently inflicted between wife and husband, related to a more conventional act of passion, there would have been less cause for suspicion; the forearm however is a different matter. But now Will Liddell presents an explanation that frustrates them. Of course, he has had some time to think of this – but still it leaves DS Leyton rather stymied. With no assistance from Skelgill, he resorts to a somewhat predictable and hackneyed line of questioning.

'Perhaps you would just remind us of what took place between when you last saw your wife and when you discovered her – that was together with Mrs – er, Mrs Duff, I believe it was?'

Will Liddell is watching DS Leyton closely – he seems intrigued that the officer is plainly labouring. Perhaps he draws the comparison with a business meeting – and concludes that he does not find his adversary especially challenging. Equally, while he has been asked before, he shows no impatience at being required to replicate the detail.

'She was still in the drawing room with the other girls when I went upstairs. That was some time after five. It could have been a quarter past.'

DS Leyton interjects.

'Did you speak to her, sir – tell her that you were leaving?'

Will Liddell shakes his head.

'She was holding court. Besides – it would have been pretty obvious where I had gone. All she had to do was come through to my suite.'

'But she didn't do that, sir?'

'If she did, it was when I was sleeping – or, I suppose in the bath.'

'Would it have been her habit to disturb you, sir – in either of those situations?'

Will Liddell looks keenly at his questioner.

'Yes.'

Now there is a pause; DS Leyton seems surprised that the man answers so definitively.

'So you would be quite certain she didn't come through.'

'My bathroom door may have been locked. I don't remember. But in that case I might not have heard her. I was listening to music.'

'Do you normally lock the bathroom door, sir?'

'It depends what I am doing, Sergeant.'

DS Leyton gives a somewhat indiscreet *ahem*.

'You said you fell asleep – and dressed in a hurry for the Murder Mystery event – and that was when you found your wife's room apparently empty. What time was that?'

'Just after seven. On my way out I grabbed my watch – I remember checking on the stairs as I put it on – that I was only a couple of minutes late. I had intended to be first in the library – in my capacity as what you might call 'host'. As it turned out, only Kevin was there.'

140

'That's Mr Makepeace?'

'Correct.'

'And you remained in the library until – as you have described – you first went up to find the external door of your wife's room locked – and then you went back up the other staircase with Mrs Duff.'

DS Leyton looks expectantly at Will Liddell; but the man merely nods.

'And has anything come to mind, sir – about those moments – now you've had time to reflect.'

'As I said – we found her – we tried to revive her – we failed.'

Will Liddell speaks in a tight-lipped manner. He stares at DS Leyton – coldly it seems, through his pale blue eyes – and then transfers his gaze to Skelgill – who seems to be thinking about something else – for, becoming conscious of Will Liddell's scrutiny, he starts, and rocks forward in his seat. DS Leyton seems unsure of where to go next – but now Skelgill tugs his left ear lobe – which might be another cue. Indeed, he interjects.

'Right, sir – we'll just leave it there for the time being.' He looks at DS Leyton with a faint inclination of his head in the direction of the interview room door. Then he glances back at Will Liddell. 'We appreciate your patience, sir.'

Will Liddell for his part nods curtly and reaches for his briefcase – as though he intends to fill any time with work that he has brought with him. The detectives depart in a somewhat shambolic fashion – as if they are trying to exit before the man asks when he might be invited to leave.

*

'There was no chance of detaining him, Guv – we're skating on thin ice as far as those injuries are concerned.'

Skelgill is staring across the rather nondescript open-plan hotel lounge to where DS Jones is engaged in conversation with a young bartender who looks like he is trying to chat her up. He releases the breath he has been holding and turns to DS Leyton.

'That's as maybe, Leyton – but we needed that medical evidence. Much longer and those scratches will be healed. Better thin ice than melt-water that slips through the net.'

DS Leyton is making the most of his heavy jowls in looking gloomy.

'Do you reckon he's reacted normally, Guv?'

'What's normal, Leyton?'

'Well – if you were innocent – wouldn't you have asked more questions? Wanted to know what we were up to? Apparently he didn't even query being lifted – just came along like a lamb – like he knew he was bang to rights.'

Skelgill's expression is one of scepticism.

'He's a poker player, Leyton – a businessman. It's his MO. Besides, start asking questions – what do you do?' (DS Leyton looks blank.) 'You lead the other person – give them ideas they've never had.'

DS Leyton shrugs despondently.

'He's got a flamin' neat get-out for those scratches on his arm, Guv.'

'Not necessarily.'

Skelgill is stern faced. He is again watching DS Jones. When he does not elaborate, DS Leyton offers a prompt.

'How's that, Guv?'

'Scarlett Liddell wasn't in his team.'

'Blimey, Guv – that's interesting.' DS Leyton ruminates for a moment or two and appears to perk up. 'I suppose we've got a few little cards up our sleeve.'

But Skelgill is looking doubtful. If Will Liddell is the poker player that he makes him out to be, then this small conflicting fact concerning the scratches is unlikely to prove to be some kind of ace. He knows the other so-called 'cards' to which DS Leyton refers are that Scarlett Liddell was wearing no underwear, and that she was pregnant – issues on which they have chosen not to challenge Will Liddell. Even so, Skelgill has no sense that they have some kind of 'strong hand'. As he wrestles with their predicament, his mind's eye seems to prefer other metaphors – are these straws in the wind – or is he clutching at straws? The latter seems more apposite – and yet it recalls his experience on the loch before breakfast: just what is the background sibilance that won't go away?

His thoughts are interrupted as DS Jones rejoins them bearing on a small circular tray their drinks and generous measure of hand-cooked potato crisps, the bowl overflowing cornucopia-fashion. She dispenses the beverages, and places the snack within closest reach of Skelgill. However, she sees that the beer, which is rather anarchically labelled as *Banana Boat IPA*, brings on a look of disapproval. She gets in her defence as Skelgill inhales to pronounce.

'The barman said it's a trendy real ale, Guv.'

'It can't be real ale if it's in a bottle – it's not physically possible.'

DS Leyton makes an effort to defuse the minor tension. He lifts his own pint experimentally.

'I just stick to the cooking lager – you know what you're getting.'

'Aye – pasteurised pop.'

DS Jones has what may be plain tonic water with ice – but she takes her seat and stoically raises her glass. Rather by conditioned reflex Skelgill grudgingly drinks, directly from the bottle; but he is apparently pleasantly surprised by the effect, for his scowl dissipates. The bar is furnished in lounge style with modern square-cushioned sofas surrounding knee-high chrome-framed tables with smoked glass tops. DS Jones opens her notebook and positions it on the polished surface so that her colleagues can both see it. It is the page with the sketch of Greenmire Castle, and the list of suspects and motives.

She looks up and grins optimistically; Skelgill's body language is not the most auspicious – yet this parley is called at his behest – he would not use the word 'brainstorming', but the logjam that he feels they have drifted into has prompted him to command something of the sort. However, it is evident he lacks enthusiasm for the process.

'Leyton – you kick off.'

With a grunt DS Leyton pitches forward and inspects the page with a look of consternation.

'Thing is, Guv – if Scarlett Liddell were killed – and her stair door was locked on the inside – it's hard to see past Will Liddell – I mean, literally, like – if it were some other geezer he'd have needed to sneak past him.'

Skelgill promptly breaks the first rule of brainstorming by lobbing in a little cluster of objections.

'Not if they waited in the bathroom, Leyton – and not if Will Liddell misled us about the external door being locked. Besides, how do you know it was a *'geezer'*?'

DS Leyton looks somewhat crestfallen.

'But why would he make that up, Guv – about the lock? It just looks worse for him?'

Skelgill's expression darkens.

'You tell me, Leyton – we're supposed to be having ideas.'

DS Leyton's countenance is pained – but he takes a gulp of lager and, suitably refreshed, tilts again at the windmill that is a mirage on the horizon of Skelgill's imagination.

'What if it were all the other way round, then, Guv? What if Will Liddell went into Scarlett Liddell's suite and found her canoodling with someone?' He holds up a finger to silence any protests, and perhaps also to demonstrate his fighting spirit. 'The geezer – *ha!* – he scarpers – does one. Will Liddell locks the door after him – turns round to demand of his wife what's going on. She backs away – he follows her into the bathroom. Takes it too far. Panics – tries to make it look like suicide.'

But Skelgill is quick to retort.

'Then the mystery *'geezer'* has conveniently not mentioned it, Leyton. Nor has the wife – or ex-wife, in the case of Kevin Makepeace – whose suite he'd likely go through to get back to his room.'

DS Leyton receives this rebuttal phlegmatically – as though it is in fact a plausible explanation – but Skelgill sees that DS Jones appears troubled by the idea. However, as he watches her, something gains her attention behind him; her eyes narrow appraisingly. DS Leyton, in a vaguely similar manner, is equally captivated.

'Reckon you might have company, Guv.'

Skelgill swivels around in his seat to see a young woman standing about eight feet away. She is wearing close-fitting gym gear that is visibly damp with perspiration – likewise a headband that restrains a shock of red hair, though strands of it have escaped and are plastered across her forehead. Her bare shoulders glisten with sweat, and heave gently, as if she is still recovering her breath. Her pose is defiant – yet she bites her lower lip to suppress what might be apprehension. It is Catriona – aka Miss Brodie of St Salvator's School For Girls. Her voice, when it comes, is husky, almost a whisper.

'May I have a word, Inspector?'

Skelgill feels two pairs of eyes burning into his back as he rises and stalks across to face her. He stands directly between the woman and his colleagues and blocks their view. He raises an eyebrow in lieu of a direct question.

'Sorry to disrupt your meeting, Inspector – I seem to have made myself unpopular.'

Skelgill gives an indifferent shrug.

'How did you find me?'

'You told me you were lodging here.'

'Aye – but I didn't plan on staying tonight.'

'I'm a member of the health club – I saw you through the glass.'

'You came to the gym?'

What Skelgill questions is the suggestion that her first intention was not to meet him. By way of response she glances down at her *Lycra*-clad figure – it is self-evident. Now there is a tremor in her voice.

'I thought I should act – while my endorphins are in the ascendancy.'

Skelgill is unsure of her motive.

'Sounds like the sort of thing my old biology mistress would say. I never did know what she was talking about.'

She flashes a patient smile – but her features quickly regain their serious cast.

'Is there somewhere private?'

Skelgill glances back at his sergeants – as if for a moment he is thinking of dismissing them to free up the seating area. But he grimaces.

'I've got a bedroom. If you can stand the mess.'

Again she forces a grin – and seems to waver in her determination. Skelgill waits.

'Ok.'

*

'Bears and cracks.'

'Guv?'

'It's beginning to make sense.'

Skelgill, grim-faced, has returned to their table. He stands over DS Jones, holding out the little branded wallet that contains his room keycard.

'This is one for you, Jones. Take your notebook.'

'What do I do, Guv?'

'You feel a pull – you strike – remember?'

It is evident that no more explanation will be forthcoming – but DS Jones understands enough that she is to take over whatever interview has begun – and that for reasons of his own her superior wants her to treat it as a blank canvas. Skelgill reaches down for his bottle of IPA, and then steps aside to allow her to pass. He swigs the bottle's contents – glances at the state of DS Leyton's pint – and stalks away to the bar.

*

'She's agreed to press charges, Guv.'

If Skelgill were a man that suffered 'high-fives' he would probably raise his palm now, as DS Jones nears their table – but in any event he detects something in her manner that holds back celebration – the look in her eyes, while triumphant, is also

146

disturbed. That upon resuming her seat and first reaching for her drink and taking a large gulp (maybe not plain tonic, after all) is an action that chimes with his intuition. There is a moment's silence – and now both of the males lean forward to rest their forearms upon their thighs, and gaze expectantly at their female colleague.

'She said it was about a year ago, Guv – she wasn't sure of the exact date but she has it in her school calendar. Will Liddell had been to watch a hockey match. It was his daughter's year group. Catriona Brodie wasn't coaching – she was supporting, and scouting. She was wearing the staff sports kit – so it was obvious she was a teacher. The first thing she really knew about him being there was during the second period. She realised he was standing beside her – she said although she recognised him, they weren't formally acquainted – but of course she knew his daughter – at some point he introduced himself and they exchanged small talk. Then towards the end of the game he told her that he ran a company and he was wondering if he could sponsor the school kit. She explained that St Salvator's like most private schools had a policy not to display company logos and advertising – but that his daughter's local club would probably take his hand off. He didn't seem very interested in that idea. Meanwhile she was feeling conflicted – the school was in the middle of a fund-raising campaign to pay for the new sports pavilion – so she decided to mention it. He didn't say anything at first – but then a few minutes later he asked her if the school held charitable status. Her answer was yes. He said he had a transaction on the horizon – that he was looking for a capital investment – a good cause – to take advantage of a tax break. She said the sum he mentioned had her head spinning. It seemed like a gift horse – and she doesn't mind admitting that she saw a chance – if not to cover herself in glory, at least to gain some kudos with the Head and the Board of Trustees. He invited her for a drink to discuss it.'

'Oh-oh.'

It is DS Leyton that supplies this belated warning. Skelgill silences him with an impatient glare. DS Jones continues – still working from memory.

'After the game he waited for her in his *Range Rover*. He drove them across to Morningside – to a cosy pub where he was obviously a regular. He used the excuse that he didn't like to drink in the vicinity of the school – his first wife lived in the area and he might bump into her or people whom he knew from when they were together. Catriona Brodie said she was feeling nervous – but in an excited way – and she drank more than she normally would. He didn't say much about the technicalities of the donation – other than he seemed to be trying to work out just how big he could legitimately make it. She said he was polite, if enigmatic – but she never felt like he was trying to chat her up. It got to about 7.30pm and she was feeling a little bit drunk and that she ought to get home. But he didn't give her an easy opportunity to break away – and the barman seemed to bring fresh drinks every time her glass was nearly empty. Then suddenly he announced that he wanted to write a proposal and send it to his accountant – that night – there was a Board meeting the next morning and it was essential to get it on the agenda before the tax year-end deadline. He asked her if she'd come round to his house – just to help him with the wording – information on the background of the school and the pavilion project – and that when they'd done he'd call her a taxi on his company account. He also said he'd made bolognaise earlier – that he'd like it if she joined him and his wife for supper. She said a little warning bell rang in her head – but he asked her in a way that was hard to refuse – not least there was the big deal on the table. So she said yes.'

DS Jones pauses for breath – but she need have no fear of any waning in her audience's attention. Skelgill nods for her to proceed.

'When they got to the house – apparently he lives in what is virtually a mansion in one of the wealthiest districts – she realised there was nobody else home. He said something like Scarlett Liddell would be back shortly. But anyway he fixed them some food and opened wine. When they'd finished she told him she didn't have much time – he said that's no problem – and he led her to his study on the first floor – overlooking mature gardens at the back of the property. He gave her the seat at his desk and a pad and a pen and asked her to write a list of reasons why the school would benefit from the funding – when you think about it, something they could have done in the kitchen – or the pub come to that. He slipped away, saying he'd be back in a minute – and he went through an interconnecting door into what she glimpsed was a master bedroom.'

Though DS Jones's colleagues do not know precisely what is coming, Catriona Brodie has told Skelgill what the gist of her 'confession' will be – and he has imparted this skeleton outline to DS Leyton. But the gradual unfolding, the sinister methodology, has brought revulsion in equal measure to their faces.

'She was writing, as requested. She heard him re-enter the study, quietly. He came up close behind – as if not to disturb her, but to look over her shoulder to see how she was getting on. She was seated on one of these ergonomic stools that has no back. She felt him press against her. For a second she just thought he'd misjudged his position. But he didn't step away. She realised his breathing was heavy. Then he started stroking her hair. She said whatever she thought she'd do in such a situation – fight or flight – she didn't. She froze. She said she was entirely paralysed by fear. He was wearing a dressing gown. He was naked underneath. He crooked an arm around her throat. He tried to swivel her around – but she kept her feet planted and held onto the desk with her fingertips. Nevertheless – what took place constitutes a serious sexual assault. He never spoke a word.'

DS Jones's mouth is dry and she reaches for her drink and drains the glass. Her expression is one of dismay – while looks of vengeance crease the faces of her colleagues. DS Jones puts down her glass. Skelgill sees that her hand is trembling.

'Then they were disturbed. There was a noise downstairs – Scarlett Liddell had returned – it was late-night shopping and she'd been buying clothes. Catriona Brodie said she'd noticed a bathroom off the landing – as Will Liddell was distracted she ran through and took refuge. She doesn't really remember how long she was locked in there – but after a while she heard voices – it was Will and Scarlett Liddell laughing. She went downstairs and they were in the kitchen. Will Liddell was dressed – sitting on a barstool – they were both drinking champagne. There was a stack of designer-label carrier bags – and he was admiring an outfit that Scarlett Liddell was holding up in front of her. She looked daggers at Catriona Brodie, and put her arm around Will Liddell and made some boast about how they were going to a VIP ball at Gleneagles at the weekend. Will Liddell was acting completely normally – she didn't know if he'd explained why she was ostensibly there – but she realised in that instant she couldn't say anything about what had just taken place.'

'What did she do, girl?' This is DS Leyton, his voice hoarse with concern.

'She mumbled some excuse and left. She ran home across town – a couple of miles. She lives not far from the school – in one of the new flats beside Roseburn.'

'And – what – she's never told no one?'

DS Jones regards her colleague intently.

'She says she confided in her flatmate – on the same night – but she made her promise never to speak of it. Apart from the humiliation and the trauma – she had a boyfriend at the time – she was sure he would have done something that would have got her sacked – and the huge sum of money was on the line – she's still terrified of losing her job, and that the donation will be withdrawn.'

Skelgill's features are like cold granite – but rage burns deep in his grey-green eyes. As if it would be worth the price! He grinds his left fist into the palm of his right hand.

'Aye – Will Liddell's ex said he came up with the money. A million. And now we know it was probably a tax dodge, to boot.'

That he refrains from bringing the words 'hush money' into his rejoinder does not stop DS Jones from raising the sentiment.

'She's simply kept quiet about it, Guv. Of course she's done everything she can to avoid Will Liddell when he has appeared at the school. But she says if their paths do unexpectedly cross he acts as though absolutely nothing has happened.'

DS Leyton shifts uncomfortably in his seat.

'So – what's made her speak now?'

DS Jones turns interrogatively to Skelgill.

'Maybe something you said, Guv. Some effect you had on her, anyway – gave her the confidence that we'd believe her and act upon it.'

Skelgill is wondering – ironically Catriona Brodie had invited him for coffee – at least coffee is what she said. *Can they trust her account implicitly?* And yet, when he had declined – there was something about her manner – as if he had passed a little test. Perhaps it was never an invitation in the first place – one that would have been immediately rescinded had he accepted. Was she testing herself, too – to see if she could take the first step towards baring her soul?

'You know me and my silver tongue.'

Skelgill says this sardonically – and his subordinates dutifully smile, if mirthlessly under the circumstances. Now DS Jones elaborates as far as she can.

'She heard about Will Liddell being 'arrested' – as she put it. She said it was all over social media this afternoon – there are various school-related chat groups – hockey mums – that sort of thing. Someone from his company must have let the cat out of the bag. There was the suggestion that it was connected with Scarlett Liddell's death – naturally she drew her own conclusions about events at Greenmire Castle. In the gym she got mad with herself – that she'd have it on her conscience – if there were another offence. As she was leaving she saw you, Guv – and she plucked up courage. Maybe tomorrow she'd have changed her mind.'

DS Leyton lets out an extended sigh.

'Let's hope the girl don't lose her bottle.'

Skelgill makes a sharp scoffing exclamation.

'We're in Scotland, Leyton – I haven't noticed it's in short supply.'

'Right enough, Guv.'

But Skelgill is pensive. His brow is furrowed as he addresses DS Jones.

'Where is she, now?'

DS Jones looks just a trifle uneasy beneath her superior's scrutiny.

'I let her go home – her flatmate's there – she phoned her. She says she'll be fine – that it's a massive weight off her mind. And she said she's got your number, Guv.'

Skelgill's gaze flickers. A little distractedly he checks his watch.

'The local CID will have to deal with this. I'll get hold of Cammy – make sure their top team's on it first thing in the morning.'

DS Jones remains apprehensive.

'The only possible fly in the ointment is that she thinks Will Liddell is still in custody.'

'He will be, soon enough.'

Skelgill's retort is terse – and DS Leyton is looking sympathetically at DS Jones – for it is plain the episode has been an ordeal for her, too. He reaches across and lifts her empty glass and then hooks Skelgill's bottle by its neck with his little finger.

'I reckon another drink is in order.'

DS Jones nods gratefully – her colleague levers his bulk from the seat and propels himself in the direction of the bar. A small silence follows, during which Skelgill makes a mental effort to step back from the immediate disclosure.

'We're going to need corroboration.'

DS Jones regards him keenly.

'Guv – she's preserved the top she was wearing – it was a school polo shirt. She also claims there's an identifying birthmark – of Will Liddell's.'

Skelgill nods broodingly.

'And you say she told her girlfriend on the same night? That might count for something.'

Rather than affirm his remark, DS Jones glances anxiously to see if DS Leyton is about to return – but it is apparent he is yet to be served.

'Guv – there's something I need to tell you.'

'Aye.' Skelgill's flat intonation suggests he half knows what to expect.

'When I went for a drink with Will Liddell.'

Now he simply stares at his colleague.

'On reflection – he was very presumptuous – in a subtle way. For instance, he didn't ask me what I wanted – he just ordered a bottle of wine and two glasses. I tried not to drink – I asked the waitress for tap water when she brought the wine. But it was after we'd been there a while...'

Skelgill seems to be nodding, almost imperceptibly.

'He said I should come for supper – to his house. That he'd made a bolognaise – *yes!*' She raises her hands in a gesture of self-reproach. 'He said he'd come across something about Scarlett that he wanted to bounce off me – something that he was struggling to understand, but that he thought I might be able to figure out. And again he didn't really ask – whether I would go – it was more an assumption – it put the onus on me to raise an objection.'

DS Jones is looking disconcerted. But so is Skelgill. He swallows – and speaks first.

'Just as well you prefer Indian to Italian.'

But Skelgill's black humour does not allay her alarm. She checks to see DS Leyton is now preoccupied with placing their order. Wide-eyed she reaches across and presses her hand on Skelgill's wrist.

'I'm only seeing this now, Guv – since hearing Catriona Brodie's account. Will Liddell's got this way about him – insidiously reassuring – he makes you feel important.'

'I must try it on the Chief.'

Again his flippant rejoinder is ineffectual. There is a rising note of desperation in DS Jones's voice.

'Guv – I was falling for it. It's a kind of grooming.'

Skelgill stares at his subordinate.

'Jones – Catriona Brodie's a tough cookie – and *she* fell for it.'

Now DS Jones agonises.

'Guv – what I'm saying – I doubt if she's the only victim.'

15. LONDON

Friday, noon

'I recognise this street, Leyton.'

DS Leyton chuckles.

'I'm not surprised, Guv – it's where you walloped that knifeman – that time you got your mugshot in the *Evening Standard*.'

Indeed, Skelgill is subsumed by a flashback – a blur of action and adrenaline – as they pass the vaguely familiar entrance to a restaurant that is guarded by a burly doorman, built like a rhino, incongruous in his pristine fur felt top hat and smart *Crombie* overcoat – and yet Skelgill overhears him greet in dulcet tones an uber-trendy young couple who make a dash from a taxi that has pulled up with a jolt at the kerbside.

'Look at that, Guv!'

DS Leyton's words are hissed, his voice awed.

'What, Leyton?'

'That was Jamie Knobble – you know – plays for Spurs?'

As the two detectives continue past, Skelgill cranes his neck – but all he gets is a glimpse of the girl's long tanned legs beneath a micro-skirt as she totters on high heels after her famous companion – and a black look from the doorman who thinks he is ogling her.

'Can't say I do, Leyton.'

'He's just broken through into the England team, Guv – they reckon he'll be our saviour – deadliest striker since Jimmy Greaves – scored a hat-trick on his debut in that World Cup qualifier against Gibraltar.'

Skelgill scowls. He supports the national side out of patriotic duty, but has little detailed knowledge of the goings on in football – or most popular sports, come to that. And certainly he has long given up any hopes of England ever again winning the World Cup.

'What are we doing playing Gibraltar? I thought that was supposed to be part of Britain.'

DS Leyton flashes his superior a sideways glance, uncertain if he is taking the mickey.

'Well – so's Scotland part of Britain, Guv – but we still play 'em. In fact we're in the same group as the Jocks an' all.' He shakes his head despondently. 'I'm not happy about that – they always raise their game against England – it's not fair competition. Our lot should have let them win more often, back in the day – not just that consolation Bannockburn malarkey – then maybe they wouldn't be so desperate to beat us now.'

Skelgill does not respond. He experiences a moment of reflection. To a degree, there is merit in carrying something of the underdog in one's soul – it does indeed enable the fighting spirit to draw upon some deep well of inner resilience. But it is a trait best kept to oneself. Allowed to manifest itself in public, it rapidly decays – like an apple cut in two that oxidises in the air – becomes bitter, a chip on the shoulder; it loses sympathy. It is a battle he fights in almost every unsolved case. Clearly, at the outset, the detective *is* the underdog – often there is little to go on – and all concerned appreciates this. But in his game patience quickly wears thin. The 'powers that be' are fickle, one day supportive, the next harbouring unreasonable expectations of progress – perhaps having made brash commitments to their own bosses, or the media and the public. At such a juncture Skelgill knows there is little point in pleading underdog – or bad luck or lack of resources – not least when he has promoted the case.

In the first hours of the death of Scarlett Liddell becoming a police matter, he felt strongly there was something awry. It was not a sentiment he could quantify – but he carried with him some echo of the young woman's vitality when she called out to him from their pleasure boat – having no idea who he was, or that forty-eight hours later he would be investigating her apparent suicide. And this initial discord – characterised by consensus with DS Jones as an all-pervasive sibilance – it kept him going. Further, when some intuition drew him to Catriona Brodie (did he experience subliminally some inexplicable incarnation of Scarlett Liddell?) – there ensued *prima facie* a vital breakthrough. But it is a breakthrough only of sorts.

Will Liddell has perhaps been exposed – and this unmasking might account for some fraction of Skelgill's unease: in particular the guardedness of Will Liddell's coterie. It would be natural to close ranks – even if they did not really know themselves for what purpose. But Catriona Brodie's revelation – now a statement signed and sealed that sees Will Liddell confined in custody while matters proceed – has merely opened up an entirely new front on Scottish soil – under the jurisdiction of the Scottish police, a charge of sexual assault, which Will Liddell flatly denies. It has shed no new light whatsoever on the death of Scarlett Liddell. Skelgill and his team are no closer to disproving suicide, to which the circumstantial evidence overwhelmingly points. And thus the rapidly growing burden of intolerance that Skelgill feels heaped upon him from above.

Hence, today's arrangement. While DS Jones is delegated to desk research on various unspecified aspects of the Greenmire case (reluctantly accepting her superior's decision that she is best equipped for such), Skelgill and DS Leyton have travelled to London to see what they can unearth. Although Skelgill's optimism is roughly on a par with his hopes for the national football team, Jamie Knobble or not, DS Leyton is by comparison chipper. Back on home turf, he swaggers through Covent Garden, specifically the irregular maze of narrow streets between Charing Cross Road and – ironically, it seems to Skelgill – their destination of Bow Street, where the London branch of *Liddell Acorns Incorporated* is domiciled.

*

'So is this in fact the head office, madam?'

Marina Vanity, Director of Human Resources – an exceptionally well-groomed suntanned blonde in her mid-fifties –

casually tilts her head to one side. Beneath a composed exterior (which may not be entirely natural) Skelgill detects caution in brown eyes that are watchful and shrewd. This is despite that the detectives have made it clear they are investigating the death of Scarlett Liddell – and that they have no connection to the separate inquiry occurring north of the border, which has seen Chairman and Chief Executive Will Liddell detained by the Scottish force.

'The holding company is registered in Edinburgh, Inspector – however, many of the senior functions are based here in London. There are significant economies of scale when it comes to sourcing external resources, such as finance and advertising, for which London is an international hub.' Her vocabulary and clear enunciation tells she is an intelligent and educated woman. 'And then, if an organisation is to retain the top talent, there are personal factors that cannot be ignored.'

'What would they be, madam?'

She appears to suspect Skelgill of being disingenuous; however her reply is delivered in a matter-of-fact tone.

'For higher earners there are significant tax disadvantages of moving to Scotland, especially if one intends to own property.' She reaches out, immaculately manicured fingers seem to hover above an electronic tablet that lies upon the coffee table between them; she squints at the display. 'And today it is 18 degrees in London, 4 degrees in Edinburgh.'

These are not the answers Skelgill has anticipated – and any mention of the climate is likely to lure him off track, not least the uselessness of the compressed Celsius scale if one is an angler, when a degree or two of water temperature can mean the difference between success and failure. However, he refrains from responding along such lines, or even mentally converting the figures to his favoured Fahrenheit.

'That didn't put off Scarlett Liddell from transferring to Edinburgh.'

The woman regales him with a look of what might be mild annoyance, mostly but not entirely concealed.

'Paradoxically, for a more junior employee the cost of living would be significantly less than London.' She flashes a half-smile that seems constrained by the taut skin of her cheeks. 'Regardless, when ambitious young people are building their careers they will set aside personal considerations.'

'And you would describe Scarlett Liddell as ambitious.'

Skelgill's tone is insistent; however on this point she does not demur.

'Certainly, Inspector – but we would expect nothing less – it is a key criterion of our selection process. There is little like ambition to drive superior performance.'

Skelgill perhaps inadvertently glances at DS Leyton, who sits hunched at an angle to him – and who looks decidedly on the defensive.

'And what was the background to Scarlett Liddell joining the company?'

The woman now raises the tablet and manipulates the screen – she gazes at it for a moment, and then lowers it, as though she has sufficiently refreshed her memory.

'She was Scarlett Robertson, then of course – as indeed she was during her entire employ.' She looks inquiringly at the detectives. They know this fact from their records, but it has not been a matter of conversation – although at this juncture Skelgill wonders if a different name casts her in a different light, and speaks of a life independent of Will Liddell. Meanwhile Marina Vanity is continuing. 'She obtained a First in French from St Andrews and an MBA with Distinction from INSEAD-Sorbonne. She joined our graduate scheme four years ago, aged twenty-four. It was her first job from university.'

Skelgill ponders this information.

'Mr Liddell studied at St Andrews University.'

Marina Vanity's resolute gaze seems to flicker. Will Liddell is probably the one person who does *not* have a CV on the company system.

'So I believe, Inspector – though of course they would not have overlapped, by any stretch of the imagination.'

There is perhaps the faintest note of irritation in the woman's tone – could it be that a reminder of the age gap between Will and Scarlett Liddell irks her? Or something along such lines? But rather than explore this notion, Skelgill simply nods.

'Happen Scarlett Liddell would have known what she was letting herself in for.' Skelgill says this rather absently, and indeed he seems to be trying to read a certificate mounted on the wall behind Marina Vanity, so he does not see the fleeting look of alarm that crosses her features. He turns his sights back upon her. 'Weather wise.'

'Ah – I see what you mean, Inspector.'

The woman is once again composed. Unblinking, she awaits the next question. Skelgill duly obliges.

'How about her employment record, madam?'

Asked of a head of HR this is a somewhat open-ended inquiry. But her answer is succinct.

'In a word, impressive, Inspector.'

Skelgill does not respond, other than after a few moments he gives a nod of encouragement. She proceeds without referring to the tablet.

'She completed our induction programme in half the normal time. She was promoted twice in a year while based here in London – and again when she got the move to the spirits division in Edinburgh. The subsequent assignment to Will's acquisition unit also involved an upgrade. She was by all measures a high-flyer.'

Skelgill is looking pensive. He wonders if beneath the professional exterior he detects once again a hint of resentment.

'How would a person get all these promotions?'

He poses the question in a rather self-deprecating manner, indeed almost forlornly – and yet Marina Vanity seems to read some innuendo into his words, for her countenance stiffens.

'Good old-fashioned hard work, Inspector – the secret weapon of many a successful executive.'

Indeed her tone is a mite disparaging – a subtle antipathy that may be aimed at the two men who sit before her; in their late thirties, they cannot in her estimation have excelled in their chosen careers – and by the standards of their conversation their progress up the corporate ladder has been excessively laboured. Skelgill, however, does not let her manner derail him.

'Could you elaborate on that, madam?'

That Skelgill persists perhaps obliges her to moderate her attitude.

'Of course – I did not have day-to-day contact with Scarlett.' She straightens in her chair, a little self-importantly. 'But she established a reputation for delivering projects ahead of schedule to an impeccable standard – working long hours – whatever it took. She was single – so she had the luxury of choice in that regard.'

'But she was a commuter, was she?'

'She lodged with a relative – an aunt – at Beaconsfield, I believe.'

Skelgill racks his brains for rivers that might help him get his bearings – he has in mind that Beaconsfield is within striking distance of the Thames – which would place it somewhere west of the capital. DS Leyton clears his throat to attract his superior's notice.

'M40, Guv. A good hour or more in a motor – could be double on a bad day. Best bet's the train to Marylebone. Then Bakerloo and Piccadilly lines to Covent Garden – or Shanks's pony from Piccadilly Circus.'

Thus enlightened, Skelgill turns back to Marina Vanity; she is watching DS Leyton through narrowed eyes, as though she may hitherto have underestimated the inspector's largely silent and brooding companion.

'Where do your executives stay when then come down from Edinburgh?'

She tilts back her head and regards Skelgill a little superciliously.

'Will is a member of a club – *The Dickman*.' She says it as though of course he must know it – but that she probably thinks he doesn't, and it has the effect of a put-down. 'Otherwise there is no shortage of local hotels.'

'In the year she was here – who did Scarlett Liddell work for?'

Marina Vanity looks like she might be about to correct the errors in Skelgill's grammar.

'She – she was in the European marketing department in our fragrances division. That's headed up by Andy Organ.'

'And he's still with you?'

'Yes – he's Marketing Manager.'

'Perhaps if we could have a word with him.'

Skelgill's response is more demand than question, and for the first time he sees a wrinkle in her smooth brow. But she picks up the tablet and begins to tap out some words. When she has finished she inhales through the narrow reptilian slits of her nostrils.

'I have messaged him on our internal system.' She glances again at the screen and swipes a couple of times. 'I can see he is in a meeting with the advertising agency for another half an hour – but he should be free after that.'

Skelgill nods.

'And what about someone at the same level as Scarlett Liddell – someone she worked alongside?'

Again Marina Vanity interrogates her tablet. It is half a minute before she finds a solution to her satisfaction.

'Leonora Cornock-Wilson was on the same graduate intake – and she still works in Andy Organ's team. Would you like me to see if she is available, Inspector?'

*

'*So* – we have a pyramid organisation – one joins as a graduate trainee – that is called Junior Brand Manager – and then a series of potential promotions: Assistant Brand Manager, Brand Manager, Senior Brand Manager, Group Brand Manager. The next job above that is Marketing Manager. Since we have so many companies in the group, it is not a case of 'dead man's shoes' – there is usually an opportunity as soon as one is ready for the next level of responsibility.'

'And you're what, Miss?'

The young woman looks a little disconcerted, being called 'Miss' by Skelgill – perhaps it emphasises the gravity of the interview – that these are the police and a meeting with them can never really be a casual chat.

'*So* – I joined as a graduate – I'm now a Brand Manager – I look after Male Grooming in the Eurozone countries.'

Skelgill is unable to suppress a scowl. That there can be two prominent explanations – personal and political – rather hides that it is most definitely in relation to the former – 'male grooming' being an oxymoron in Skelgill's lexicon. He glances at DS Leyton, of whom it must be said also has a look of some trepidation going about his unmoisturised jowls.

'You worked with Scarlett Liddell – Scarlett Robertson, as she was?'

'*So* – we were on the same induction programme – subsequently we were both placed in fragrances – we had similar tasks and responsibilities – we just worked on different brands.'

Skelgill's frown persists. It is dawning upon him that the young woman – aged 26, she has told them – has probably thought through the idea that she might be interviewed about Scarlett Liddell – perhaps even wished for it – for she seems eager with her replies. But he has also realised she has a most annoying trait – to preface each reply with a stressed '*so*' – a modern affliction that has joined usage such as 'absolutely' when a person means 'yes' and 'literally' when they mean 'almost' (but not literally!) – and it further adds to the impression that her answers are rehearsed. While she explains exactly which brands of snake oil she and Scarlett Liddell purveyed, Skelgill half-listening assesses her appearance and deportment. She is well dressed – certainly in what he imagines would be called 'trendy gear' – and she has an expensive haircut and manicured nails – and she wears subtle make-up. But to his eye she is plain looking, rather thin and flat-chested, tall – indeed when she stood up to shake their hands in the meeting room assigned for their discussion she seemed stooping and self-conscious of her height. Moreover something in her manner betrays an underlying anxiety – she glances away each time to complete her answers. She is clearly bright and probably highly competent – but if the impression he is forming is correct she is probably the sort of competition that the ambitious Scarlett Liddell would have swatted aside fairly mercilessly.

'How did you get on with her?'

She seems surprised by this question; perhaps its unexpected informality.

'We had a perfectly civil relationship.'

Skelgill picks up on what he senses is a rather euphemistic description.

'But you wouldn't say you were friends?'

'Scarlett didn't really socialise with the crowd.'

'What – you mean with her colleagues?'

The girl nods.

'There's a bit of a tradition to go for a drink after work on the last Thursday of the month – you know, payday? People live in such disparate places – that's how it works in the West End – decamp to a bar and get the last train home.'

'But Scarlett Liddell didn't do that?'

Now she shakes her head. Skelgill has a follow-up question.

'Perhaps she had a boyfriend elsewhere?'

Leonora Cornock-Wilson looks doubtful.

'She never spoke of anybody. My impression is that she would rather work late.'

'And was she alone in doing that?'

'Oh, no – it's a hard-working culture – and the more senior one gets – there is something of an expectation – but Scarlett did it from the outset – and then as time went by she became quite obsessive.' She pauses and reaches the long spread ringless fingers of both hands to adjust her hair, although to Skelgill's eye it does not appear to need such attention. 'I have seen her desk light on from the street when I have been heading for Covent Garden tube.'

Skelgill is pensive and silent for a moment. She has abandoned the conjunction 'so' – perhaps because he has moved her away from the stock questions she might anticipate. He casts an even more speculative line – like he would try an unpromising swim he has drifted past a couple of times, just in case he can draw an impulsive take. It is a variant on his earlier question.

'What was she like?'

Perhaps predictably this also unsettles her. Clearly, there is a wide range of possible answers, from personality to appearance, from endearing character traits to irritating habits. Under scrutiny Leonora Cornock-Wilson bows to some felt obligation and rather blurts out her response.

'She liked to be noticed.'

'You mean by her bosses – for her quality of work?'

'Actually – no – I mean that she dressed rather provocatively.'

'Aye?'

The northern adverb carries sufficient inflexion for her to understand it is a request for more information.

'Well – although she didn't attend nights out – she always wore the sort of things one might get changed into for a special occasion – shorter skirts, silky tops, hair and make-up done – perfume – *hah.*' She gives a little laugh – and then backtracks. 'But – of course – at any time there were a dozen sample bottles on her desk.'

'What about in the company, then – there must be plenty of single chaps wooing you young ladies?'

Leonora Cornock-Wilson folds her hands upon her lap and furrows her brow; it is the kind of body language that smacks of a schoolgirl caught writing rude words in a game of 'Consequences'.

'We have an unwritten rule – pro – er, discouraging staff relationships.'

Skelgill notes the modification of what might have been 'prohibiting'.

'Seems a bit draconian to me, Miss. What's the harm – especially if you're at the same level?'

His devil's advocacy draws the return of the dreaded conjunction. It sounds like a well-versed rebuttal.

'*So* – counter-intuitively it is a rather popular policy. Two people at the same level may not remain thus for very long. And once there is a disparity it brings scope for accusations of favouritism. I think everyone would rather work in an environment in which progress is based upon merit and it doesn't feel like a perpetual speed-dating event.'

*

'Scarlett Liddell must have been quite a loss, sir – when she got promoted to the job in Edinburgh?'

European Fragrances Marketing Manager Andrew Organ has something of the look of the proverbial rabbit in the headlights. Yet on the face of it, Skelgill's question is perfectly reasonable – it is merely a restatement of facts they have gleaned in their discussions. Perhaps it is the man's thick-lensed spectacles, which make his eyes appear to bulge, or the warmth of the afternoon sun on his back, this time of year sufficiently high in the sky to penetrate the west-facing office above surrounding buildings and spotlight Andrew Organ at his desk. However, Skelgill would not read too much into appearances – as he frequently reminds his colleagues, the sight of a police officer does strange things to some folk, guilty conscience or not. More salient to Skelgill is that the man seems to glance by reflex at a framed photograph on his desk – it faces away from the detectives, who have been invited to pull up chairs that are probably intended for junior staff when impromptu meetings are held. In his late thirties, Andrew Organ is of a birdlike appearance – probably he would be described as 'geeky' by uncharitable colleagues – he is tall and thin, with features that are all rather too large for his face, and protruding teeth too large for his mouth. His attire, though a new-looking ensemble of suit, shirt and tie, seems unhappy on his angular frame. He has rather unstylish lank black hair, and a pale though now flushed complexion.

'Well – I, er – it is important for the organisation – that talent is allowed to develop.' He wipes a hand across his brow. 'It would be a bigger loss if someone in whom the company has invested felt their progress was thwarted and went instead to a competitor.'

He speaks quietly with a nondescript southern accent, his words clipped, perhaps out of anxiety.

'Scarlett Liddell seemed to get promoted at record speed.'

'I think you'll find she held her own each time she moved up, Inspector.'

It is hard to tell from Skelgill's expression whether or not he doubts this statement. However, he senses he should not discomfit the man more than is necessary – much as he seems a ripe candidate for bullying.

'So what did Scarlett Liddell have that others didn't?'

Andrew Organ leans his elbows on his desk and brings his hands together. There is a nervous flurry of fingertips – as if he is solving an imaginary Rubik's Cube. His eyes acquire a glazed look, and he speaks while still wrestling with the invisible puzzle. It seems he does not dispute Skelgill's assertion.

'Well, er – she was certainly an achiever – she came here with uniform top grades.' He pauses, and frowns – as though he is actually wondering himself – realising in hindsight that she did in fact progress with unseemly rapidity. 'I suppose some people are innately more competitive than others – they have a will to win.' He gazes at the detectives – he blinks behind the lenses, as if a little surprised to find them there. 'They don't just do a good job – they do it in a way that gets them noticed.'

Although Andrew Organ is the second person this afternoon to use the phrase, Skelgill does not appear happy with his analysis. In consequence, the man rather shrinks back – as though unwilling to fight his corner.

'How did the move to Edinburgh come about, sir?'

Andrew Organ's features become distressed; he looks perplexed, as though he is slightly panicked by his inability to recall basic detail.

'I, er – we, er – we have a system of, er – 'management by objectives', we call it – everybody gets a monthly review from their line manager – so individual progress is monitored – and, er – at the same time there is a space on the company intranet that lists vacancies – we have hundreds of employees across many different subsidiaries.' For a moment he resumes his work on the transparent Rubik's Cube. 'I moved from a market research role myself – I was previously in Fempro.'

'Come again, sir?'

'Oh, er – feminine protection – towels and tampons, you know?' He looks inquiringly at the two detectives to see that they clearly don't – indeed now they are showing signs of distress. This seems to bolster his confidence. 'It's a very significant market – we estimate 40 billion dollars worldwide by the end of the decade – it grew by twice the global GDP rate last year – most, er – most men outside the industry are unaware of it. Combined with my research background – it meant I was able to bring an understanding of the female consumer – to my role in fragrances.'

He looks hopefully to Skelgill as if for his approbation – but Skelgill, unhappy in the pincer movement of 'fempro' and 'fragrance' is eager to get back on track.

'You were saying, sir – how Scarlett Liddell moved to Edinburgh.'

Andrew Organ appears a little dejected.

'Oh – yes – er, well – I can't honestly remember which came first – you know, chicken or egg? But I recall speaking with Kevin Makepeace – at a departmental heads meeting – that she was in the running for a Senior Brand Manager's job in his team. He was saying he doubted she'd have the experience necessary.'

Skelgill nods.

'So, what – it was Scarlett Liddell that applied for the job – it wasn't the company that moved her?'

'Well – it was probably an element of each – I mean, er – obviously no one would be transferred if they didn't want to go – especially when there's a geographical upheaval involved.' He glances again at the frame on his desk.

'Did she have other choices?'

'Oh – I dare say there were other vacancies. But I really can't remember – it would have been about three years ago.'

'And you were upset to see her leave, sir.'

Even Skelgill is a little surprised that his words come out lacking the inflection that would make the phrase a question. But if it is a subconscious insight it seems to strike its target.

'Well – yes – I was.' Andrew Organ appears defensive and at the same time flustered that Skelgill apparently knows this. 'Not least – I, er – I was ready to promote her onto our flagship fragrance brand – but she decided quite reasonably that experience of a different market would stand her in good stead in the longer term.'

'Did you try to get her to stay?'

With what is thus far uncharacteristic decisiveness the man shakes his head.

'I could see her mind was made up.'

Skelgill is silent for a few moments.

'How would you describe her – as regards being cooperative – say, on a scale of one to ten?'

Andrew Organ seems to react to this challenge – he produces an awkward smile that displays his piano-key array of teeth.

'One would normally use a five-point scale for that sort of question, Inspector.'

If it is a diversionary tactic it is a curious one – and the man's tone and demeanour are nothing if not ingenuous – as though he cannot let pass the professional discrepancy, no matter that he gainsays the uncompromising police inspector.

'You see – a ten-point scale has no midpoint – and a significant proportion of respondents to a research questionnaire will wish to select what is effectively the 'neither/nor' option – viz. number three in the case of a five-point scale.'

Skelgill glances at DS Leyton, who appears to have tuned out and is mooning at the buildings on the opposite side of Bow Street. Meanwhile Andrew Organ is looking rather quizzically at Skelgill. Skelgill sighs and obliges with an appropriate prompt.

'On a scale of one to five, then, sir?'

'Actually, there is no single answer, Inspector – it would vary by occasion.' He presses his fingertips together but this time there is no Rubik's Cube, just a still void – perhaps a fortune-teller's orb. He flashes a nervous grin at Skelgill 'Mainly ones and fives.'

'Why would that be, sir?'

'Well – she, er – she was a charismatic young woman – just at times rather headstrong.' He ponders for a moment, and shakes his head introspectively. 'I suppose the two naturally go together in personalities that forge their way to the top – George Bernard Shaw's 'unreasonable man', and all that.'

He continues to reflect upon this, ruefully it seems – perhaps that he is in life's more reasonable camp – and that as such he harbours some regrets.

'Was she a quitter?'

'Oh, never, Inspector.' The sharp question rouses him from his reverie. 'Thwarted, she was more likely to come back at you twice as hard. That's why it all seems so improbable.'

'What does, sir?'

Andrew Organ looks at Skelgill almost impatiently, as though he considers he has not been paying proper attention.

'That she committed suicide.'

Skelgill stares back severely.

'When did you last see her, sir?'

The man lowers his eyes, somewhat submissively, as if the little outburst has exhausted his capacity to be combative.

'To speak to – not since she left London. I saw her at a distance at the next annual conference – just over two years ago – but she was seated at the top table – she was working in Will Liddell's corporate unit by then.'

'So that's a lot of water under the bridge, sir.'

The man twists his bony shoulders; his frame seems to writhe with discomfort, independent of the ill-fitting suit jacket. He shrugs despondently.

'Who knows what demons a person conceals.'

But he offers no further explanation – and gazes once more at the picture on his desk; it seems to be the default for his woes. Skelgill rather impatiently stretches his arms behind his head – and in fact he rises and flexes his troublesome back – and then seems to notice something out of the window, where DS

Leyton's gaze has been preoccupied – he strides quite purposefully across, behind and a little to one side of Andrew Organ, and rests the heels of his hands on the sill – and looks out, down at the street level, for a moment or two before returning. However, he remains standing beside his chair. He glances at DS Leyton – before addressing Andrew Organ.

'Happen we'd better get our skates on, sir – if we're to get out of London before the rush hour. Looks lively down there already.'

The man's expression seems to conflate relief with alarm.

'Unfortunately rush *hour* is something of a misnomer, Inspector.'

Skelgill inclines his head towards DS Leyton, their designated driver.

'Aye, well – we've got half of the M1 and most of the M6 to deal with after that.'

'You might try the M40 to the Umberslade Interchange. Thence the M42 link runs directly onto the M6 Toll. With a fair wind you could be north of Birmingham by five-thirty.'

Skelgill looks at DS Leyton for corroboration. DS Leyton turns out a fleshy bottom lip and gives a non-committal shrug of his broad shoulders. It is an expression that speaks of 'six-and-half-a-dozen' – though he does not voice the sentiment. However he raises his bulk from the chair with an expiration of breath concomitant with the effort required. Skelgill does not compose any particular words of departure, or thanks, or future reference, but as he reaches for the door he turns to look at Andrew Organ – who has half-risen, appearing ungainly and gangly – and once again rather indecisive.

'How did you get on with Scarlett Liddell – at a personal level, sir?'

The man seems to start – and his eyes dart about his desk, as though some answer might be gleaned from its contents. He looks up almost pleadingly at the detectives, as if he would rather not be asked.

'I should have liked Scarlett to answer that question, Inspector – but now I shall never know.'

16. DETOUR

'Oh, no, my dear – I'm not a blood relative. We were neighbours of the Robertsons before they moved to France – when Scarlett was aged seven or eight. We had no children of our own and we used to take her out sometimes – and we had a little Pug of which she was rather fond. He was called Winston – after Winston Churchill – and she would insist on dressing him in her dolls' clothes – which Winston never seemed to mind – although of course I don't imagine the real Winston Churchill wore floral dresses.'

Skelgill nods amiably. The woman, Mrs Camelia Ivybridge, sole resident of a substantial and rambling half-timbered Buckinghamshire property constructed in mock Tudor style, perhaps in her late sixties, is the archetypal English elderly lady, a rather plump and fluffy concoction of grey hair and woollens moving slowly and serenely within an almost tangible cloud of rose water. Her voice possesses a soft West Country burr, and she has won his approval by insisting they partake of tea and cakes – the latter a tiered arrangement that would surely feed half of the Women's Institute at this evening's gathering – for which she insists she has baked a surplus. However, the rather worrying lack of irony in her tone – and, he senses, a propensity to waffle (of the non-cake variety) – has him skirting around the subject of cross-dressing prime ministers.

'So what led to her coming back as an adult, madam?'

Before answering Mrs Ivybridge leans forward from her needlework-upholstered winged armchair and rotates the cake stand to indicate that having finished a Chelsea bun Skelgill should avail himself of a slice of her Bakewell pudding. He sees no reason to disoblige. DS Leyton makes his apologies, citing his 'diet' – and earning a reproachful glance from his superior.

'Well – there was an open invitation for the family to stay if ever they visited the area – and when George – that's my late husband – passed away and not long after there was mention that Scarlett had a job in London – her mother and I always exchanged Christmas cards, you see – I thought, wouldn't it be nice if Scarlett came to live here – at least until she found her feet – because George had always worked in London and he found the commuting quite convenient. And I would have some company.'

She blinks slowly several times, her doughy features mournful beneath a floury powder coat. Her account is informative, if a little verbose, and it leaves Skelgill wondering what exactly it is that he wants to find out – and how he might do it without offending her kindly sensibilities. However, fortified by the sugary bun he decides to cut to the chase.

'And how did that work out for you, madam?'

She does not seem perturbed by his question.

'Oh, well – Scarlett was a model lodger – so tidy – never a plate left unwashed nor a cushion not straightened – she did all her own laundry and took care of her own catering.' At this juncture she gazes rather sadly at the cakes – the inference being that, unsurprisingly, her lodger was probably not quite as appreciative as Skelgill. 'But, of course, she worked such long hours – she would often go back into the office at weekends – that company certainly got its money's worth out of her, I can tell you – so I didn't really see a great deal of her – and then of course she moved rather suddenly to London – and she promised she would pop back and visit – but it was only a couple of months later that they sent her to Scotland. I never saw her again.'

She sniffs and produces a paper tissue from the sleeve of her fluffy cardigan. It is hard to judge whether she displays genuine emotion, but Skelgill's antennae have pricked up regardless. There appears to be a fact of which the company is unaware.

'You say she moved to London, madam?' (The woman nods, still dabbing at her nose.) 'What was that about?'

'Well – it was quite understandable – nothing to do with any problems here, you see, officer? She got the chance of an apartment close to her work – what with the long hours – it made sense, I suppose.'

'Did she happen to leave an address?'

At this the elderly lady looks a little distressed; she wrings the tissue between plump fingers.

'I don't believe she did, my dear – she began to tell me the address – but – that's right – she didn't know the postcode – and she was going to let me know – and then it must have slipped her mind – and then when she moved again I suppose it didn't matter.'

Skelgill is nodding sympathetically.

'We're trying to understand why Scarlett might have committed suicide.' (Now the woman does appear to be holding back tears. She inhales and exhales more heavily.) 'How did she seem to you, madam – her personality – her behaviour – whether she had any troubles – whether there was anything that gave you cause for concern – in her private life?'

It is question that invites an admission of prying; however the woman remains phlegmatic in this respect.

'She was charming, well mannered. She often must have been tired – and she always made an effort to be polite.' But now Mrs Ivybridge plies Skelgill with what might be considered a conspiratorial look. 'Of course – I heard her giving someone a dressing down over the telephone now and again – but that's the way it goes in business – a *doggy-dog world*, my George always used to say to Winston when he pushed him out of his armchair.' She gazes rather forlornly at the chair in which DS Leyton sits, his forearms resting upon his ample thighs; he seems discomfited. 'They're very clever at getting their own way, dogs, aren't they?'

Her anecdote strikes Skelgill as ambiguous, and he wonders just who pushed whom out of the preferred seat; however, he resists the urge to invite a potentially long-winded clarification.

'Did she have any close friends that you were aware of – a boyfriend, for instance?'

The woman shakes her head quite decisively, though her reply is more oblique.

'Of course, modern youngsters have their mobile phones – there's no need for a fellow to telephone the house or knock on the door with a red rose – you wouldn't know what your children were getting up to, would you? I shouldn't like to be a parent nowadays.'

Skelgill's expression becomes rather pained.

'It's not cheap living in London – the flat she moved to – would that have been shared with somebody?'

The woman regards him rather blankly; she blinks several times.

'I'm sure she told me she would be living on her own – she liked to have things the way she wanted them – I don't think she would have been keen on a flatmate – besides, she was happy with her own company.'

The mournful expression returns, and with it the suggestion that perhaps in her time here Scarlett Liddell did not socialise as much as her 'aunt' would have liked. Skelgill is pondering this subject when she volunteers a piece of information.

'There was a gent – came to collect her.'

'Aye?' Skelgill tries to make his inquiry sound casual.

'She said he was a colleague, helping her out – I suppose a taxi driver would have abandoned her in London on the kerb with her bags – they're very rude these days – in too much of a hurry – what do they call themselves, *Hoover* drivers?'

'Do you happen to know who it was – what he looked like?'

She shakes her head.

'If Scarlett mentioned a name I don't remember it, I'm afraid, my dear.' Now she glances at the bay window, its latticed panes lined by net curtains. 'It was evening, you see – it was dark outside – and what with the hedge – and Scarlett having her suitcases ready in the porch.'

Skelgill ponders for a moment.

'Did she keep in touch with you – after she moved to Edinburgh?'

The woman makes a fussy movement with the fingers of both hands upon her lap.

'Oh – she was very busy – I know that – there was her work – and then all those wedding arrangements and a big new house to look after – and I didn't expect to go to the wedding – like I say – George and I – we weren't her real uncle and auntie – that's just what she used to call us – besides they only had a handful of guests – it was held on her new husband's boat, in the Virginal Islands, I believe – her mother put a little note about it in the next Christmas card.'

Skelgill notices DS Leyton surreptitiously checking his watch, and shifting impatiently in his seat. While there have been some minor additions to their insight – it seems the relationship was conducted at arm's length, very much landlady and tenant; little intimate knowledge was shared – and it is an account that ends abruptly over two years ago. However, Beaconsfield has proved to be only a minor diversion from the route suggested by Andrew Organ – and constitutes the kind of refuelling stop Skelgill would have insisted upon anyway. He eats the remainder of the homemade cake from his plate, and swallows the last of his tea. The woman correctly interprets his actions as those of 'wrapping up' the interview – though she contrives to look disappointed when he refuses her exhortations to sample her Victoria sponge. (DS Leyton looks relieved.) At the end of a beamed hallway the woman rather struggles with the great blackened oak front door – and DS Leyton darts forward to assist. Skelgill, perhaps chastened by his colleague's show of chivalry, thanks her for her hospitality, and commiserates with her for her loss. Though she continues to look sad, she becomes distracted, and speaks musingly, as if to herself.

'You know – when she was a little girl – she used to think we were very rich – I don't know why – perhaps it just seemed a big house to her then.' She gazes wistfully at the detectives as they wait off balance, straining to set off down the curving path. 'She always said, *Auntie Cammie, when I grow up I'm going to marry a millionaire.* Such a shame how it turned out for poor dear Scarlett.'

*

'I'm cream-crackered, Guv. That'll be the thick end of six-hundred miles round trip by the time we're done.'

'Aye – we'll stop for a mash in a bit, Leyton. What's the next services?'

In the dark interior of the car, part-illuminated by light from oncoming vehicles that throng the opposite carriageway, DS Leyton's shoulders can be seen to sag. He shifts position to check details on the dashboard – clock and odometer.

'Sandwich.'

'Come again?'

'Sorry, Guv – I mean Sandbach – don't know what I was thinking.' What he *was* thinking – optimistically so – is that they could grab a sandwich from the petrol forecourt and keep moving, but 'mash' – a pot of tea in Cumbrian parlance – in Skelgill's own vernacular generally comes with some version of all-day breakfast. Skelgill regards sausage, egg and beans as 24-hour staples; meanwhile the long-suffering sergeant's wife is waiting with dinner in the oven. He makes a sound of private exasperation, and then tries to cover it up with conversation. 'We must be in Cheshire. Sandwich is down in Kent, ain't it.'

'Aye, happen it is.'

'Mind you, Guv – Sandbach sounds like it's something to do with a sarnie – cross between a sandwich and a roll – *batch* is what they call a roll round the Midlands, if I recall.'

Skelgill is silent. It is hard to say if he is engaged with this idea – or simply thinking about food. DS Leyton adds a rider.

'Then there's Tebay, Guv.'

'It's a bit far, Leyton – we'd be nearly home.'

'Naw – I meant it's a good name for a services, ain't it? Sounds like it's what you get. *Tea bay.* Like *pit stop.*' He gives a strangled chuckle. 'Like they called it that on purpose.'

'It's named after the village, Leyton. Hamlet, anyhow.'

DS Leyton ponders for a few moments.

'Hamlet, Guv – that would be a good 'un an' all – sounds like it's short for ham omelette.'

Skelgill makes an unfairly scornful sound in his throat.

'Well let's make sure we don't stop at one called Grubgone.'

A collective silence descends. All northbound lanes of the motorway are dense with traffic to the point of saturation. The M6 between Birmingham and Manchester is not for the faint-hearted, the mere thought of a journey has motorists in their thousands reaching for tranquillisers. Not that DS Leyton is daunted, he cut his driving teeth on London's mean streets – but, on a Friday evening, the scope for epic delays is never more than a slight lapse of concentration away; "are we there yet?" becomes infinitely futile. However, although they are barely averaging 45 mph, at least they are moving, and it is in this respect that DS Leyton comments.

'The M40 route turned out alright, Guv. That Organ character knows his motorways.'

Skelgill is still brooding over something – or perhaps now this new suggestion – and his sergeant continues.

'Mind you, Guv – when you think about it – a bit of coincidence – that it was the way to Beaconsfield. Double handy for us as it turned out – once you decided we should see the old biddy.'

'Happen Organ was trying to tell us something.'

Skelgill says this cynically – as though he does not mean it – and certainly that he does not intend to sound like he is pinning some hopes on a rather tenuous coincidence. But they have little to go on – and DS Leyton is sufficiently quick-witted to see the implied connection.

'You mean he was the mystery geezer – that picked up Scarlett Liddell when she moved into town?'

Skelgill pulls a series of faces, like he might have bitten into a lemon.

'Reading between the lines, Leyton – she had him wrapped round her little finger.'

Unwittingly mirroring his boss, DS Leyton also contorts his features; they look sculpted, heavy and craggy in the flickering half-light.

'Mind you, Guv – he was the boffin type – they often come across a bit jumpy.'

'Jumpy – he was waiting for us to drop a bombshell, Leyton. He kept staring at that picture on his desk. That's why I got up to take a deek.'

Now a rising note creeps into DS Leyton's voice. 'It wasn't Scarlett Liddell, Guv?'

Skelgill, however, bridles at the suggestion.

'No, Leyton – you donnat. It was his wife and kids.'

'Oh, right, Guv.' DS Leyton makes a mumbling sound of acquiescence. 'Right enough – she could probably have taken her pick, Guv – like you said to that Leonora girl, there must be plenty of fanciable young lads – why would she have a dalliance with a queer-looking old cove like Organ?'

In the gloom, Skelgill's countenance is conflicted. It is a few moments before he responds.

'What's the Chief's favourite word – a matter of *expediency?*'

DS Leyton also takes a while to consider his next contribution.

'You saying Scarlett Liddell found a way of jumping the queue, Guv – when it came to getting promoted?'

'It wouldn't be the first time in human history, Leyton.' But Skelgill, as is his capricious wont, now seems uncomfortable with such a prurient line of thinking. A yawn comes upon him and he stretches awkwardly in the limited passenger accommodation. 'What's to say they didn't just ship her off to Scotland – dressed it up as a promotion.'

'What – to get shot of her, Guv?'

Skelgill shrugs.

'She might have been effective, but that doesn't equal popular. It's all very well having a superstar – but if they play the prima donna and pee-off the rest of your team, what use is that? High-flyer or not, she was still a small cog in a big wheel.'

DS Leyton nods. He bites his lower lip, and his eyes dart about his mirrors as he manoeuvres from one lane to another – and then he curses as the traffic in the lane they have left suddenly picks up speed.

'I suppose the one thing that don't fit is her moving out of London, Guv. I mean – I know Edinburgh's technically their head office – and no disrespect to the Jocks, like – but if you want to get on, London's where it's at.'

Skelgill makes a disparaging exclamation.

'That's why you moved out, Leyton.'

DS Leyton squints more intensely into the oncoming lights. His features take on a determined cast.

'Like I've said before, Guv – we done it for the kids. Where would you rather have your nippers knock about – the Lake District – or Lakeside? It's a no-brainer.'

Skelgill, too, gazes ahead, eyes narrowed. It is less than a no-brainer; it requires no neural activity whatsoever on his part to reach this conclusion; he is hard-wired to know it, and as such it is one aspect of his relationship with DS Leyton in which there is unanimity. Thus deprived of any opportunity for recalcitrance, he sinks into a brown period. It is therefore DS Leyton, evidently continuing to mull over the scenario, who chimes up after a while.

'Mind you, Guv – I suppose you can't say it didn't work out for her in the end – she only went and married the owner – married her millionaire.'

'Aye – just the wrong kind of millionaire.'

17.

BASSENTHWAITE LAKE

Saturday, 7.10am

S till picking particles of London from his nostrils, Skelgill sits watchfully in his boat. While it has been light for well over an hour, only now does the sun penetrate his position. He is tucked beneath old crack willows at the shallow southern reaches of Bassenthwaite Lake. Skiddaw, like a slumbering brindled bear yet to wake from winter hibernation, lies brawny and robust, seeming to breathe as the sun's heat upon its steaming flanks causes rising air to play tricks with the transmission of shimmering light. Skelgill feels reassuringly Lilliputian by comparison. A light breeze, a welcome south-westerly, creates a ripple on the water surface and keeps Skelgill honest, the corduroy collar raised of his trusty threadbare *Barbour*. All about him birds, largely invisible, make their presence known. The blackbirds were at their dawn chorus when he awoke before first light, their lazy morning melody percolating through his open window and pre-empting his alarm; still some of their ilk persist, now joined by a whole spring cacophony that comprises the likes of stock dove, coal tit, robin, nuthatch, chaffinch, wren and mistle thrush. From the reedbeds to his right emanates the irregular cackle of mallards indulging in some horseplay, and the occasional plaintive *kirruk* of a solitary moorhen.

His thoughts drift back to his last visit when, floating not far from here, he experienced for the first time the paradox of

Scarlett Liddell. Something of her capricious nature was displayed even in that fleeting pass. Engaging while he was the novelty of the moment; dropping him abruptly as soon as he had served her whim. What did Andrew Organ say – mostly ones and fives? Never a three.

Except a carrion crow *craws* three times, energetically – in this season a sound that triggers alarm, a warning ingrained into his psyche, since boyhood days tagging along at the heels of shepherds out on the windswept fells. He looks shoreward for vulnerable lambs. In the direction of Greenmire Castle there is rough pasture and a grazing flock – but it is a human figure that catches his eye, immediately incongruous, an awkward movement at the end of the rickety wooden landing stage. Skelgill squints. It is Thomas Montagu-Browne, and he appears to be fly casting, badly.

Skelgill watches for a minute or so; then he winds in his own line and takes up his oars. The breeze is with him; two minutes more finds him backing alongside the pier. Thomas Montagu-Browne, a seemingly permanent startled expression etched into his features, has stopped 'fishing' and leant his rod against the handrail. He understands however that Skelgill is about to toss the painter to him, and makes a satisfactory catch.

Skelgill heaves himself onto the splintered boards by the heels of his leathery hands, and performs a half-roll and springs lightly to his feet.

'Morning, Tom.'

'Good m-morning, Inspector.'

'Were you trying to get rid of the midges?'

'P-pardon, Inspector? There are n-no midges.'

The man looks slightly terrified.

'I saw you casting.' Skelgill gestures at the fishing rig. 'That's a half-decent new rod – but you'll get nowhere thrashing an imaginary cuddy.'

It seems to dawn on Thomas Montagu-Browne – perhaps Skelgill's informal greeting has sunk in, and his focus upon angling, and now a rather artful grin – that perhaps the policeman is not about to accuse him of some criminal misdemeanour – and in fact harbours a genuine interest in what he has been doing.

'Oh – oh – L-Lavinia wants to offer fly fishing as p-part of our package – that I should be some kind of g-ghillie? Also that we provide a free experience to local youth groups – scouts – g-girl g-guides. She's advertising an Open Day.'

Skelgill has not interviewed Thomas Montagu-Browne – that task fell previously to DS Leyton – so he is not sure if the man's stutter is habitual or simply borne out of nerves. He recalls the aforementioned Lavinia's warning – that her half-brother was unintentionally ill mannered. He detects none of that – but perhaps he has the jump on the man in the 'bluff Northerner' stakes.

Skelgill reaches to pick up the rod. He inspects the arrangement – a nylon leader is correctly attached via a braided loop to the heavy fly line – he suspects the tackle shop of setting this up; it looks a professional job, secured with a spot of super glue. Sensibly, for practice purposes, no hooks have been tied on. Skelgill digs into his pocket and pulls out a large rusted steel washer. Deftly he secures it to the leader and draws in the line by hand until it is stopped by the rod tip ring.

'Why do we cast, Tom?'

Without waiting for an answer, left-handed Skelgill flicks the rod and sends the line shooting across the water. The washer disappears with a splash, maybe twenty yards from their position. Thomas Montagu-Browne watches, blinking.

'Er – t-to reach the fish?'

Skelgill does not reply – but in his manner there is sufficient to indicate the affirmative. He reels in, holding the rod wrong-handed, the reel uppermost.

'See how easy it is with a weight on the end. But in fly fishing –'

Thomas Montagu-Browne realises he should complete the sentence.

'There is no weight on the end.'

'Exactly. The weight's all in the line. And you can't push a line.'

Skelgill strides down the pontoon towards the grassy bank, biting off the washer and pocketing it as he goes. Now he produces a crumpled scrap of paper towel and tears off a corner. This replaces the washer on the end of the nylon leader. He holds it up; it twists in the breeze.

'Fly – right? Safety version.'

Skelgill strips out maybe ten yards of line, allowing it to pile up in a loose coil at his feet. He hands the rod to Thomas Montagu-Browne. Now he picks out the false paper fly and draws it away, five or six feet, and lays it upon the turf.

'Trap the line above the reel against the rod with your right index finger.' He watches to see that the man follows his instruction. 'Now cast in one sweep.'

Thomas Montagu-Browne does as asked. There is a flurry of line as the first few yards rise out of the heap, but otherwise the cast is a failure; the line collapses and the fly does not move. Skelgill looks pleased with this result. Now he picks up the fly and walks away; he does not stop until he has stretched the line to its full extent.

'Try again.'

This time there is a swish and the fly lifts off and hurtles past Thomas Montagu-Browne's head and out across the meadow. The man turns, a look of amazement on his face. He brings the line back. It lands close to Skelgill. He repeats the action. Then he makes a kind of forced grin, keeping his lips pressed together.

'You can't push a line, Inspector.'

Skelgill approaches.

'You get it?'

'I do – it's obvious really, isn't it?'

Skelgill makes a conciliatory motion with his hands.

'Happen it's not so obvious as you'd imagine. Folk see a fisherman casting with a single-handed rod like that – they think what you do is this back-and-forward business. If everyone learned by casting a double-handed salmon rod – they'd get the principle of loading the rod in five minutes. You just did it quicker.' Skelgill pauses to inhale; he notices that Thomas Montagu-Browne looks suddenly discomfited – the unaccustomed praise, perhaps? 'When you fish for salmon you're out in the river. You can let the line lie on the water. You've got a big rod with the leverage to lift it in one movement. But with a little trout rod you need to keep the line airborne while you extend it – if you let it drop, the water creates too much resistance – and if you're bank fishing it'll snag behind you.'

The man nods obediently. He has the demeanour of one who is accustomed to taking orders, and seems content with this state of affairs. But when Skelgill casually asks him what sort of team of flies he proposes to use, the worried look returns.

'I've n-never fished before, Inspector.'

Skelgill can't help but to smile again – however, it is with uncharacteristic benevolence. There is a new-looking traditional canvas-and-leather fishing bag suspended by its shoulder strap from a post. He retrieves it and squats down to examine its contents. Thomas Montagu-Browne watches anxiously.

'I asked the tackle shop to give me a s-selection of everything I might need.'

Skelgill nods appraisingly – it is a good mix. The store has not taken advantage of his novice status.

'Especially if you're in a boat, it's usual to use a team of three flies.' Skelgill is about to expound further when there is a sudden flash of boyhood memory – on the riverbank, being taught to fly fish by his mentor, Professor Jim Hartley. He always began with a question. 'Can you think why that might be?'

'Well – I suppose you can offer different types of – *b-bait?*'

Skelgill raises an eyebrow at his use of the word; however, he nods.

'Aye – that's about the length of it. Your point fly sinks the deepest – then you'd have two droppers. The nearest one to you comes back through the surface film. So you might even use a dry – one that mimics a laying adult.' He has hold of a plastic fly box that has a transparent lid, and jabs a finger at one of perhaps thirty artificial lures. 'The point fly – maybe a swimming nymph – the middle dropper – perhaps a rising pupa – we call that an emerger.' Skelgill glances out across the lake, squinting into the low morning sun. 'Obviously – you look around – see what's hatching – if you catch a fish and you're keeping it to eat – slit open its stomach – see what's on the menu today.'

'So that is why the flies are referred to as 'naturals', Inspector?'

The question tells Skelgill the man is catching on.

'Aye – although there's plenty that are not – you'll hear talk of *boobies* and *dog nobblers* – but that's a cop-out in my book – and they're banned by a lot of waters.'

'I should prefer to do it by the book.'

'Good man. What do you know about knots?'

'I know a nautical mile is approximately 1.15 land miles.'

Thomas Montagu-Browne says this with a straight face – Skelgill is about to react as if the man is being ironic – but again he recalls half-sister Lavinia's remarks, and is not so sure.

'I'll take that as a no. *Tying* knots – I'm talking about.'

'Yes. I m-mean – no – I'm afraid I don't.'

Skelgill rummages in the bag – he finds what he seeks – a spool of leader line. He locates the loose end and bites off the first twelve inches and keeps a grip of it between his teeth. Then he strips out a yard more from the spool.

'You have to make the droppers before you tie on any hooks. I'll just set one up so you can see what we're aiming for – then I'll show you the knots more slowly.'

Skelgill places the two lengths of line parallel to one another. There is a blur of fingers as he creates a loop, passes the loose ends through repeatedly, moistens the interwoven section with his lips and draws the whole arrangement tight. The short strand is now tied perpendicular to the main line, forming a cross, and Skelgill bites off one half and holds up the result.

'Dropper. Like all good knots it gets stronger under tension. You'd put one about ten foot from the point fly – and the other about half way. Next – to tie the flies on – I use a tucked half blood knot.'

He selects a *Peter Ross* from the fly box and feeds the tip of the line through the eye of the hook. There is another whirr of movement as he winds the loose end round the standing part five times and feeds it through the formed loop. Then he makes a second tuck, moistens the arrangement and – holding the loose end clear with his teeth – draws the knot tight, one hand pulling the line, the other grasping the fly tightly between finger and thumb.

'Wish I'd had a pound for every time I've hooked myself doing this.'

Squinting sideways Skelgill sees that Thomas Montagu-Browne's eyes are alert; they differ from those of his half-sister, they are pale blue and guileless. Skelgill raises his little demonstration piece – a point fly tied on, and a dropper ready for a fly.

'So that's what we're aiming for. Obviously spread over a longer length of leader.' As his student nods Skelgill bites off the fly and returns it to its place amongst the ranks of others. Then he bites off the used section of nylon and feeds it into his jacket pocket. 'Right – let's have a look at the knots – more slowly.'

Thomas Montagu-Browne makes a nervous clearing of his throat.

'I – I think I can do it.'

Skelgill glances at him doubtfully – he recalls his own clumsy first efforts, with the Professor gazing on patiently – *"Less haste more speed, Daniel!"* But Skelgill shrugs and hands over the spool of line.

'I sh-shan't bite it – if you don't mind – I don't think my teeth are up to it.'

Thomas Montagu-Browne has a pair of clippers on a retracting zinger affixed to his quilted gilet, and he uses these to snip off a short length. He places the two strands together and then without hesitation replicates Skelgill's dropper knot – in only marginally more time. He extracts the same fly – the *Peter Ross* – from the box and promptly reproduces the blood knot. Skelgill watches wide-eyed as the man even remembers the second tuck – a little 'Skelgill speciality', that as far as he knows few anglers employ. When Thomas Montagu-Browne holds up his efforts for inspection, Skelgill swears under his breath.

'Excuse my French – but I think you've cracked it in one, Tom.'

A reluctant grin temporarily occupies Thomas Montagu-Browne's somewhat lopsided countenance; he looks away self-consciously, and red patches form upon his pallid cheeks. For a moment his cadaverous demeanour seems to get an injection of life. His blue eyes brighten and he steals a sideways glance at Skelgill.

'I think you must be a good instructor – you would be much better at this than I, Inspector.'

Skelgill scowls and rises to gaze pensively over Bassenthwaite Lake. He flexes his back, driving his fists into the base of his spine. A few moments pass before he responds.

'If your guests come to fish – those that know what they're doing – you can leave them to it – concentrate on being the boatman. The beginners – looks to me like you'll be able to put them right.' He indicates the rough pasture with a sweep of his arm. 'Get them to do a bit of false casting over the grass. Set the team of flies up. Easy as pie. Just make sure folk wear sunglasses and a cap. So's you can't be sued for lost eyes.'

He notices a sudden change in Thomas Montagu-Browne's expression. Something of the earlier look of bewilderment returns. Skelgill jerks his head in the direction of Greenmire Castle.

'Have you got folk staying now?'

'Oh – n-not until next Friday, Inspector.' Suddenly he grimaces, a tormented expression that bares two rows of somewhat irregular teeth. 'But Lavinia is not letting out Lady Anne's chamber for the time being.'

18. PENRITH, HQ

Monday, 10am

'**A**lright, cock?'

Skelgill has entered his office to find DI Alec Smart holding court before his two sergeants. He is taken aback that the skinny inspector is lounging in his chair, feet up on the corner of his desk. He wears pointed crocodile shoes, the leather of the soles barely worn, as if they might be brand new. But Skelgill has no intention of admiring the Mancunian's no-doubt trendy attire. He looks more like he might have come directly from his boat; an impression reinforced by a large dog-eared cardboard box that he carries – from the interfolded flaps of which snakes a stray coil of fine nylon line. Unceremoniously he dumps the carton on his desk, raising dust from his in-tray. DI Smart seems to take the hint. He swings his legs down and steps around the far side of the desk to stand beside DS Jones, where she sits beneath the window. Skelgill notices that he sidles disturbingly close. As he bends to brush his designer suit a sly grin lingers at the corners of his narrow mouth.

'What can I do for you, Smart?'

DI Smart raises his hands, palms outward – it is a gesture intended to amplify Skelgill's unfriendly undertone.

'Just passing your door, Skel – thought I'd drop in to say well done.' He cranes his neck to squint at DS Jones, as if he is demanding corroboration. 'The Chief was telling me you've nailed a creep – done the *Keystone Jocks'* work for them.' He sniggers at his own little play on words.

Skelgill's belligerence is somewhat stymied by this apparent praise. He slumps into his seat and scowls indecisively.

'There's nothing certain – they've not charged him yet.'

DI Smart in turn leans back against the window and folds his arms. He narrows his eyes as if accustomed to squinting through a veil of cigarette smoke, and he plies Skelgill with an old-fashioned look.

'Come off it, Skel. Word is there's glory seekers coming out of the woodwork like maggots.'

DI Smart's tone is disparaging – but his meaning seems to suggest some development of which Skelgill is unaware. Inexplicably absent this morning, he has missed both his regular Monday briefing meeting with his superior and an update from his team. He glances, unable to conceal his alarm, at DS Jones. She appears reluctant to respond – she realises her answer will only confirm her boss's lack of knowledge – but Skelgill nods for her to continue.

'Guv – news of Will Liddell's arrest has got out on social media – I'm talking nationwide – not just a local chat group like before. I don't know how – it makes you think there was a deliberate leak – it started with a blogger for an Edinburgh newspaper.' She pauses – and visibly grits her teeth, the muscles beneath her prominent cheekbones flexing. 'Three women have come forward – to report allegations of historical sexual assault.'

There is a cynical cackle from DI Smart. He preens at his clothing and grins salaciously at DS Jones.

'I bet they didn't complain while they were necking his champagne, eh? Admiring his etchings.'

There is a silence – brought on if anything as much by DI Smart's distasteful remark as the news itself. Skelgill's features contort as if he is trying to find some rejoinder. However, it is DI Smart who is first to speak.

'That's no help to you, though, eh, Skel?' He flicks the fingers of one hand through his rather lank hair. 'The Chief's getting all uppity – that your little Greenmire victim's floating unclaimed round that lake of yours.'

Now Skelgill is driven to an ill-considered retort.

'Happen it *were* just a suicide, Smart.'

DI Smart once again simpers – as though he is not convinced – and that Skelgill is being disingenuous. Meanwhile the two sergeants appear variously alarmed and disconcerted that their own superior is being driven into a corner. DI Smart presses home his advantage.

'I can't see the Chief buying that, Skel – not now this billionaire sex pest's in the frame. She'll be getting questions from above – from the media – why hasn't her team pinned the missus on him? Reading between the lines she's talking about a fresh set of eyes.'

DI Smart pushes off from the wall at his back and slinks across to the open door. He pats DS Leyton condescendingly on the shoulder. 'Fresh pair of *mincers*, eh, geezer?' He imitates DS Leyton's East End accent. 'I'd have him by the short and curlies – that'd make him squeal, eh, Emma?' And he departs with sleazy wink at DS Jones.

The trio is left in brooding silence. Skelgill has a face like thunder. But he might do well to wonder if DI Smart's little incursions – always seemingly well timed to rub salt into his wounds when a case is in the doldrums, with thinly veiled threats of displacement conveyed apparently from the Chief – have more method in them than madness – and if DI Smart, far from being, in the Chief's eyes, some saviour in waiting, is nothing more than a pawn in her game. However – anger blinds him to any such speculation. He lifts the mug that has been cooling upon his desk, and takes an angry pull, followed by a face of disapproval.

'Fresh cup, Guv?'

DS Jones shifts forward as if to rise. There is a glint of determination in her eye – perhaps that she uses the word 'fresh', a refusal to allow it to be appropriated by the departed Machiavellian DI Smart. Skelgill shifts uncomfortably in his chair.

'Aye – in a bit.' He empties his mug, cold or not, and bangs it down in a small act of defiance. 'Where were we?'

Now DS Jones grins. She waves her sheaf of notes.

'Fresh mince pies, Guv?'

She flashes a grin at DS Leyton – permission to hijack his lingo – and then plies Skelgill with an optimistic gaze. 'That was your brief for me on Friday.'

She hands a stapled copy to each of her colleagues – Skelgill immediately puts his down on the surface before him.

'Also, Guv – I loaded it onto the system on Saturday.'

Skelgill looks rather like a schoolboy being asked by his maths tutor to explain Pythagoras' theorem, when what is running through his mind is the best angle to hold a fishing rod to retrieve a pike lure. For his part, DS Leyton is also looking rather sheepish – as though he, too, has overlooked his homework. However, he evidently decides to inject a small dose of topical humour into his excuse. He expels air through his rubbery lips and sinks back into his seat resignedly.

'We've got the old dragon staying – the wife's ma – she's only gone and broke her flippin' foot – she's stuck up the apples – barking out her orders on the dog – the flamin' trouble's had me in a right two-an'-eight.'

DS Jones lets out a peal of laughter at DS Leyton's contrived Cockney rant – and even Skelgill is obliged to grin. DS Jones waves her papers.

'I suggest I start from fresh, then, Guv?'

Skelgill picks up his copy of the report and casually flicks through it. Now he makes a face of trepidation.

'Jones – happen I will have that tea.'

'Sure, Guv – back in two ticks.'

She rises and moves lightly to the door.

'Jones.'

She turns and regards him obligingly.

'Guv?'

'Bacon buttie?'

'Food for thought, Guv.'

*

'So –' (Skelgill's eyes flicker – there goes the '*so*' again – now it's DS Jones – though on reflection at least she is reprising). 'The new developments concerning Will Liddell?'

Skelgill, however, nods his approval. DS Jones regards him earnestly.

'DS Findlay phoned looking for you, Guv – he said he tried your mobile first thing – and that he wouldn't mind a chat when you've got a minute – but he gave me a summary.'

She refers to Detective Sergeant Cameron Findlay – "Cammy" – Skelgill's long-time ally in the Scottish force. Skelgill looks momentarily disconcerted – presumably that he was absent when the call came through on the police landline. He glances at the box on his desk and shoves it a little more to one side. 'Aye – I must have had no signal.'

DS Jones seems unperturbed; there is nothing new in Skelgill's unaccountable movements. She sees that he is not looking at the notes but is watching her, waiting for her to begin.

'The three females that have contacted the Scottish police – two are in their late twenties and were employees of companies in the *Liddell Acorns* group. The alleged incidents both occurred when they were working late and were called to his office suite. The time frame is within the last three years. The third person is a woman in her early forties – but the incident took place at a dinner party at Will Liddell's house over ten years ago. It seems he used the excuse of showing her his art collection, to separate her from the others and lure her into a bedroom.'

There is a small risk at this juncture that DI Smart's flippant remarks might strike a chord – but it is far too serious a matter for that – and Skelgill and DS Leyton both regard DS Jones severely – and it is DS Leyton who utters an oath that sums up both their feelings.

'Makes you want to ring his flippin' neck, Guv.'

Skelgill looks inclined to share this sentiment – perhaps even that it would be too good a fate for the man – but his ingrained recalcitrance brings out the devil's advocate in the guise of official protocol.

'Let's not get too excited – it's not going to be easy – one person's word against another's.'

But DS Jones looks ready to disagree.

'Guv – what I said to you – about Catriona Brodie?'

Skelgill seems to become distracted.

'Just remind me?'

'That she wasn't the first.'

Skelgill regards her almost genially.

'So you were right – well done.'

DS Jones passes quickly over the rare compliment.

'Guv.' She taps her papers with the back of her fingers. 'I believe these three are just the tip of the iceberg. I think it's going to be one person's word against many. There are successful precedents for gaining a conviction.'

DS Leyton interjects.

'I take it he's denying it?'

DS Jones nods, and her expression becomes introspective. She no doubt recalls what she now suspects was the introductory phase of Will Liddell's method. The memory is raw. Her voice gains a note of controlled anger.

'And he'll be good at that.'

DS Leyton picks up on her pent-up emotion. He looks appealingly to Skelgill and extends his meaty hands, oversized for a man of his limited height.

'Surely this means we can nail him now, Guv – for the murder of his missus?'

'Leyton – you sound like Smart.'

But DS Leyton is not deterred by the slight.

'Well – we keep saying, Guv – what with her outside bedroom door being locked – he was the only one that could easily have done it. He had the injuries on his arm. She had his skin under her nails. She was wearing no underwear.' He rubs a palm absently on the back of his sturdy neck. 'Now we know what we do about him – why would we be surprised if he strangled her?'

But Skelgill is squinting doubtingly.

'I'll be surprised when two and two make five.'

194

The retort is somewhat unfair, but he leaves it hanging. He regards each of his subordinates in turn. DS Jones makes an effort to be positive.

'From these new leads, Guv – maybe something will emerge – some connection with what happened at the castle?' However, her tone is short on optimism. 'If only she hadn't been his wife –'

She tails off – and there is silence – for Skelgill is nodding. Any imagined scenario of a coercive nature involving Will and Scarlett Liddell just does not seem to stack up. After half a minute it is DS Leyton that speaks, a cautious and yet faintly manic note having entered his voice.

'What if she threatened to blow the gaff, Guv? What if she knew about him? His dodgy antics? For all we know he tried it on *her* one time – before they got hitched.' But now DS Leyton, too, seems to have second thoughts – he brings his hand up to cup his chin. 'Then again, would you marry a geezer who'd done that to you?'

He looks inquiringly at DS Jones, as though she might be the oracle on such a matter. She does not respond – though she regards him reflectively for a moment before turning to Skelgill.

'What if she were about to 'blow the gaff' on someone else?'

Skelgill does not appear fazed by this suggestion.

'Such as?'

DS Jones turns over the first page of her notes, the addendum concerning the latest allegations. Beneath is the main body of the report. She raises it illustratively.

'When you went to London – I decided to forget about Will Liddell and concentrate on the backgrounds of the others.'

The two men look on, DS Leyton hopefully; Skelgill is more taciturn.

'Can I start with Derek Duff?' Her colleagues nod, rather blankly now. 'Of the three – let's call them *husbands* for the sake of simplicity – he was the first that I interviewed last week. On the face of it he's a really nice guy – affable, laid back – yet despite that I came away feeling as if there was something not quite right.'

She glances at Skelgill – who gives a small approving nod – after all, this statement chimes with his own unfathomable methodology. She continues.

'Displayed around his office there were posters and samples of products that his company had worked on.' She expounds for DS Leyton's benefit. 'He organises marketing campaigns – you know, like in a pub they give you a scratch-card – and you might win your next drink free, or a prize or something?' DS Leyton nods comprehendingly. 'So – I looked on his website – and at press releases – and marketing industry media reports. Altogether I found mentions of about twenty different brands – spirits, beer, cosmetics, confectionery, toiletries.' Now she pauses to take a breath – the result is a heightening of the attention of her audience. 'Every single one of them – no exceptions – was a brand owned by one of Will Liddell's companies.'

DS Leyton is looking puzzled.

'So what are you saying, girl?'

'That – in effect – he only has *one* client. The *Liddell Acorns* group. He might be running his own company – ostensibly he's an independent businessman – but he relies for all his income on Will Liddell.'

DS Leyton gives his colleague an admiring look.

'Struth – so you reckon Scarlett Liddell was about to say something that would put him in Queer Street?'

Skelgill interjects.

'Hold your horses, Leyton – let the lass finish.'

However DS Jones looks rather strained. She lays her papers on her lap and holds up her hands in a brief gesture of retreat.

'Well – that's really all there is in relation to Derek Duff – maybe if I explain about the others?'

Skelgill is nodding. DS Jones recovers her place in her notes – though again she begins to recite mainly from memory.

'As you'll recall, the next person I interviewed in Edinburgh was Mike Luker. You couldn't really get more like chalk and cheese than him and Derek Duff. While Derek Duff – *I think* – is candid, by comparison Mike Luker is cagey to the point of making you feel he isn't going to tell you anything – and certainly not about his business – especially if you don't know the right questions to ask.'

DS Leyton gives a self-deprecating harrumph.

'Hah – that'd be me, girl.'

DS Jones regards him magnanimously.

'So I asked a contact in the Met's corporate fraud office – we were on the same graduate intake – to run a few checks on Mike Luker's firm. It's called *Luker Investments*. He'd mentioned to me that he started doing some work for Will Liddell about five years ago. Up to that point it looks like he was more or less flying solo. But since then turnover has doubled each year – and now he's got quite a little operation going. Not to mention a healthy profit. As with Derek Duff's firm – it looks like the bulk of the increase in revenue has come from working as a consultant for *Liddell Acorns*. There are numerous press releases that refer to *Luker Investments* handling 'M&A' – that's merger and acquisition – projects for them. So far so good – except when my contact requested a credit rating it came back as just one notch above junk.' She glances at her notes. 'They call it being highly geared – inadequate share capital and loans supported by other loans. It takes just one investment to go bad – or the firm's underlying funding to dry up – and the whole lot could come down like a house of cards. And *Liddell Acorns* is listed as a major preferential bondholder for *Luker Investments*.'

The detectives fall silent. The penny – or perhaps, rather, the pound – is beginning to drop. DS Jones takes a sip from her glass of water.

'Finally, on the face of it, you might think Kevin Makepeace is most dependent of all upon Will Liddell – he's his employer, after all. However, I searched his job title and there are hundreds of good positions advertised at his level – admittedly mostly in the South-East, fewer in Scotland. As a Marketing Manager with extensive blue-chip experience he's a saleable commodity. I don't think he'd have much to worry about, as far as making a good living is concerned.'

'So *what?*'

Skelgill's intonation suggests he detects some contrary sentiment underlying her assessment. It seems to him that she errs towards Kevin Makepeace.

'I don't know, Guv – I suppose he was quite standoffish about Scarlett Liddell. I mean – I can see how Mike Luker could justifiably claim that he distanced himself from her – he was a company outsider, dealing with confidential tax and investment issues for Will Liddell – but Kevin Makepeace worked for the *Liddell Acorns* group for the entire duration of Scarlett Liddell's employment. He surely had passing contact with her when she was based in London – and certainly he approved her promotion to his department in Edinburgh. From what we know, she wasn't easily overlooked.' DS Jones glances from one colleague to another in turn. 'And my impression of Kevin Makepeace is that he isn't the sort of guy that would ignore her.'

Skelgill nods pensively – her earlier description of the man's narcissistic traits has remained with him. Were Kevin Makepeace and Scarlett Liddell something of the proverbial 'birds of a feather'?

'When was he divorced from Felicity Belvedere?'

DS Jones narrows her eyes – but Skelgill knows she is too diligent to have overlooked this fact.

'Their *decree nisi* was registered about three-and-a-half years ago. That would have been before Scarlett Liddell moved to work for him in Edinburgh.'

Now DS Leyton glances at Skelgill – as if to check whether he is about to comment – when it appears he is not, the sergeant makes his own contribution for DS Jones's benefit.

'The girl we spoke to – that Scarlett Liddell worked alongside in London – she had her marked down as flashy, flirty – liked the look of herself. And her previous boss – he let slip that she was quite a handful – Guvnor and I even wondered if she were messing him around – leading him on, know what I mean? Like the London crowd weren't too sorry to get her out of their hair. But what's to say she didn't carry on being a troublemaker once she moved to Edinburgh? She might have got some juicy dope on Makepeace. We know she'd been drinking on the Saturday afternoon when they got back to Greenmire Castle – maybe she got a bit loose-tongued – put the wind up him – next thing he's throttling her.'

DS Jones is looking uncertainly at Skelgill. Though she is partly responsible for her fellow sergeant's pursuit of a rather sensational line of thought, she is reminded of the facts that constrain their suspicions.

'Guv, I was re-reading the pathology report. If she were strangled by another party, against her will – then the medical consensus is that there would have been far more signs of a struggle.' She glances tentatively at each of her colleagues. 'It comes back to the suggestion that she was voluntarily engaged in whatever took place – such as the romantic encounter that went wrong.'

Despite his sergeant's use of the euphemism Skelgill looks discomfited. He rises and turns to gaze rather aimlessly at the map on his wall. It seems unlikely it will provide subliminal inspiration; not when the critical locus – Greenmire Castle – is a microscopic rectangle infilled with beige ink – and not when events that came to pass therein have their formative roots anchored well off the map, in the capital cities of London and Edinburgh.

'How many times have we jumped on the same roundabout that brings us back to Will Liddell.'

He intones this as a statement. His team know he refers to the 'Murder Mystery' evening – and the realisation that, with hindsight, they have been left with an incomplete set of clues. The participants, the emergency services – and even the initial police reaction – were all conditioned by the belief that they were in the midst of a drama – an attempted suicide in which the victim may still have been alive. Called to the scene the following day, Skelgill found the stage abandoned, the actors' lines forgotten – their memories impaired by alcohol and inattention.

When Skelgill turns around he sees his sergeants are valiantly racking their brains for ideas. DS Jones is scanning line by line through her report, and DS Leyton has his notebook open and is awkwardly thumbing over pages of his trademark small neat print, a style that belies his hulking demeanour. It is he that speaks.

'There's only a short window, Guv – between her death and when she was last seen alive – barely ninety minutes. If we could nail that down.' He squints at the page and jabs a thick finger in frustration. 'I mean, she was alive and kicking, in the drawing room until – what? – 5.21pm.'

Skelgill regards him broodingly.

'Remind me where you got 5.21 from.'

DS Leyton makes a pained face.

'That Montagu-Browne cove, Guv – remember I said he's a bit of queer one? I was trying to write, "at about 5.20pm the ladies left the drawing room" and he got quite uppity – like it stressed him that I was rounding – I could see he even watched me write it down. I reckon he's got that thing the missus wishes I were more like – what do they call it, sounds like CID?'

Still standing, Skelgill gazes at DS Leyton, but he seems not to see him. Then he leans over his desk and takes hold of the sides of the cardboard box with both hands, and stares at it as though it is some alien object that has materialised during their meeting without his noticing. Now he mutters under his breath.

'I'm not a good instructor.'

His subordinates exchange looks of familiar resignation; there can be little new in their boss's repertoire of erratic behaviour. But Skelgill breaks out of his trance – and he appears surprised that his colleagues are still present. Then he picks up the carton and purposefully tucks it under one arm.

'Skates on.'

The others begin to rise dutifully. DS Leyton speaks on their behalf.

'Where to, Guv?'

Skelgill flashes him a glance that suggests the answer ought to be obvious.

'To do what we should have done a week ago, Leyton – to ask the butler.'

Skelgill disappears through the door as his colleagues hasten to follow.

'What's in the box, Guv?'

'What?' Now Skelgill shrugs and answers somewhat absently without looking back. 'At Greenmire Castle – they're starting up fishing classes – some for local kids' charities – this is a load of spare tackle. A donation.'

It is with no little bewilderment on their faces that the two sergeants, on Skelgill's coattails, slip past DI Smart – who loiters in reception with his usual air of casual nonchalance. Yet there is something in their bearing, their determined gait that disrupts the disparaging sneer that creases his weasely features. A fly on the wall might speculate that the Chief's ploy has worked – Skelgill is energised.

19. WHAT THE BUTLER SAW

Monday, 11.30am

'Y-yes – they called me *M-Memory Man* at school.'

Skelgill casts what might be interpreted as a reproachful glance at DS Leyton. Accordingly his sergeant's head retracts tortoise-like into his broad shoulders. But on reflection he was not to know about Thomas Montagu-Browne's aptitude for detailed recall – the remarkable skill that often accompanies other less socially desirable traits possessed by people with his so-called 'disability'. Even Skelgill did not realise in the first instance – when the man faithfully replicated his instructions to fly cast, and to tie intricate knots. Perhaps subconsciously he put it down to him being more comfortable in the role of novice, when in fact he did have some experience under his belt; it was an arrangement that pandered to Skelgill's ego. Now, the three detectives (two with pens and notebooks poised, not leaving matters to memory) sit with Thomas Montagu-Browne in the library of Greenmire Castle; it is a second chance to break the deadlock. Skelgill is conducting the interview – and he has assumed the same presumptive yet informal manner that served him well during his impulsive stint as angling instructor.

'Tom – on the night of the Murder Mystery – you were here in the library the whole time – from before the first person arrived – until you ran to alert your sister to call an ambulance.'

'Y-yes.'

'And where were you stationed?'

'J-just opposite the main door.' He indicates with a nervous glance. 'I had a drinks trolley – with the classic c-cocktails. And ingredients to make more.'

'And you were watching the clock.'

'I always keep a c-close eye on the t-time – you see – Lavinia is very particular about the smooth running of her events.'

The man shifts his gaze to the bracket clock on the mantle above the hearth. Indeed now it strikes the quarter and Skelgill checks it against his wristwatch and sees that it is accurate. He rather suspects that Thomas Montagu-Browne leads a life browbeaten by his authoritarian sibling. And now he surely finds the presence of the plain-clothes officers intimidating. His eyes dart about anxiously and fine beads of perspiration coat his broad forehead.

'Could you run us through the sequence of events – I'm particularly thinking of who came and went – and when.'

The man nods urgently. They are seated on the pair of chesterfield sofas, the two sergeants opposite Skelgill and Thomas Montagu-Browne. The police are trying to look relaxed, but he sits bolt upright, uncomfortable in a tweed suit. He has his hands loosely together resting on his thighs – his fingers make little movements that might almost be counting – although it strikes Skelgill that he could be subconsciously tying knots.

'When I came in with the trolley it was 6.54pm.'

Skelgill flashes a glance at his subordinates – immediately the specific time reminds them of the nature of the information they are about to receive.

'Mr Makepeace was first to arrive – at 7pm exactly. I sounded the gong just as the clock was striking the hour.'

'What did he do?'

'He took a cocktail and drank it immediately and asked for a refill.'

Skelgill seems to hesitate for a moment.

'How did he appear?'

'He was dressed in a white dinner jacket with black lapels, buttons and pocket hems. A black bow. Black trousers and black patent leather shoes.'

Now Skelgill seems to start – this was not the answer he banked upon – but of course Thomas Montagu-Browne deals in particulars and not sensibilities.

'And Mr Liddell was next to arrive.'

'Yes – at 7.03pm. He collected a drink – and Mr Makepeace approached him – and they walked over to face the eastern window.'

'Did you happen to hear what they were discussing – since there was just the three of you in the room?'

Skelgill adds the rider by way of exonerating Thomas Montagu-Browne from any accusation of eavesdropping – but the man does not seem perturbed.

'Mr Makepeace was telling Mr Liddell about the recall of a batch of malt whisky that had been incorrectly labelled. The logistics of recovering the stock from retail outlets in different countries and a programme of reimbursement – and then the reworking of the product with new labels.'

Skelgill raises an eyebrow.

'Did Mr Liddell engage in the conversation?'

'He listened and nodded – but they were soon interrupted – Mr Duff and Mr Luker came in at 7.05pm. They chose drinks and joined the other two gentlemen. Mr Duff made a toast to Mr Liddell – concerning his birthday.'

'So that was all the chaps here.'

'Mrs Duff arrived a minute later – it was 7.06.'

'What did she do?'

'She accepted a cocktail and walked over to the gentlemen. They f-formed into a semi-circle – and they were admiring her d-dress.'

Skelgill notes that while the man has been reciting straight facts his stutter has been largely absent – as if he is more confident with exact detail. Only now does he stumble over his image of Suzy Duff and her dress – or was it the admiring thereof?

'Did you hear anything that was said?'

Thomas Montagu-Browne gives a sideways jerk of his head.

'Mr Duff turned up the volume on the sound system. One of the speakers was placed just behind me. After that I couldn't hear anything clearly.'

'Who was doing the talking?'

'It was mainly Mr Duff – he seemed to be telling jokes – or at least recounting amusing anecdotes. Then Ms Belvedere and Mrs Luker arrived – at 7.11pm.' He glances at Skelgill – who provides an encouraging nod. 'I think the group were then discussing the costumes that the ladies were wearing. The three ladies moved away to take a photograph of themselves in front of the fireplace.'

Skelgill is reminded of the selfie shown to him by Felicity Belvedere. It occurs to him that the clock might be in the background.

'What about Mr Liddell – what was he doing at this point?'

'He was watching the ladies. Then when they had taken the photograph he went across to speak to Mrs Duff.'

'What – he interrupted them?'

Now Thomas Montagu-Browne shakes his head in a more conventional manner.

'She moved away from the other two ladies – she noticed him coming towards their group.'

Skelgill glances briefly at DS Jones and DS Leyton; they diligently take notes.

'Tom – now think carefully about what happened next.'

Thomas Montagu-Browne frowns; he does not need to think carefully. 'They spoke for a few minutes – the clock chimed for a quarter past seven – Mrs Duff noticed it. I think she pointed out the time to Mr Liddell. He handed his glass to her and went out through the door to the tower on the ladies' side.'

'What did Mrs Duff do?'

'She waited alone. She sipped her cocktail – and tasted the drink given to her by Mr Liddell. It was a *negroni* – she didn't appear to like it.'

Skelgill recalls the revealing dress worn by Suzy Duff – as captured in the photograph. He does not wonder that the butler's attention was easily held by her presence. The man's eyes fall upon his hands, and his fingers stop moving.

'Carry on, Tom.'

'Y-yes. Mr Liddell returned almost immediately – the minute hand on the clock was still on the quarter hour. Mrs Duff gave him his glass. They spoke for a moment and then they both finished their drinks and left the room together.' He indicates with a raised finger. 'Through the door to the staircase on the gents' side.'

'Did they speak to anyone else – tell them where they were going?'

'Mrs Duff smiled at the two ladies. The other three gentlemen were laughing together about something and didn't notice. Mr Liddell went ahead of her by a few paces.'

'And the time?'

'7.16pm.'

'Did anyone else leave the library after that?'

'No.'

'What were the rest doing?'

'Mr Makepeace and Mr Duff came for more drinks – but otherwise they were all talking together in a group in front of the fire.'

Skelgill regards the man evenly – it strikes him that, by now, most people would understand they are to read between the lines of the interactions, to provide a more subjective insight into what was afoot – but Thomas Montagu-Browne continues faithfully to replay the movements of the participants. Skelgill tries a more oblique tack.

'And how did you feel about what was going on?'

'I began to be concerned that the time for the Murder Mystery was approaching and that I would need to warn Lavinia that not everybody was ready. And then Mrs Duff came crashing back through the ladies' stair door – at 7.21pm – and she screamed at me to c-call an ambulance.'

Now Skelgill remains silent. Indeed there is a hiatus such that his colleagues look up expectantly from their notebooks. After a

206

few moments more, it seems that DS Leyton can hold his tongue no longer.

'Mr Montagu-Browne – did she speak to you directly – Mrs Duff – about the ambulance?'

'She was staring right at me.'

DS Leyton sees that his superior is still disengaged, and continues in his lieu.

'When I questioned you previously, sir – you said the other guests thought it was part of the Murder Mystery.'

'Yes – some of them were laughing at her – Mr Duff – and Mr Luker.'

'What did you do?'

'I did as asked. I knew that Mrs Liddell was not the intended murder victim.'

DS Leyton's brow creases.

'But you didn't know she was dead, sir.'

Thomas Montagu-Browne looks suddenly alarmed – as if he realises the interview has been a charade – and that the police are tricking him – into making a confession – he shrinks away from the pugnacious sergeant like a cornered animal.

'B-b-but –'

The man's reaction causes Skelgill to snap out of his reverie. He leans sideways to slap Thomas Montagu-Browne on the shoulder.

'That's all, Tom – very helpful.'

Skelgill rises purposefully and jerks a thumb in the direction of the main door of the library.

'Tom – that cardboard box I left in the porch. It's got a load of tackle inside – for the kids you're having up to fish – you might want to go and have a sort through it. We've just got a couple of things to do – in private. Aye?'

Thomas Montagu-Browne is plainly accustomed to being dismissed for such trivial purposes – and does not appear to take offence; indeed he might be greatly relieved, although his features have regained the startled look that seems to be their default setting. When he has gone, Skelgill addresses his sergeants collectively – though his gaze seems to favour DS Jones.

'Get all those times?'

DS Jones replies in the affirmative – but DS Leyton seems a little crestfallen – and looks askance at his own notebook, as if his was a futile exercise. Moreover, Skelgill torpedoed his interrogation tactic. But now his superior points a decisive finger at him.

'I want to do an experiment. Leyton – you can be timekeeper.'

*

'One minute sixteen seconds, Guv.'

DS Leyton mops his brow and draws in a couple of lungfulls of air. Climbing the four floors from the library to enter Lady Anne's chamber from the ladies' stair has taken its toll. He looks expectantly at Skelgill, who has not yet enlightened him regarding the purpose of their exercise – and now Skelgill seems distracted.

'Where's Jones? I asked her to come back up with you.'

'Oh – thing is, Guv – just after she burst into the library – and I stopped the watch – Lavinia Montagu-Browne appeared saying there was a call. DS Jones went to her office. Seems the station's been trying to get us on our mobiles – but of course there's no signal. George on the desk must have guessed we'd come here.'

Skelgill makes a face that acknowledges the fact.

'Aye – he saw me arrive with that box – he accused me of bringing a ferret to work so I had to explain what was in it. Turns out he's got a grandson in the scouts – I promised I'd tip him the wink once they start up these free fishing classes.'

DS Leyton makes a superficial attempt to appear interested – but he is plainly preoccupied with his part in the 'experiment' – a recording of the time it took for Skelgill and DS Jones to leave the library together, ascend the spiral staircase on the gentlemen's side, enter the 'Lord's chamber' – what had been Will Liddell's suite – pass through the interconnecting dressing rooms into

208

Lady Anne's chamber – formerly Scarlett Liddell's room – for Skelgill to peer into the bathroom – and for DS Jones to hare down the ladies' stair and break into the library – at which point DS Leyton was to stop his watch. Now he waggles the handset at shoulder height to attract Skelgill's attention.

'What about this time, Guv?'

'Take it away from five minutes and what have you got?'

Somewhat out of condition, DS Leyton is still panting – and this mental challenge compounds his discomfort.

'Cor blimey – now you're asking me, Guv. Seconds and minutes – always does my head in – arithmetic with sixties instead of hundreds.'

'Leyton – it can't be that difficult – if it were racing odds and I said work out your winnings at sixty-to-one you'd tell me in a flash.'

DS Leyton half closes one eye.

'Strictly speaking, Guv – that's even more confusing.'

'How come?'

'Well – *sixty-to-one against* means that means that if a horse ran sixty-one times it would be expected to win once. If you wanted the odds out of sixty you'd need to say *fifty-nine-to-one against*.'

Skelgill looks like he is regretting his question.

'Leyton, just work it out.'

'Yes, Guv.' DS Leyton scowls at his handset. Little oscillations of his head reflect some inner machinations. 'Three minutes forty-four seconds, Guv.'

Skelgill gives a condescending nod.

'That's what I thought. Have you got a countdown timer?'

'It's got everything, this, Guv – more features than they landed on the moon with, so they say.'

Skelgill makes a disparaging scoffing noise in his throat.

'Set it for 3:44 and let it run.'

'Righto, Guv.'

DS Leyton does as bidden. He props the handset against one of the mirrors of the Queen Anne dressing table so that they can both observe the display. But Skelgill turns away and wanders across to the west-facing window, whence there is a view of

Bassenthwaite Lake. Behind him, DS Leyton shuffles about, and begins to make little fretful groans as his body recovers from its exertions.

'It seems like ages, Guv.'

'Watched pot.' Skelgill stares at the lake, perhaps wondering when he'll get back out there, free of any burden, when waiting in anticipation of a bite becomes a sheer pleasure. 'You'll never make a fisherman, Leyton.'

'You know me and water, Guv.'

Skelgill is about to respond but the timer breaks in – and a second later there comes the rattle of the door handle from the ladies' stair – and then another rattle followed by a tentative knock – and then DS Jones's voice.

'Guv – are you in there? I'm locked out!'

Skelgill scowls at DS Leyton.

'Did you lock it, Leyton?'

'Nope. Definitely not, Guv.'

Skelgill strides across to the door. He turns the handle and simultaneously gives it a sharp tug, but there is no response. He tries again, this time putting his body weight behind it, tug o' war fashion – but still to no avail. The lock is a traditional mortise set into the darkened oak, and a large blackened iron key protrudes from the keyhole. He turns the key and there is a click, and then DS Jones pushes through. She is breathing noticeably; she must have run back up the spiral staircase. She appears eager to speak – but Skelgill pre-empts her with a terse statement.

'We never locked it. I've been nowhere near the door – and Leyton just came in and shut it normally.'

DS Jones parks whatever news she bears – she has her notebook open in one hand.

'Well – obviously – I went *out* – I couldn't have accidentally locked it – not with the key on the inside.'

DS Leyton gives a nervous laugh. He looks cautiously about the old room.

'Must be that ghost, Guv – Lady Anne whatsername?'

210

Skelgill's retort is dismissive, one that relates the phantom to a part of his anatomy, around the median posterior. Addressing DS Jones he points an index finger at the door.

'Go back out. Close it.' When DS Jones does as instructed, he raises his voice. 'Now come in.'

She opens the door – she seems a little disappointed – as if expecting it to have foiled her.

'Do it again.'

'The same, Guv? Right outside?'

Skelgill gives a curt nod. DS Jones duplicates the procedure. Again the door swings smoothly open.

'Keep going. Pull it snappier when you shut it.'

DS Jones glances a little sheepishly at DS Leyton, who has moved backwards by a couple of paces and is looking baffled; he might almost be thinking of the maxim attributed to Einstein that to repeat the same action and expect a different outcome is a sign of madness. He lets out a long sigh.

But at what must be the eleventh or twelfth salvo by DS Jones, just as she is beginning visibly to flag, the door does not open. Her voice comes as an echo from the stone stair.

'Guv?'

Skelgill darts forward and tries the door himself. Sure enough, it is locked – despite that the key has not been touched, and is in its normal upright or neutral position in the keyhole. However, he twists it clockwise and it serves to free the lock. He pulls the door open to reveal a wide-eyed DS Jones.

'Wow.'

But Skelgill does not wait for any praise. He drops to one knee and, with the door ajar, he turns the key anticlockwise and takes hold of the protruding deadbolt between his left thumb and forefinger.

'Look at this.'

As his subordinates crowd over him, he demonstrates that there is play – not much, but about a quarter of an inch – in the direction of travel of the deadbolt.

'This lock's ancient. The springs must be work-hardened.'

Now DS Leyton pipes up.

'So what, Guv – what's happened?'

Skelgill stands up and flexes his spine. Then he gives the door an illustrative shove.

'I reckon each time someone closes it, that deadbolt creeps out a fraction more. Eventually it's just enough to catch in the strike plate – bingo – it's locked.'

There is a moment's silence – but it is not long before DS Jones speaks, her voice tending towards a whisper.

'But, Guv – this means when Scarlett Liddell died – it might not have been locked from the inside.'

There is a more prolonged silence as they each process the implications – at their respective rates – and it is DS Jones that states what is perhaps the most salient aspect.

'Someone could have come in and out this way – without needing to pass Will Liddell. When they closed the door – it locked itself.'

'Whoa – that's opened a can of worms. Now it could have been any of the beggars!'

DS Leyton's interjection is rather too flippant for Skelgill's liking.

'Tom included, eh, Leyton? Or Lavinia?'

There seems to be sarcasm in Skelgill's tone – and perhaps DS Leyton takes what he himself might call 'the hump' – albeit he would pronounce it minus the initial 'h'. He contrives a rather grumpy sounding retort.

'It is like the flippin' *Adams Family*.'

Skelgill flashes a surreptitious grin at DS Jones.

'Never mind the *Adams Family*, Leyton – if it weren't for you and your flippin' 5:21 we wouldn't be standing here now. I'll settle for the can of worms.'

DS Leyton appears to be a little placated.

'So what, Guv – surely it's still back to the drawing board?'

There is a substantial pause before Skelgill replies.

'Back to school, Leyton.'

20. RETURN TO EDINBURGH

Monday, 3pm

'**G**uv – I think this is potentially significant.'
DS Jones settles back in the passenger seat of Skelgill's car. Two-handed she holds to her breast the report she has just read; she makes an expiration of breath, her lips pursed against the top edge of the pages, and the papers vibrate like the reeds of a wind instrument. Her gaze becomes clouded; rain is lashing down and the wipers fight a losing battle against the hammering onslaught that is bolstered by spray thrown up by a convoy of trucks that chokes the middle lane of the motorway. Having left DS Leyton to hold the fort at headquarters, departing forty minutes ago they have crossed the border. Signposts to Lockerbie are imprecise in the mist, and the landscape begins to assume a rolling character, hinting at more barren country to come. But they can see little of this – a blessing perhaps for DS Jones – for at least Skelgill cannot so easily be distracted by thoughts of fishing each time they cross some swollen beck or – now that they are in Scotland – swollen *burn*.

'Reckon you'd better fill me in.'

The report – the headline of which DS Jones was about to impart to her colleagues when the lock of Lady Anne's chamber jammed, prompting the about-turn that has them heading north – concerns a separate matter. A delving into Scarlett Liddell's mobile phone account has unearthed some irregular activity.

'The top line points are these.' DS Jones remains in her semi-recumbent pose, and does not refer to the notes. She continues to stare ahead, as if hypnotised by the metronomic swish of the

213

wipers. But her voice is clear and her phrases economical. 'Scarlett Liddell had been contacting an unregistered number – a pay-as-you-go mobile. The calls date back three years – towards the end of the period that she worked in London – and the most recent was two weeks ago. Typically one call per week – usually on a Friday. The calls were of short duration – under a minute – often just a few seconds. There have been periods of several months when there were no calls. There was a particularly heavy cluster about a month ago. All of the calls were outbound from her mobile. The receiving handset and SIM card were purchased in a *Tesco* supermarket in Edinburgh a few days before the first call from Scarlett Liddell. The buyer paid cash – likewise for subsequent top-ups.'

'Sounds like it's her dealer.'

Although Skelgill is merely sarcastic DS Jones's brow is furrowed, and patently his suggestion goes against the grain of her thinking. Besides, not only had Will Liddell dismissed any such notion, but also no alien substances had been found in his late wife's bloodstream.

'The majority of the calls were received in Edinburgh – but occasionally London – and the earlier calls were made from London. More specifically, the recipient was invariably either in the Covent Garden area – or what they call the East End of Edinburgh.' She pauses for a moment. 'We can probably request more accurate triangulation – but these locations correspond to the offices of *Liddell Acorns.*'

Skelgill gives a casual shrug that travels as a shudder down his arms to the steering wheel and causes a wobble in the vehicle's trajectory.

'Happen Will Liddell's got another phone.'

But DS Jones has thought this through.

'Guv – I could buy that – maybe while they were having a clandestine relationship – but why would it continue afterwards – for another two years?' Skelgill does not respond, so she continues. 'And I could buy that Will Liddell might have a private number – separate from his business line – but surely it would still be on the company account – and why these strange one-sided calls?'

'So, what's your theory?'

'Unlike texts, phone calls leave no incriminating trail of words. I think she was arranging to meet. I think she was having an affair – with someone as keen to conceal it as she was. We know about the company policy on relationships. We know Will Liddell is regarded as controlling.'

In his professional life, at times like this, Skelgill's natural recalcitrance is probably an asset, for it acts as a check on what he regards as the blinkered enthusiasm of others.

'Aye, but she was having an affair in the first place – *with* Will Liddell. What you're telling me – that would mean she was having two affairs.'

'Actually, Guv – the longest period when the calls temporarily stopped corresponds to just before she left the company – when her relationship with Will Liddell became public knowledge. You could construe that she got herself hitched to him – and then reconnected with the other person. Someone from Edinburgh. Maybe someone who was at the Murder Mystery weekend.'

Skelgill makes a disparaging growl in his throat.

'You're talking Kevin Makepeace, obviously.'

Surprised by his direct prompt, DS Jones feels obliged to backtrack.

'Well – it's a fact that Derek Duff and Mike Luker are both regular visitors to the *Liddell Acorns* building in Edinburgh – several times a week for meetings. But the earlier calls made by Scarlett Liddell from London, and received *in* London – surely that rules them out? Whereas we know Kevin Makepeace travelled south for meetings with other marketing heads, and his various advertising agencies. And he gave her the job.'

Skelgill ruminates for a moment or two.

'I take it we've tried ringing the number?'

'It's switched off – although not deactivated.' She gives a little ironic laugh. 'And no personal greeting.'

A silence descends – as they each ponder the possible implications – although while DS Jones thinks along lateral lines, Skelgill simply waits to see what happens. It is a method that he has refined through angling. There are times when trying too hard yields a blank day on the water; when sitting tight, drifting with the breeze, not allowing himself to be distracted by an intrusive stimulus is the best response. In his experience, fish – or at least bites – come along of their own volition, frequently in little clusters. The London bus phenomenon. And, now, the capital connection breaks the calm surface of their contemplation. It begins with the disembodied Cockney voice of DS Leyton, who calls DS Jones's number; she engages speaker mode. He sounds animated.

'Guvnor – that old biddy we went to see – Scarlett Liddell's auntie – well, not auntie – but you know what I mean – you ate all her cakes?'

A scowling Skelgill glances to see that DS Jones is grinning – but he can only fleetingly take his eyes off the indistinct road ahead.

'Get on with it, Leyton.'

'Yeah, Guv – what it is – she found that address that Scarlett Liddell moved to in the West End – a mail redirection notice that she'd hung onto – the Post Office sends it to your old address to stop any Tom, Dick or Harry diverting your mail without you knowing?'

'I'll take your word for it, Leyton.'

'Anyway, Guv – she phoned it through earlier – I've had the address checked. It's a flat in Shelton Street – that's just behind Long Acre – and not far from Bow Street.'

Skelgill does not need reminding that the London offices of *Liddell Acorns* are located in Bow Street. But this simply fits with the information they already possess – that Scarlett Liddell moved to an apartment close to her work. However, DS Leyton's next revelation is one he does not anticipate.

'Guv – London Borough of Camden's got a landlord registration scheme. The owner – for the last nine years – has been a Mr K. Makepeace. Can't be too many of them around.'

Into the silence that ensues DS Leyton enters some conjecture.

'How about that, Guv – he must have been the mystery geezer that turned up that night at Beaconsfield – gave Scarlett Liddell a lift to his gaff? Helped her move in.'

Skelgill continues to stare ahead. A look approaching alarm has slowly gripped his features – as though he is being forced progressively to accept something he is not comfortable with. Again he snatches a glance at DS Jones – she makes a brief fanning motion with a hand in front of her face, as if to suggest this news is too hot too handle. DS Leyton pipes back up – that he has a DC trying to extract the historical council tax records so that they may confirm that Scarlett Liddell was indeed the occupant – but Skelgill appears sufficiently convinced – if inexplicably crestfallen. When he offers no rejoinder DS Jones intervenes by relating to their colleague the discussion of the 'mystery mobile' – and her suggestion of a relationship. DS Leyton is quick to respond.

'Cor blimey – sounds to me like Makepeace was the middle rung of the ladder.'

Now Skelgill interjects.

'What are you talking about, Leyton?'

'Well – you know, Guv – everything we've heard about Scarlett Liddell – in a nutshell – it's naked *ambition*. Like the old auntie told us – it ended up with her hooking her millionaire. Seems to me like she weren't too fussed about who she had to trample over on the way. For starters there's that sad case, Organ – so she moves on to Kevin Makepeace – chews him up – gets to Edinburgh – spits him out – on to the main course, Will Liddell.'

Skelgill seems momentarily defeated by such blatant logic. His rudderless craft has become sucked into turbulent waters. With a hint of desperation in his voice, he contrives to cast an anchor.

'Leyton – these calls have been going on right up until the last few weeks. How does that fit with your theory of her dumping

Kevin Makepeace – if it even *were* him? Like I've just said to Jones – what if it's Will Liddell's spare mobile?'

DS Leyton is evidently a little flummoxed by his superior's somewhat agitated retort – via the loudspeaker curious hemmings and hawings come down the line – like the sound of a baffled pupil determined to convey to his schoolmaster it is just a matter of time before his brain clunks ponderously into gear.

'Oh, sh--!'

But it is DS Jones – and there is nothing ponderous about her reaction. Indeed she appends her exclamation with an uncharacteristic profanity – it is an oath of self-reproach. But on rarity value alone it wins the attention of her colleagues. She flicks urgently through her notes.

'Guv – what you just said – about the calls continuing until recently.'

'Aye?'

She finds the page she seeks. Her eyes dart about the columns of figures. She tentatively places a manicured index finger on the paper as though she feels for some invisible embossing.

'This cluster – about four weeks ago – calls that were made from Scarlett Liddell's mobile and received in Edinburgh.' Now she turns to look directly at Skelgill. 'It's just struck me – Will Liddell was in Shanghai. He was there for a month – covering that whole period.'

Skelgill pulls his face into a grimace. 'So – they weren't to him, then.' But if he continues to play devil's advocate, he no longer sounds convincing.

In the background DS Leyton clears his throat – perhaps a reminder that he is still there – and keen to hear what his colleague has to say. He senses there is more; and he is right. She takes a deep breath.

'But, Guv – it's not that – it's not the phone calls –'

'What is it then?'

'While Will Liddell was in China, six thousand miles away – Scarlett Liddell didn't just make an unusually high number of

218

phone calls.' DS Jones licks her lips as though her mouth has become dry. 'Guv – think of the timings – *she also got pregnant.*'

*

'You not eating, Guv?'

Skelgill sniffs morosely. He has ordered just a mug of tea. DS Jones has opted for water.

'Thought I'd better save myself – In case we end up in that *Laldhi* joint again tonight. It's a waste not to finish a banquet when it's paid for.'

DS Jones grins. It is not often her boss eschews a snack – and not least that they are seated inside a busy Moffat café that she has heard him laud for its bacon rolls; if she recalls correctly, "The best this side of *The Horn*" (which had turned out to be a roadhouse located alongside the River Tay). Their present location is just thirty miles north of the English border – the halfway point of their two-hour journey – and that Skelgill has stopped at all is in some respects a surprise – but DS Jones has detected an air of fretfulness about him since their conference call with DS Leyton. True enough, the steamed-up car was becoming claustrophobic – but his caged demeanour she has witnessed before, when evidence piles up and the facts don't fit his feelings – more than once he has climbed out of his office window, protesting the need for fresh air. But the café stuffy with the cloying aroma of roasted coffee beans mingled with sundry cooking smells is not exactly the great outdoors.

Certainly Skelgill is disquieted. Just as DS Jones's news of the calls became temporarily subsumed at Greenmire Castle by the discovery of the faulty lock, so did his own line of inquiry – more permanently. But a doubt continues to dog him. Yet he cannot dispute the new understanding that points to Kevin Makepeace as some key actor in the drama of the Murder Mystery weekend. While there is not yet proof that the mobile phone belongs to him, there can be no doubt about the Covent Garden flat that Scarlett Liddell – then Scarlett Robertson – had temporarily occupied. And of the interview with Thomas Montagu-Browne,

Skelgill's sergeants were quick to remind him that – while the butler was no reader of emotions – his account of Kevin Makepeace arriving solo in the library, downing a cocktail and taking another, was surely pertinent. And not forgetting that, on the fateful evening, while the Duffs on the first floor and the Lukers on the second had kept open their adjoining dressing room doors, on the third floor Felicity Belvedere and her ex-husband Kevin Makepeace had not. If Kevin Makepeace had wished to leave his room unnoticed, he could have done so. He could have descended the gentlemen's stair, crossed through the empty library, and ascended to Scarlett Liddell's suite via the ladies' stair. Adding weight to such conjecture is one simple fact – omitted at the time, but now confirmed by a retrospective telephone call to Thomas Montagu-Browne. While the other members of the house party entered the library from the tower doors that corresponded to their respective sides of the building, *Kevin Makepeace had entered from the ladies' stair.*

Skelgill, however, has insisted that the rampant speculation that threatened to take hold of their debate be held in check. The corollary of DS Jones's startling deduction about Scarlett Liddell's embryonic pregnancy is the question of paternity. But this is a matter of fact – and one that can be established – subject to the correct and sensitive protocol. *If necessary.* His reticence has puzzled his subordinates – and his vehemence in this regard he does not fully comprehend himself. Does his unrest have its roots in that the idea was not his? The issue of the timing of Will Liddell's trip abroad had eluded them all in the first instance – albeit in hindsight it is glaringly obvious. But with the subject off limits, DS Jones seems to struggle to find common ground for discussion, and something of an awkward silence settles between the pair. In fact it is Skelgill that now resurrects the conversation, but only to the extent that he outlines his thinking about their next steps.

'Tomorrow – you see Makepeace.'

'On my own, Guv?'

Skelgill's expression becomes somewhat pained. They have contacted DS Cameron Findlay in order to set up on their behalf the interview. Skelgill considers for a moment that the experienced Scots officer could sit in – however, he dismisses the idea on the grounds of unfamiliarity with the case. Besides, if anyone, it should be him, but he feels an aversion that is hard to put into words.

'You've interviewed him once.'

'But not under caution, Guv. As it was, he was bolshie, remember?'

'Aye – but he was also trying to impress you – so you're halfway there.'

DS Jones looks doubtful about this suggestion.

'Do I ask him outright?'

They both understand that she refers to Scarlett Liddell's pregnancy.

'See which way the wind blows.'

That Skelgill will rarely plan an interview – the occasional secret signal between colleagues excepted – is of no great comfort, and the cliché a piece of rather empty advice.

'I feel it's more likely that he won't have known about it.'

'Whatever.' Skelgill shrugs indifferently. 'When he finds out – he's smart enough to realise it's not going to be difficult to identify the father.'

DS Jones nods reflectively. If this is an ace they hold up their sleeve, then she wants to deploy it to best effect – but what is the desired outcome? Some kind of confession from Kevin Makepeace? But to show their cards risks handing over the advantage – and simply providing their opponent with the means to mount a defence. If there were a clandestine relationship, then only one person is alive to write its history. And circumstantial evidence alone will not prove that Kevin Makepeace was involved in the death of Scarlett Liddell any more than her husband – or any of the other members of the party, come to that. Perhaps she must resign herself to 'seeing which way the wind blows'.

'What about you, Guv? What will you do?'

It takes a while for Skelgill to answer. When he does, it is with another from his repertoire of slippery clichés.

'I'll sleep on it.'

21. *IUNCTA SORORIBUS*

Tuesday, 6.15am

'**G**ibbons, Inspector?'

Skelgill takes a seat on the bench above the stone wall, below which the elderly man, David Balfour performs his Tai Chi before the great vista of Edinburgh, the city's spires and stacks wreathed in a smoky mist that recalls its epithet *Auld Reekie*. The newly risen sun picks out the distant Bass Rock, and Skelgill is reminded that he has not checked his boat for evidence of its erstwhile epithet, *Covenant*. For this is the man that might well say, "Ah kent yer faither."

'Something like that, aye.'

This is a white lie – for the zoo's primates were curiously silent this morning – and Skelgill's wakefulness stemmed from some internal source. He was alert with the nervousness of an impending challenge – for many people an examination, albeit not for him – but a fell race, perhaps or a cricket match – though neither of these are activities in which he has much formal involvement these days. It can only be the Liddell case. That this might be the crucial day. But even so – he is not the one going into bat, so to speak – for DS Jones pads up to face Kevin Makepeace at 10am at Fettes Avenue police headquarters. Skelgill's strategy is that she has, if not exactly his trust, then the man's cooperation – but perhaps more importantly she has his measure – and thus Skelgill's presence might clip the wings of one who tends to preen before the fairer sex. Though he was guarded before – maybe Kevin Makepeace will reveal to DS Jones a chink in his shining armour.

'I never got very far with the Sallies girls.'

Skelgill starts. David Balfour has broken off from his exertions and has turned to face him. A sympathetic grin seems incongruous on the lopsided features. Yet – though he obviously speaks of bygone times, and of a matter of a different nature – there is perspicacity in his words – and he seems to sense something of Skelgill's discontentment.

'It's not the lasses I've been speaking with.'

Now the old man raises a sagacious finger.

'But their mothers will be Sallies girls.' Skelgill must look puzzled – for the man elaborates – if in obtuse terms. *'Iuncta sororibus.'*

'You've got me there, I'm afraid.'

'Their motto. I'm not sure that whoever came up with it was all that hot on Latin – but it just about passes muster. The infamous wall of silence!' He frowns and shakes his head reflectively. *'Sisters side by side.'*

*

Skelgill is looking at what appears to be a row of nondescript females in old-fashioned long smock uniforms. There is something of the domestic servant about their appearance – although this strikes him as paradoxical, since surely these carved images are meant to represent the daughters of wealthy Victorian merchants. They stand straight, arm in arm, and their sandstone eyes look vacantly over the grassy quadrangle as they must have done for the past 150 years. He wonders that he did not notice the commemorative tablet on his last visit – it must be six feet by three, and it tops the central portico of the old school building. Beneath the static figures, sure enough, is the motto, *Iuncta sororibus,* a new addition to his smattering of Latin, to go with *Esox lucius, aurora borealis* and *et cetera.*

His attention is distracted by a proletarian cry, "Hallo, there!" – it is the janitor – some distance away – but distinctive in his high-visibility vest – displaying a palm of recognition above the cropped head. However, if the man intends to conduct some shouted conversation he gives up before he has begun – a small cavalcade of showroom-fresh 4x4s lumbers into view along the school entrance road, and he jumps out to intercept them.

Skelgill is reminded of a clip he has seen on television, of a protestor valiantly trying to face down a column of tanks. By the look of it, the janitor has a similarly futile mission. But now the clatter of hockey sticks and a sudden crescendo of high-pitched cries tell him the 'push-back' (another recent addition to his knowledge) has taken place.

*

'You weren't at this school.'

Suzy Duff blinks but does not look away from the hockey pitch.

'I grew up in Hamilton – south of Glasgow. I attended the local state academy. Over here in the east they consider me a *Weegie.*'

Skelgill nods, perhaps commiseratively. He is familiar with this regional appellation for anyone vaguely Glaswegian, generally well meant – like Scouser, or Geordie, or Cockney – but he suspects in these more exalted circles it carries a hint of disparagement, and class differentiation. Her accent alone probably divulges this is not her *alma mater*. To look at, however, there would be nothing especially to distinguish her from the other well-heeled mothers who bask in the luxury of watching their daughters play hockey on a weekday morning. When last he saw her she was a little dishevelled – just out of the shower, her hair damp, with casual wear thrown on for a dog walk. Now her hair is brushed and glossy, and she sports a navy quilted knee-length coat that is tailored at the waist and hints at her shapely athletic figure; beneath she wears black leggings and calf-length boots. The coat looks new, although the boots on reflection are perhaps a little scuffed. He wonders if she has invested any thought of meeting him into her appearance; certainly there is perfume – but the warm, tactile manner of their walk on the wooded hill has deserted her. She had sounded a little flustered on the telephone – that she was about to leave for hockey – her daughter Poppy has been drafted into an older year-group to play an important cup tie. Skelgill had offered to meet her pitchside; and here they stand, in the cool, bright morning, the sun still low, streaming through bare treetops between south and east. She has pointed out to him that Lulu, the Liddell girl is also playing; but Skelgill sees no sign of her mother along the touchline; he wonders if the arrest of Will Liddell is keeping her away. Out on the pitch the action is as frantic as before, although – he notes – more precise. This is the under-16s squad, and he sees Catriona Brodie across in the home dugout, animated, engrossed, making each sweep and block, silently cursing at each infringement; he wonders if she has noticed his presence.

'What about the others?'

'The others?'

It is a stalling rejoinder. Patiently, Skelgill elaborates.

'Mrs Luker. Ms Belvedere. Mrs Liddell – *Muriel* Liddell.'

Her response is overly slow.

'Yes, I believe they did – attend Sallies.'

In this feigned doubt Skelgill detects a note of foreboding.

'Another reason to send their bairns here.'

'Yes.'

For a man often impatient and too self-absorbed to be a master of social niceties, Skelgill can be crafty. But he is less than comfortable in dealing with platitudes such as they exchange now – and it must be obvious to Suzy Duff that these are facts of which he is well aware. As a silence descends – it feels like for several minutes – they watch the play; they are both still, and seem absorbed in their thoughts; but Skelgill gets a growing sense that Suzy Duff is waiting for him to make his move. Her face has taken on a mask of impending doom; she seems resigned to her fate; yet Skelgill is an unwilling executioner. But there is a lighter moment – a vigorous tackle just a couple of yards from them. It involves Poppy Duff and her opposite number. The ball ricochets up – in their direction – Skelgill half-ducks and simultaneously flings out his left arm to make a decisive catch. The umpire signals it is Sallies' ball – Skelgill holds it out to the girl – who regards him with her cold blue eyes – but as she takes it there is fleeting yet endearing smile. Suzy

Duff – when she might be expected to encourage her daughter – does not speak. As the play surges down the wing, it is Skelgill who does.

As the words come to Skelgill he feels like they have been with him for a long time – not exactly on the tip of his tongue – somewhere more visceral – and that they are ancient words in themselves – and that these were the words that he slept on – albeit fitfully, the disquiet would not leave him – letters that formed like embryonic tadpoles and finally spelled out the uncomfortable truth that has nagged at his subconscious.

'She's Will Liddell's.'

He does not employ further explanation – or even a hint of inquiry in his intonation – such is his phrase borne with the certainty of gut feel – and it is a conviction that is thus conveyed to Suzy Duff. She continues to gaze out over the pitch, her eyes no longer following the play, or even her daughter, come to that.

'Is it so obvious?'

In the dizzying instant Skelgill can only just hear her words, such is the sudden pounding of blood in his head, his heart rising up in his chest. When he speaks, his voice sounds disembodied, as though it cannot be his own. But he feels a great weight lifted from him, as though an angel has swooped unseen.

'I shouldn't say so. She's got your sparkle in her eye.'

That Skelgill describes a maternal tempering of the icy blue paternal eyes might just as easily be interpreted as a slight as the compliment he intends; however she accepts his observation with apparent equanimity. It is a little while before she replies.

'Will is a very old friend – of Derek's – a very good friend.'

Skelgill too continues to gaze out over the pitch, as if to face her will prick the little bubble of confidence that has enveloped them. Indeed, his demeanour might be considered overly passive, but a fellow angler would recognise a focus in his eyes, a possession that prevails in that interval between a bite being indicated and the quarry to be discovered floundering in the net. But he does raise an eyebrow at the remark.

'That's one way of putting it.'

'It's the truth.'

227

'Strikes me Will Liddell's got an interesting take on friendship.'

There is more silence. Out of the corner of his eye Skelgill can see that Suzy Duff is biting her lip. Does she hope that he knows less than she fears? She does not respond to his observation.

'When Scarlett Liddell didn't come down to the library – and Mr Liddell found the door locked – it was definitely you that suggested you should accompany him back up – not the other way round?'

She does not seem surprised that Skelgill has fast-forwarded to this question. Still she does not look at him; however there might be a sign of relief, a relaxation of the shoulders. Certainly her tone is unguarded.

'Yes – my idea.'

Skelgill inserts another pause before he poses his next question – but she waits patiently.

'Me and my sergeant – DS Jones – we did a reconstruction. To get up one stair, through the rooms, and down the other. You took about three-and-a-half minutes longer than us.'

At last she turns her head to face him – but he detects no sign of panic in her eyes. She seems to understand that he requires an explanation.

'Inspector, have you asked Will about this?'

Skelgill grimaces.

'I hear that Mr Liddell has been advised by his lawyer to answer "No comment" to all questions at the moment.'

Suzy Duff is plainly interested that Skelgill is honest about this point – when he could have resorted to subterfuge. Could he be on her side? To Skelgill, it seems apparent she is wrestling with divided loyalties, yet she is not rushing to cover her own tracks, a condition he would recognise in an instant.

'Naturally, we go back a long way, Inspector.'

Her tone carries neither bitterness nor affection; neither regret nor yearning. It is wholly empty of emotion.

'Long enough for Scarlett Liddell to come between you?'

'Oh, no – no – nothing like that.' Now her features become alarmed. 'We entered Scarlett's room – it was exactly as I have described. Will immediately looked into the bathroom – he cried out – and I ran for help.'

Skelgill again takes a few moments to compose his rejoinder.

'You just took longer to get there in the first place.'

'There's no crime in that – surely, Inspector?'

Still her tone is matter of fact, when he might expect it to be pleading.

'It can be a crime to withhold evidence – to hinder a police officer in their line of duty.' He inhales and lets out the breath more slowly. 'But there's no rule I can think of that says you had to take one minute or two minutes or three minutes or more to reach Scarlett Liddell's bedroom.'

'If we'd had any inkling that Scarlett had been in trouble – of course we would have raced to her assistance.'

'And that goes for Mr Liddell?'

'Undoubtedly, Inspector. He worshipped the ground she stood upon.'

'He had a funny way of showing it.'

Now there is another pause – and she does not contend the assertion, but merely sighs.

'Nothing is quite what it seems with Will.'

'Evidently.'

Skelgill is thinking that if Will Liddell had taken a witness to the 'discovery' of Scarlett Liddell, having killed her earlier, it would have required an extraordinary degree of callousness to dally with Suzy Duff for the best part of four minutes. But now her voice interrupts his reverie.

'I don't for a moment believe he killed her.'

Skelgill regards the woman intently.

'Would Scarlett Liddell have known about his – what are they calling it – his peccadilloes?'

But now she surprises him with a small act of resistance.

'Is anything proven, Inspector?'

Skelgill's features become severe.

'I'm told another four alleged victims got in touch overnight. We're approaching double figures.'

Suzy Duff's gaze falls away.

'I can't speak for Scarlett, Inspector. But she hadn't known him all that long. In the scale of things they were virtually a new couple.'

'That didn't appear to be a deterrent on his part.' His gaze seeks out Catriona Brodie. 'We know of at least one reported incident in the last twelve months.'

Suzy Duff looks downcast. She nods slowly.

'Maybe not.'

'What about the first wife – Muriel Liddell – we're talking what – fifteen years together? She must have been aware of something.'

'You'd have to ask her, Inspector.'

Skelgill senses that a measure of reticence has entered Suzy Duff's manner.

'I thought wives knew everything about their husbands? And then confided in their friends.'

'I suppose you can choose *not* to know certain things. And there are degrees of friendship.'

Skelgill nods contemplatively.

'Then what about Belinda Luker and Felicity Belvedere – what would they say if I asked them about Will Liddell – now the lid's been lifted?'

Suzy Duff's eyes dart about, as though she is measuring the distances between the white lines on the playing surface.

'I don't think it's fair to ask me these questions, Inspector – I mean – we've not done anything wrong – not against the law. Have we?'

Skelgill appears momentarily perplexed by her response; that it is in the plural. But he proceeds with his intended question.

'Suzy – why did you go upstairs with him?' He looks at her and gestures with a restrained sweep of his arm towards her. 'You've got nothing to prove.' He might wish to add more – but he is already alarmed that he has used her first name, and one further step could constitute uninvited attention.

Nonetheless, Suzy Duff blushes. She shifts on her feet. When her response comes, it is curiously oblique, her tone one of resignation.

'Derek is still living the dream – he still thinks he's a professional footballer – a local celebrity – that all he has to do is to turn up in some potential client's office and they will hand him a blank cheque. But that was all two decades ago, near enough. The young people in marketing – they've never heard of him – and winning ways don't get you very far in today's cutthroat business world.'

Skelgill is nodding – but he is thinking of DS Jones's deduction – that Will Liddell's businesses were almost certainly the sole source of Derek Duff's income. And now the corollary of that circumstance stands all around him – the hockey pitches, the floodlights, the pavilion, the manicured grounds, the beautifully maintained buildings, the happy pupils and motivated staff. Suzy Duff already has one child at this establishment – and three more knocking on the great oak doors. What sort of household income is required to send a brood of four to private school? But what mother, having sent the first, could deny the others?

Skelgill wonders if the picture is becoming clearer – or more confused. One speculative line of his sergeants has been that Scarlett Liddell may have threatened to come between Will Liddell and the livelihood of one of the males who depend upon him. But which is the most dangerous animal in the jungle – of course, a tigress with her cubs.

And yet this is not the imagery that dominates his thoughts – what he sees is the photograph of the three women – Suzy Duff in her low-cut gown – and, 'sisters' either side, and each strikingly attractive in their own way – Belinda Luker and Felicity Belvedere. He sees the paradox.

*

'Where are you, Guv?'

Skelgill glances around but does not break stride. He is following his nose from the school through well-to-do suburbs. Ahead, perpendicular, runs a tree-lined avenue of detached residential properties. He has the impression that this more significant thoroughfare crests the ridge that runs down from the 'Rest & Be Thankful' viewpoint; it is a road he recognises. He wheels left from the cul-de-sac that he misreads as 'Crazy Avenue' – opposite there is another sign on a boundary fence.

'Heading west along Ravelston Dykes.'

It must be sufficiently evident from Skelgill's description that he is not en route to join his colleague – albeit that he is only a mile from her location at police headquarters.

'Oh.'

'What is it?'

'Before I tell Kevin Makepeace he can go – I thought you might want to see him.' She gives an apprehensive cough. 'He confessed!'

Skelgill stops dead in his tracks. His expression becomes one of dark dismay. He appears dazed and does not answer. At the other end of line, DS Jones detects his confusion. She too seems conflicted, for her zeal is tinged with an undertone of dissatisfaction.

'Not to *murder*, Guv – not to causing the death of Scarlett Liddell – otherwise I'd be asking you about locking him up.' Again she clears her throat. 'He admits they were lovers – for most of the last three years – right up until – when she died.'

This qualification seems to be welcome to Skelgill. He recommences walking, albeit more circumspectly, his eyes picking out irregularities caused by tree roots that corrupt the fabric of the tarmac path before him.'

'Is he lying?'

'I don't think so. I decided to challenge him with the pregnancy head on – no build up – and he just kind of folded – he's blaming himself – saying that she wouldn't have committed suicide if he'd believed her – but he thought she was bluffing and –'

Now Skelgill interrupts.

'Hold on, hold on – what's the full story – start at the beginning.'

DS Jones sounds like she is reorganising herself at a desk, perhaps finding the right place in what may be voluminous notes.

'What we thought about the unregistered phone – we were right – it's his – he bought it when they started seeing each other – when Scarlett Liddell was Scarlett Robertson – based in London. He was in the middle of his divorce proceedings – plus there was the issue about inter-staff relationships being prohibited. So it seems they were both happy to keep it under wraps. They had a simple system – she would call him to arrange to meet. No voice messages or texts. If she didn't get through she tried again later. And he admits to owning the flat in Shelton Street – originally his bachelor pad. When he married Felicity Belvedere he moved in with her – she had a larger apartment in Hammersmith that was closer to where they both worked at the time. He rented his place out – when Scarlett Robertson came on the scene it just happened to be between tenancies, so he offered it to her.'

Skelgill, though listening intently, is also scowling. His tone is rather scathing.

'Where does this lovebirds business fit with her marrying Will Liddell?'

A nervous laugh escapes DS Jones. To Skelgill it seems she harbours some sympathy – but for whom it is impossible to tell. That Kevin Makepeace lost out – or that Miss Robertson found it impossible to resist the allure of becoming Mrs Liddell?

'He said her head was turned. So he thought it was all over between them. But after she'd left the company and married Will Liddell she started calling him again. She told him she realised she truly loved him. They picked up where they'd left off.'

'Except by now she's having her cake and eating it, too.'

'She insisted the marriage had been a mistake – and she told him there was a more sinister reason why she couldn't stay with Will Liddell.'

'But not what it was?'

'Not at the time – obviously he's put two and two together since Will Liddell's arrest.'

'Did Will Liddell know anything of this – affair?'

'Kevin Makepeace claims not, Guv. He says he wouldn't have lasted five minutes in his job if he had.'

Skelgill's pacing becomes rather ponderous, his head nodding with each footfall.

'Remember Muriel Liddell told me it was a good time financially for Scarlett to have married Will Liddell. Kevin Makepeace would have known that, too.'

Skelgill hears a hissed intake of breath.

'Guv – are you suggesting it was a conspiracy?'

'Why not? Marry Will Liddell just as his wealth doubles – ship out with a tidy sum – settle down happily ever after as the new Mrs Makepeace.'

'But, Guv – a plan like that – it would tilt the motive for murder back in favour of Will Liddell.'

'Happen it might.'

There is a period of radio silence – but in this interval DS Jones replays Skelgill's proposition and concludes it is not underpinned by any great sense of conviction.

'Guv – on the evening of the Murder Mystery – Kevin Makepeace says he went to see Scarlett Liddell – he says he left his room before 7pm – he doesn't know the exact time, maybe ten minutes to – he went down and through the empty library, and back up the ladies' stair – like we thought someone might. She had been putting pressure on him during the previous week – she wanted him to confront Will Liddell – to tell him that he and Scarlett were in love. He couldn't understand why it had suddenly come to a head as far as Scarlett was concerned – he tried to dissuade her from rushing into it. Of course – if he didn't know about her condition, it's understandable that he felt she was acting rashly. He says she became really insistent – and mentioned it several times during Saturday – that if he didn't do it, she would. He tried to persuade her it would be catastrophic – to break the news over the weekend of Will Liddell's birthday celebration. But at teatime she began drinking heavily – she threatened to announce it later in the library in front of everyone – saying what could Will Liddell do then? Kevin Makepeace said he'd be forced to deny it. Her response was to warn him that she'd do something even more drastic – something he'd regret for the rest of his life. He thought she was just posturing – what could she actually do? Except there was a kind of manic intent in her manner that scared him. So he went to her room to try to head her off.'

'And what happened?'

'Ah – that's the thing, Guv. He got no answer. He knocked multiple times – waited seven or eight minutes – in case she was in the bathroom or dressing room and hadn't heard him. Eventually he tried the door – and it was locked. Probably it had locked itself when Scarlett Liddell went up after tea. He said he couldn't do much else – she may have been through in Will Liddell's suite – breaking the news. When the gong sounded at 7pm he gave up – he didn't want to be caught on the wrong stair by one of the other guests. He said he was shaking – he went straight for the drinks – and downed one, just like Tom Montagu-Browne described.' DS Jones pauses reflectively. 'You know – he may not have trusted Scarlett Liddell to see it through – it's one thing to tell Will Liddell – but another altogether to leave him. Or maybe he was getting cold feet – he might have preferred to carry on with the clandestine affair. Despite the outward bravado I think he's a bit of a coward at heart. He admitted he was terrified when Will Liddell marched into the library – and so he launched into the account of the whisky labelling problem – though he quickly realised Will Liddell couldn't yet have known anything – and then others began to arrive and it defused the situation – except he says he was still on tenterhooks in case Scarlett carried out her threat of a public announcement. Then came Suzy Duff's dramatic intervention – and it suddenly hit him – her suicide is what he would regret. Although of course, with hindsight, we know that may not be what she meant.'

Skelgill does not seem inclined to differentiate.

'Why didn't he come clean?'

'He claims he was planning to – when he'd composed himself – but then he got wind from the others – Derek Duff and Mike Luker – that the police were treating it as possible foul play – and he realised that he'd be the prime suspect. He says once he'd not spoken out in the first place, he felt he had no choice but to keep quiet – and that in any event he'd done nothing wrong. He knocked on her door and went away.'

Skelgill's brows are knitted. This excuse of protested innocence has a familiar ring to it.

'So who does he think did it?'

'He looked genuinely shocked when I asked him that, Guv. He said surely it was suicide? When I pressed him – the only scenario he could come up with was if Scarlett had told Will Liddell – and that he killed her in a jealous rage. But he felt it implausible – what kind of psychopath would murder his wife and then behave normally towards her lover, just minutes apart?'

Skelgill looks like he can think of what kind – but he has a more salient question.

'What did he have to say about the pregnancy?'

'He was totally bewildered – she'd promised him she was using contraception. He's genuinely distressed about that, Guv. He was really quite emotional. And I think today's interview is the first time he's been able to express his feelings for Scarlett to another person.'

Skelgill makes a cynical growl in his throat.

'Bear in mind he's had going on a fortnight to rehearse his excuses.'

DS Jones inhales – although she hesitates as if carefully to select her words.

'Look, Guv – I thought he was our best bet for a murderer. Now I find myself believing him.'

Her tone is apprehensive – and therefore Skelgill's reaction must be unexpected.

'Fine. Get it written up.'

'Oh – sure – I will, Guv.' The surprise is evident in her voice. 'I'll, er – tell Kevin Makepeace he can go, shall I?'

'Aye.'

'Er – what are you doing, Guv?'

'I'm about to relate a mystery to his ex-wife.'

*

Just as Skelgill is poised to press the button to request access to Felicity Belvedere's Ravelston apartment, his phone rings – or, rather, the *Lambeth Walk*, that most ubiquitous of jingles chimes out in the affluent Edinburgh suburb.

'Leyton.'

Skelgill backs off from the communal doorway, as if wary that eavesdroppers might hear him through the building's intercom.

'Ah – Guv – gotcha – bit of interesting news from forensics – *and* the techie boffins – on that phone of Scarlett Liddell's. Thought you'd want to know straight away.'

'Aye.'

DS Leyton evidently detects sufficient encouragement in Skelgill's monosyllable, for he launches into his explanation.

'First off, Guv, forensics. There's three sets of prints on the handset – you might have expected more, really – the way people pass their phones around these days. Scarlett Liddell's, obviously – and Will Liddell's we know about – and then another set – probably female – delicate, like – and deposited with a residue of some type of hand cream. And they're some of the most recent, kind of on top of the others, if you know what I mean?' (Skelgill grunts an acknowledgement. He has squatted upon a low wall and is staring at foraging ants.) 'Meanwhile IT have been liaising with the phone company – it seems Scarlett Liddell – or at least someone using her phone – tried to send a text at a quarter to seven on the Saturday night – and the intended recipient was that mystery number.'

'Makepeace's private number, Leyton. He's just admitted it to Jones.'

'Cor blimey – well, there you go, Guv.' DS Leyton makes a confirmatory double-clicking sound with his tongue against the roof of his mouth. 'Thing is, though – the text never got through – the file was too big, like maybe it was a photo she was trying to send – and what with the weak signal inside the castle walls – the network only barely picked up the attempt to connect.'

'It doesn't come as a surprise, Leyton – given what Jones has just found out.'

'No, Guv – but maybe *more* of a surprise – there's no trace of the text or a photo on the phone itself. They've been deleted.'

Unseen by his colleague, Skelgill is grinning, though it is with a certain severity. When he does not respond, his sergeant offers a prompt.

'What do you reckon, Guv?'

'I reckon you've just added a little twist to my tale, Leyton.'

*

'Ms Belvedere – I shan't beat about the bush.' Skelgill immediately contradicts his words by not continuing. He licks his lips, and it is apparent that his mouth is dry. It is hard to judge if it is simply because, now faced with what he has to say, he finds it unpalatable, or alternatively because he wants to create some psychological pressure. Either way, it takes a few seconds in order for him to resume. He is flexing what appears to be a Kirby grip between the index finger and thumb of his left hand. 'This is a moment to put pride or embarrassment to one side. If you can give me the answer I'm expecting – you and your daughter can get on with your life. This conversation will be entirely off the record. I have a question – and then a – a little – *story*. I'd be obliged for your opinion as to whether it's far-fetched.'

Felicity Belvedere regards him keenly with her bright blue eyes. Her naturally downturned mouth perhaps exaggerates the impression that she knows what is coming. Silently, she nods once.

'The question concerns yourself – and Mr Will Liddell.'

*

'Mrs Luker – I shan't beat about the bush.'

22. OPEN DAY

Saturday morning, 11 days later

With practised aplomb and not needing to look over his shoulder, Skelgill pulls his craft – presently referred to as plain "lass" when she does not quite behave, but once (he has now confirmed from faded lettering at the stern) the more illustrious *Covenant* – out from the narrow neck of Peel Wyke anchorage and into the main body of Bassenthwaite Lake. With his right-hand oar he backs down to turn the prow towards Greenmire Castle.

'How long will it take us to get there, Guv?'

'You complaining? You're welcome to row.'

DS Jones grins amiably.

'I'll give it a go – just say when.'

Skelgill grimaces as he hauls hard on the oars to get up to speed, his slightly superior expression suggesting that only he would have the strength to do the job – though simultaneously his gaze falls upon his colleague, as she trails the fingertips of one hand experimentally in the cool water. She is a relatively slender young woman, but her bare arms, subtly sculpted, reveal a hidden musculature – and he has glimpsed her in the gym, on the rowing machine – what she lacks in pure bulk she would probably make up in her naturally precise technique. That she is attired accordingly – close fitting *Lycra* sportswear that seems de rigueur these days, sport or not, for those females that can carry it off – owes something to the arrival of a ridge of high pressure stretching two thousand miles from the Azores to Iceland, that has brought summer temperatures to spring the length and breadth of the British Isles. For his part Skelgill is looking overdressed and already a little hot, an authentic if shambolic fisherman – though he has not any rods at the ready – indeed no tackle at all in his boat – only a crate containing his Kelly kettle, and the wherewithal for a rustic picnic of Cumberland sausage sandwiches.

'We'll be there in ten minutes – when we're done you can row back with the wind to Scar Ness – there's a nice shingle bank – we'll land for a mash.'

DS Jones grins in a way that is appreciative of his incorrigible adventurism. Why visit the comfortable refreshments tent when you can sit on a rock and brew tea with lake water fired by driftwood?

'Sure.'

She settles, seemingly happy and relaxed. They look like a couple – day-trippers on an outing – and if any local were to recognise them as police officers – they would assume they were off duty. In body, this would be a correct assumption – but in mind police officers are never really off duty – especially detectives such as these. And not least that they are now passing into waters where Skelgill is reminded of their most recent case.

'It was round about here that I saw Scarlett Liddell.'

It takes DS Jones a moment to register the context.

'Really, Guv – what actually happened?'

'They just passed me – about fifty yards off. She called out. That was it. I noticed Will Liddell didn't approve.'

Now DS Jones's memory is jogged.

'Did you see the Scottish police tweeted about the case this morning?'

Skelgill pauses mid-stroke to ply her with an old-fashioned look.

DS Jones chuckles and waves an apologetic hand.

'Will Liddell has pleaded guilty to three specimen charges of sexual assault.'

Skelgill remains still – his expression momentarily frozen.

'He's playing the system.'

'He could get fourteen years, Guv.'

'That'll do for starters.'

Now his features contract to indicate that the figure would be insufficient in his view. He resumes rowing, the splash and swish more frequent than before. However, DS Jones's voice comes lightly.

'What was she like, Guv?'

Skelgill seems to be wondering himself.

'She noticed me. The others didn't.'

His answer is abrupt, punctuated by a deep breath.

DS Jones nods. She too pauses reflectively.

'I'm glad about the Coroner's verdict, Guv. Death by misadventure. If there's such a thing – it must be much less painful for the family. I think Kevin Makepeace's testimony made all the difference at the inquest.'

Skelgill momentarily bares his teeth – it could just be the effort of rowing – although there is a hint of disapproval – but now he tempers this by making a kind of nod in his subordinate's direction, as if to convey his recognition of her role in this regard. Now he becomes a little more expansive, speaking in short bursts between inspiration and expiration.

'We were looking too hard. I should have admitted – to myself – it was a mare's nest – from the beginning. Suicide – dressed up as murder – *hah!*'

Going by DS Jones's expression this latter phrase sounds a little alarm bell – however her first response is to allay his self-reproach.

'But, Guv – the death had occurred – there was nothing we could have done about that – and if we hadn't have investigated it the way we did – who knows – Will Liddell might still be at large. Think of the potential misery we've put an end to.'

Skelgill ponders her assessment.

'But in one case – you might call that a silver lining.'

He does not appear inclined to elaborate. He has been circumspect about his informal visits on what had proved to be the concluding day of the investigation, first to Suzy Duff at St Salvator's, and thence the school's 'Old Girls' – Felicity Belvedere and Belinda Luker – and finally to Muriel Liddell. DS Jones has been obliged to read between the lines – for she is more than sufficiently perceptive to sense that, if Skelgill has withheld information, it may just be to protect her from the horns of some dilemma, caught between morality and the law.

'I take it you mean Suzy Duff?'

Like the arcing strokes of his oars in relation to the trajectory of the boat, his reply to this question is oblique.

'My guess – Will Liddell – will leave instructions – for Derek's Duff's business – to be looked after. He's a very old – friend. A very good – friend.'

That he repeats verbatim Suzy Duff's words – and hears her plaintive voice in his head as he does so – cannot be apparent to DS Jones – but the nature of his delivery supports her own, not uninformed, suspicions.

'Guv – do you think the wives will file complaints?'

Skelgill has been squinting across the surface of the lake, and now his eyes flash as they fix on his colleague. He understands that she is closer to his thinking than he has given her credit for.

'Not a cat in hell's chance. Besides – we've cleaned up their mess for them.'

Skelgill has already employed the provocative phrase "suicide dressed-up as murder" – and now this equally controversial hint. And perhaps DS Jones detects a slackening in his stroke rate, as though to postpone their arrival at Greenmire Castle's landing stage. She decides to follow her intuition.

'Guv – the way I see it – putting it bluntly – my guess is that Will Liddell basically created a latter-day harem.' She watches closely for Skelgill's reaction – he scowls but does not demur. 'Financially, he'd got the husbands in his grip – and their wives knew it – and their lifestyles depended on it. He treated them to luxurious trips – and had his pick of whomsoever took his fancy. Whether the men knew they were being cuckolded – who knows – but the females felt there was no choice but to comply – close their eyes and think of the school fees.'

DS Jones clamps her hands between her thighs and leans back, lifting her feet and balancing at her centre of gravity, but her gaze remains locked upon Skelgill's narrowed grey-green eyes, challenging him to contradict her. It is a few moments before he speaks.

'Carry on.'

DS Jones releases the breath she has been holding – it seems with relief – and now she looks away across the water.

'When you think about it, Guv – with the possible exception of Suzy Duff, as you say – the females involved in the close circle are far more independent than, say, five years ago. Muriel Liddell – she probably has a hefty divorce settlement – and, jail or not, Will Liddell can afford his maintenance. The Lukers may now be insulated – I know Mike Luker's firm depends on Will Liddell – but he'll have banked profits in seven figures. And Felicity Belvedere – her fortunes are no longer tied to Kevin Makepeace – her architectural business is expanding – and she stands to inherit from a wealthy family. Put that all together – Will Liddell's control has been weakened.' She glances at Skelgill to see that he is nodding. 'What if it had run its course – and they were about to take matters into their own hands?'

Though her words constitute a question, her inflexion conveys a good deal more certainty. Skelgill is regarding her keenly – for she seems to have fathomed his cryptic logic with some ease. As if to confirm this, she pinpoints the crux of the matter.

'Guv – what exactly did you mean – when you just said we cleaned up their mess?'

Skelgill feathers his oars mid stroke but does not return the blades to the water; instead he draws the shafts into the boat, and they glide smoothly to a halt. The light south-westerly breeze pushes ripples against the hull, creating a gentle rocking motion. They have stopped in more or less the position from which Skelgill, from beneath the anonymity of his wide-brimmed *Tilley* hat, had viewed Will Liddell's party, several of them becoming inebriated perhaps for anaesthetic purposes. How little could he have guessed what thoughts, what agonies, what schemes were going through the minds of the passengers in Abel Thurnwyke's crowded launch? Yet – ironically – Scarlett Liddell had seemed among the most carefree of them; but perhaps it was her way, rarely middling. Skelgill sighs and then inhales more deeply, his arms akimbo, his palms pressing down on his thighs – it is an indication of a forthcoming statement.

'We saw it with Catriona Brodie – she was our stroke of luck –' He pauses as if to check that DS Jones is nodding her agreement. 'It must feel nigh on impossible – for a lone woman to come out against someone like Will Liddell. Never mind the financial stranglehold – when it's one person's word against another's – you need cast-iron proof – and a concrete witness.'

That he employs a somewhat peculiar adjective owes itself to the image that momentarily occupies his mind's eye – the oblong stone tablet above the portico of St Salvator's – with its motto, *Iuncta sororibus* – 'Sisters side by side'. The thought seems to distract him, and it is left to DS Jones to insert a prompt into his nascent but stalled soliloquy.

'Are you saying they were going to set him up – a *sting?*'

'You know I don't go in for speculation.' Skelgill produces an ironic laugh that could also sound just slightly mad. 'But it's all over now. Both cases closed. So bear with me.'

DS Jones tilts her head, almost imperceptibly, as if over-exuberance might deter him. Skelgill continues.

'Suzy Duff will be best placed – despite that she's got most to lose and that she's not one of the 'sorority' – that's what they call it, aye?' (Now DS Jones nods obediently.) 'But her lass will give Will Liddell a get-out-of-jail card. He could just claim they've been having a consenting relationship for the past fifteen years. So, maybe the four of them get together – including Muriel – and agree their roles – they convince Suzy she must be part of it – there would be the shame of not acting. And though it will be a kind of deceit, entrapment, if you like – perhaps for her it will be easiest. A swansong – *hah!*' Now he looks rather sheepishly at DS Jones. 'So she won't pull any punches with her choice of outfit.'

DS Jones is listening attentively, her expression implacable – though Skelgill sees that she swallows. It seems he need not enter into any salacious detail. He moves on.

'After that – it will just be a matter of picking their moment. Now it's Felicity Belvedere's turn. She makes sure she and Will

Liddell are simultaneously out of sight of the rest of the group. The Murder Mystery probably means they'll split up and search the castle for clues. Belinda Luker will draw attention to their absence – and perhaps she'll casually go looking for her friend Felicity. And what will she 'find'? She'll 'find' Felicity being assaulted by Will Liddell. He might be nowhere near – but that doesn't matter. They may not even tell him – they'll just call 999. And when we investigate, what do *we* find? There's his DNA on Felicity's clothing. There's traces of his skin under her nails – matching scratches on his arm. And there's a concrete witness. As Leyton would say, he's bang to rights.'

'But, Guv – that was Scarlett Liddell – the nails?'

Skelgill raises a silencing palm.

'So – the time comes – Suzy Duff grits her teeth and sets off upstairs with Will Liddell – remember Tom Montagu-Browne saw her smile to her pals as they left the library. She knows what he'll want to do with her – and she's right. The first act is almost complete. But then they discover Scarlett Liddell hanging – and she's dead. All hell breaks loose. Plan A flies out of the window.'

DS Jones inhales to ask a question; Skelgill pre-empts her.

'Belinda Luker and Felicity Belvedere think quickly. Scarlett Liddell may well have committed suicide – but as they come on the scene it looks just as much like she could have been murdered – there's Will Liddell bent over her lifeless corpse on the bed – and he's probably the only person to have been with her – and in fact that's more or less correct. Suddenly they're presented with Plan B. Let's make it look like murder – if it works – problem solved – no need for them to testify – no humiliation for their partners. It's a wacky idea – but – hey – it's a Murder Mystery Weekend!

'In the commotion Belinda Luker goes into the bathroom. There's Scarlett Liddell's mobile lying on the floor. The screen had cracked – when she dropped it. She'd taken a picture of herself – tried to send it to Kevin Makepeace – to get him to come to her room – to find her feigning death – to scare the living daylights out of him. But she slipped on the wet tiles –

and choked.' Skelgill pauses for a moment, as though he feels he ought to insert a respectful interlude. 'Belinda Luker checks the phone – whether she realises what has happened – your guess is as good as mine – but she deletes the photo and the failed text – and leaves the handset beside the bed.'

DS Jones is now regarding Skelgill with a mixture of consternation and bewilderment.

'Has she admitted this, Guv?'

Skelgill casts a strange look to the heavens, his features momentarily contorted in some agony.

'Jones I can't remember what they might have said and what I might have invented. This is a mystery, remember.'

He looks back at DS Jones, and they seem to come to some unspoken accord. She blinks her continued consent to his hypothesis.

'Let's say they're all crowding around the body on the bed. Suzy Duff's giving CPR. Felicity Belvedere takes Scarlett's hand. She scrapes the underside of their nails together. Nobody would notice – it would look like she was trying to offer comfort. But now the match for the scratches on Will Liddell's arm has been transferred – aye – you were right – but remember it was Felicity Belvedere that was in his team for the assault course. She scratched him in the first place.

'Let nature – and CID – take their course. If there was foul play – aye, Will Liddell's a prime candidate. And when interviewed, the women drop subtle hints about him being controlling – about conflict between him and Scarlett – about the idea that she was a gold-digger. But nature and CID can't find any clear evidence to charge Will Liddell. The death has all the hallmarks of a suicide. We try to investigate a murder – and at best we find other equally plausible suspects. All along – it doesn't feel right. Aye – folk are being evasive – but they're not being evasive in the direction that we're looking! But because they're being evasive, we're trying to see something that isn't there. The truth is – we're looking at a tragic accident.'

DS Jones has been nodding reflectively, sympathetic to his complaint. But now she is compelled to interject.

'The truth is, Guv – a dangerous predator who's been committing despicable acts and getting away with it for years has been caught.' Her face becomes stern. Her dark eyes engage those of Skelgill. 'And the truth is – these women have suffered more than enough.'

Forcefully Skelgill slaps his palms down onto his thighs. *She* rests his case! His colleague understands – indeed concurs – that even if there were some alcohol-fuelled ham-fisted obstruction of justice on behalf of the women – firstly, that to pursue such fantastic conjecture would be futile – and, secondly, that their ordeal needs to have ended.

The pair settle in silence – maybe for as long as half a minute. Now DS Jones's gaze slips past Skelgill – and she finds a focus upon Greenmire Castle. The open day event appears to be in full swing; good numbers of visitors mill around stalls set out on the alluvial pasture between the castle and the shoreline. She sits up determinedly – and her countenance brightens – as though the sun has emerged from behind a cloud.

'Well – I suppose we solved one of the mysteries of the Murder Mystery weekend.'

'Aye?'

'The ghost, Guv – or rather – that there is no ghost that locks the door of Lady Anne's chamber!' She shakes her head ruefully. 'That was a proper red herring!'

Skelgill grins sardonically.

'Lavinia Montagu-Browne's probably already come up with another ruse to attract visitors.'

DS Jones smiles, flashing her even white teeth. She half-swivels, bringing up her feet to sit sideways upon the thwart, and hugging her knees. Skelgill regards her, admiring the athletic ease of her movements.

'Sure you're up for a shift in charge of the bouncy castle?'

'Just try to stop me, Guv – if I'm in charge, that means I get to have a shot. Besides – it sounds like I need to work up an appetite.'

She glances pointedly at his rustic crate. Skelgill shrugs nonchalantly.

'Just don't try and get me on the thing.'

'I think you'll have your hands full with the fishing, Guv.' She raises a palm in a mariner's salute – to shade her eyes. 'If I'm not mistaken that's DS Leyton's kids running rings round Tom Montagu-Browne.'

Skelgill grunts and heaves the boat back into action.

'Well – I taught Tom to cast – happen I'd better introduce him to the technique known as the skelp round the lug.'

***

Next in the series...

A RACE AGAINST THE CLOCK,
A YOUNG LIFE AT STAKE

When DI Skelgill takes under his wing a talented fell-runner – his underprivileged cousin, Jess – little does he realise in what jeopardy he places her. For Cumbria is being targeted by the infamous 'county lines' drug gangs. As turf wars break out, Jess inadvertently finds herself in the crossfire – but family ties blind her to the danger of her association with Skelgill. As the body count increases, Skelgill finally recognises the threat to his young protégé – but is it too late to save her?

'Murder on the Run' by Bruce Beckham is available from Amazon